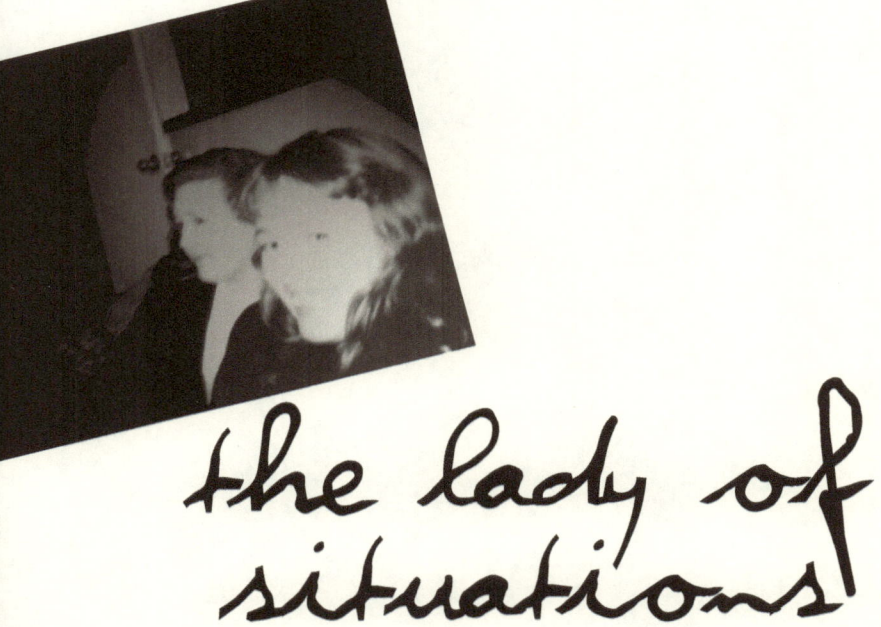

the lady of situations

the lady of situations

STEPHEN DEDMAN

TICONDEROGA
PUBLICATIONS

Thanks to

Ed Bryant, Jeremy G. Byrne, Ellen Datlow, Gardner Dozois, Scott Edelman, Russell B. Farr, Paula Guran, Elaine Kemp, Samira Keshavjee, Robert K. J. Killheffer, Keira McKenzie, Peter McNamara, Tamara Patt, Robin Pen, David Pringle, Kristine Kathryn Rusch, Tanya Schmah, Richard Scriven, Cecily Scutt, Jonathan Strahan, Sean Williams, Sheila Williams, Katharine Susannah Prichard Writers Centre, the British Museum, Bayswater Public Library, and A Touch of Strange bookshop.

To Grant Stone,
patron saint

The Lady of Situations
by Stephen Dedman

First published by Ticonderoga Publications

Designed & edited by Russell B. Farr

Typeset in Goudy Old Style and Violation

National Library of Australia
Cataloging-in-Publications entry

Dedman, Stephen, 1959–
The lady of situations

2nd ed.
ISBN 9780980353174 (hc)
1. Science Fiction.
A823.3

ISBN 978-0-9803531-7-4 (hc)
ISBN 978-0-9803531-8-1 (tpb)

Ticonderoga Publications
PO Box 29, Greenwood WA 6924 Australia
www.ticonderogapublications.com

10 9 8 7 6 5 4 3 2

contents

foreword

Read any three items by Stephen Dedman—and I do mean *any*: choose at random—and the first thing that will strike you is the range of his work. To avoid spoiling any of the works that await you in this collection, let me reach outside this book to illustrate my point. A short piece like "Optional Extras" (*Aphelion*, 1986) is a slick one-page joke; "A Walk-On Part in the War" (*Dreaming Down Under*, 1998) is a cleverly devious re-working of the myths about the siege of Troy; and his novel *The Art of Arrow Cutting* (Tor, 1997) is a fast-moving contemporary fantasy-thriller combining oriental magic and ninja intrigue with gritty streetwise urban realism. The Dedman universe seems inexhaustibly vast.

The second striking aspect of Dedman's work is his ability to make his stories resonate—to make them cast a reflective, intelligent light on our own world and times. Without sacrificing entertainment-value and without ever getting heavy with the reader, Dedman is able to take the wildest ideas and track-through to some kind of crypto-quirky linkage with our own human condition. For example, "As Wise as Serpents" (*Fantasy & Science Fiction*, 1993) is about the alien Lagva, who are locked in combat with snake-like alien parasites which leech onto the necks of their targeted victims. The Lagva are winning their struggle and their life is improving, so why is it all thrown into jeopardy because they create an interplanetary incident by killing a bunch of influential Earthmen? Does this have something to do with the fact that the Earthlings wore colourful ties on their necks? (It does—but what does that say about The Meaning of Life?)

I've said Dedman is engagingly quirky, and ingeniously devious, and I've made the point about the astonishing range of his work. Something else also needs to be mentioned: Mage. Michelangelo Magistrale is his full name, but on Brooklyn's mean streets you don't last long enough to say it all—so he's Mage. He's the central character in *The Art of Arrow Cutting*, and he's thoroughly credible (and likeable) as a fictional creation. Mage represents Dedman's other great talent: an ability to render contemporary characters in a way that resonates convincingly with the world's realities. Some of the best (and quirkiest) of those characters are waiting for you right now, queued behind this very page.

—Van Ikin

flogging a dead horse

Scene

SEAN WILLIAMS *is busy typing away at his computer. Standing by him, and occasionally looking over his shoulder, is his friend* MARK RADIUM. MARK *is a horse. A big, chestnut thoroughbred.*

  SEAN *pauses and reads aloud from the computer screen.*

SEAN: I first encountered Stephen Dedman in 1990, via the pages of *Aurealis* and a neat little tale called "But Smile No More". From that first reading, I knew that I had found an author who wasn't just telling me a story but was giving me a genuine slice of life. He was speaking to me not as a grandfather would to a young child asking for a story, but as an equal, and I felt—

MARK: (*snorting*) As an equal? You can't say that!

SEAN: Why not?

MARK: You can't fool me, you know. I've seen this Dedman character. He's no equal. Only got two legs, for one thing.

SEAN: (*sighing heavily*) That's *equus*, not equal. With those ears you should listen more carefully.

MARK: My hearing's as good as geld.

SEAN *groans and his head sinks onto his arms. After a moment he sits up and looks over his shoulder.*

SEAN: I refuse to get into a punning war with you.

MARK: Do you always address figments of your imagination in such an offhand way? Actually, don't answer that. I've seen the way you treat Uma. All flattery and batting eyelids. Just because I've got fetlocks.

SEAN: Look, I've got a job to do, do you mind keeping your insecurities to yourself?

MARK: You're going about it the wrong way. Who cares what *you* like about Dedman's work? You've got to give the reader something to latch onto; you need a hook.

SEAN: But whoever's reading this has already bought the book. They know how good Dedman is.

MARK: Maybe, maybe not. They could be glancing at this to help them decide whether or not to buy the collection. Your intro might whet their appetites. Take me for example. You could start by saying something like: "Stephen Dedman is a complete god!"

SEAN: Look, this is confusing the issue. I want to tell people why buying this book was an excellent decision.

MARK: (*with a warning in his voice*): You're disagreeing with me.

SEAN: Not at all. It's just that I think you don't understand the finer points.

MARK: Well, excuse me! I wouldn't want to cause you inconvenience. Wouldn't dream of *saddling* you with any extra work, not after the *palfrey* attempt you've made so far.

SEAN restrains himself by holding onto the keyboard.

SEAN: What I want to say is this: Dedman, for me, redefined the boundaries of what a science fiction writer could talk about. Times are changing, and the telling of stories should change with it—but at the time I found little that documented the world I felt around me. Not Adelaide, not Australia, but the *Zeitgeist* of the late 20th Century. What are the new moral codes? What is evil? What is forgivable? Is desire tamed enough, or does it need to be quenched at the source as well?

The fiction of Stephen Dedman deals with such issues. A casual reading of his work over the last decade will have encountered numerous territories familiar to many but explored in public by few in this genre. It is a pleasure now to read some of them again in a single volume—giving a rewritten script (or scripture) to this most jaded of centuries.

MARK: Comes across a bit, you know, *pony*.

SEAN: Do you want me to kill you?

MARK: In *colt* blood, I assume?

MARK *sniggers to himself, pleased with that one.* SEAN *resigns himself to the inevitable, and resumes reading from the screen.*

SEAN: Dedman's work has a style of its own. It is not Australian, although one can see its origins there: ironically forthright, and whimsically dark.

Every story is very much grounded in today. For all the glimpses of past and future in his work, he is writing for the readers of now, not yesterday or tomorrow. Stories like "Salvation" and "A Single Shadow" transcend their geographic and social origins with a clarity few writers ever achieve.

Dedman's work is rich and detailed, hinting at greater depths with every paragraph—calling to mind the playful elegance of Poulenc or Debussy, with entrancing details of melody that linger long after the complete work is finished, and just a hint of the deprecating—

MARK: Deprecating? You don't want to say that. Might give people the shits.

SEAN: *Deprecating*, for God's sake, not defecating. Now shut up and listen: —deprecating pomp of Kodaly's "Hary Janos" suite.

MARK: Bit la-de-da, isn't it? And what's poor Janos's hair got to do with it? Anyway, it's irrelevant. Who was it who said that writing about music is like dancing about architecture? They knew what they were talking about.

SEAN: (*defensively*) I'm not writing about music.

MARK: Oh, forgive me. You're talking about Kodaly the jockey, I suppose, and Debussy the bus driver. Look, mate, you're using a musical metaphor which will alienate or confuse most of your readers, assuming there are any left at this point.

SEAN: Just what are you trying to say?

MARK: More to the point, what are *you* trying to say?

SEAN: That Stephen Dedman is not just a major Australian writer, but a major writer in his own right.

MARK: Then say exactly that!

SEAN: (*ignoring him*) I go on: The landscape of the Stephen Dedman stories collected here in this book is populated by wanderers—anti-social colonists and backpackers, world-hopping therapists and vampires—all searching, sometimes successfully, for an elusive love, peace, closure or ideal, whatever takes their fancy. They don't always get what they want ("Godfather", "Double Action") and what they want might not always be the best ("Founding Fathers") but we feel their yearning in every word and every action. They are real, and we are, however briefly, part of them.

Their journeys are frequently mirrored by sexual desire in the text; indeed, one of the most noticeable aspects of Dedman's works is his free allusion to sex and sexuality. That's not to say that his work is pornographic: far from it. He is, rather, acutely aware that desire runs like a red thread through the often roughspun cloth of our lives. To ignore it would be to deny a large part of what makes us human. The beauty of Dedman's work is that he does so without constraining us. His characters set us free. They show us how it ought to be.

As such, he is not just a keen activist for women's rights. He advocates the rights of all genders (and combinations of genders) to love the ones they wish in the way they wish. "We all have the right to choose," he writes in "Miracle", and that, I think, is a key tenet to his work. Whether it be when to die or how to live, or, more topically at times, what sex to fuck or how to express the sexual desire we might feel for any gender our inclinations chooses for us, it is our choice, not someone else's, that should determine our actions.

Of course, it is never that simple.

MARK: Especially for a horse. Double especially if you're a real stallion, like me. No "do you mind" or "excuse me", it's just one mare after another and "do your duty, boy" and "keep it up, Mark Radium" and.

SEAN: Shhh! (*reading*).for Dedman's worlds also abound with conspiracies. Conspiracies to kill true love before it has a chance to blossom ("Transit"), to expose the secrets of powerful men ("The Godfather Paradox"), to hide the terrible truth behind a crime that some might not even consider murder ("Founding Fathers"), and to sell guns ("Double Action"). In response, Dedman rails against child porn, exploitation, bigotry in all its forms; he champions hermaphrodites, victims of all kinds, and the love-lorn. All his characters desire with a keenness that cuts both ways. Few writers could write a story about the "local girl [who] makes it into movies, even if you can't see the bottom half of her face" and get away with it.

Dedman, who perhaps shares the 'ethical atheist' tag of "From Whom All Blessings Flow" is not a grim realist. He would simply rather we fall 'sanely in love instead of madly', and that, I think, is a rather noble sentiment.

MARK: You're being didactic. All this guff about messages and so on—

SEAN: Look, one of the reasons I like Dedman's work so much is because he speaks from—or at least *of*—a place I'd sometimes like to be. But there's a big difference between having a message and being didactic. I enjoy Dedman's stories for more than just their message. I enjoy them for their tales, for the characters, for the craft he shows in the way he writes. Basically, I just enjoy them. Is there anything wrong with that?

MARK: I never said there was.

SEAN: I mean, to go back to music for a second, someone once said that: "If you don't instinctively want to tap your feet to it, it isn't good music. It's only rhetorical noise" and—

MARK: Hmm. That's Robert Anton Wilson, isn't it? What you mean, of course, is that sometimes you can like something just because you do. The fact that it's good will only make it better, of course, but having to explain the reasons *why* it's good can get in the way of the real message. You like Stephen Dedman's fiction. You could read it *ad nauseam.* You think this is a great book, and you want people to enjoy it. You don't have to get all literary on me to get that message across.

SEAN: You know, for a horse, you're surprisingly well-read.

MARK: You're just saying that because you know that as a figment of your imagination I have only read what you've read.

SEAN: I was being sincere. And there's one thing left to say. (*reading*) Ultimately, for me, the greatest thing about Dedman's stories is the way they can touch me. Many stories by many authors make me laugh, or think, or shiver—but "Transit", "Never Seen By Waking Eyes" and "Amendment" are three stories which, no matter how often I read them, will always move me. The gentle redemption they offer gives me comfort late at night, even in a world full of metaphoric if not literal vampires, that there is hope enough left for all of us.

MARK: What, even horses?

SEAN: Indeed.

MARK *sidles up to* SEAN's *side and sniffs the galley pages of Dedman's book.*

MARK: Well, maybe there's something in this after all. Not keen about the metaphorical vampires, mind you, but all that guff about sex had me going.

Fade.

—SEAN WILLIAMS & MARK RADIUM

the lady of situations

It was raining outside, and the hostel very sensibly lacked a television; the dishes done, we all retired to the common room. Gwen has always loved meeting new people, and travelling as we were, we met new people every night and left them behind us each day: the sort of strangers with whom you might share sex, but never your toothbrush (okay, so I'm a cynic). Tonight, there was the inevitable pair of Germans; a New Zealander, furry and clumsy as a koala bear and about as ineffectual; an amiable Australian giant named Danny; Elliot, a mathematician from the Other Place (at last, someone I *knew*, thank God)... and Jacqueline.

Jacqueline was the most exquisite creation I can remember seeing outside an art gallery, as fine as cut crystal, and with a voice to match—clear, hard, and without any colour that it hadn't stolen. You could not *not* watch her, and watching her, you could not help but imagine the body inside those carefully-worn sloppy clothes and the lily-gilding make-up, could not help but follow the lines and curves that converged between her thighs, could not help but be drawn deeper and deeper inside her... but never beyond the skin. Any deeper than that, of course, and you would encounter the soul of a ninja. Rather than look at Gwen, and risk comparing her to Jacqueline, I tried to distract myself by watching the chess game. Elliot had brought a set, of course—not his replica Lewis Chessmen, which I had murderously coveted since our first meeting, but a small board with a built-in computer. We watched him demolish the New Zealander in six moves, as though taking an *hors d'oeuvre*... well, most of us watched. Danny was lost somewhere between the headphones of his walkman, and Jacqueline was ostentatiously reading, a paperback cover-down across her thighs. Elliot accepted a challenge from Gwen; she opened with the Queen's gambit, and survived for seventeen moves.

I wondered who Jacqueline was pretending to ignore, who it was she was really interested in, and decided that it had to be Elliot. He was, after all, the best looking man in the room: slightly taller than I am, but barely half my weight, long legs and minimal hips, wavy blond hair, labyrinthine green eyes, a small mouth with generous lips, pianist's fingers... remember Dennis Christopher in *Breaking Away*? Best looking, hell; he was beautiful. I tried to remember what I knew about him. An excellent student, of course, who *should* have been a fellow Oxonian; brilliant, but also extremely serious. Single, and had been so for as long as I'd known him. Unusually for a mathematician, he had no interest in music whatsoever. He had been beating me consistently at chess, go, and (to my vast irritation) ancient and medieval wargames, every holiday for three years, and for all I knew, I might have been the best friend he had. It took me three guesses to remember his Christian name: Charles. Hell, I know more than that about Myrddin or Pelagius.

Gwen smiled, thanked Elliot for the game, and backed away from the board. Elliot glanced at the German couple, who shook their heads simultaneously. There was no way to back out gracefully, so I dropped my seventeen stone (metricise me and I will break your heathen skull) onto the chair opposite him, and tried the Danish gambit.

Elliot's king wasn't where I expected it to be: damn. Jacqueline stretched, advertising a body that it would overwork my heart to imagine, and stifled a yawn. The New Zealander, as smitten with her as I was trying not to be, hastened into the kitchen to make her a cup of coffee which I knew she wouldn't drink: he'd made the mistake, at dinner, of calling her 'Jacky' (I never did learn *his* name, but perhaps he didn't need one). She took the mug from him without thanks, or even a smile, sipped to make sure he'd remembered how she liked it (she was used to getting *exactly* what she wanted), and then put the cup on the floor.

Within a few minutes, the game was all over, and I was left staring glumly at the board. Elliot switched the computer on: no-one else in the room was likely to challenge him. He was doing a better job of ignoring Jacqueline than I was; perhaps he wasn't trying as hard. "What are you playing?" I asked.

"Modern Beroni," he replied. "Fischer vs Spassky, third match game."

"How many games does it know?"

"A hundred, plus variations."

"Wow," murmured Gwen. "You know, that's what I've always wanted."

"A chess computer?" I asked.

"No; an eidetic memory."

"No, you haven't," said Elliot, without looking up from the board. "I knew a girl with an eidetic memory, once. Better than eidetic, even: a perfect memory."

Jacqueline closed her book. "No-one has a perfect memory," she drawled.

"She did," replied Elliot.

"How do you know?"

"I knew her very well."

"*How* well?"

"She was the first girl I ever fell in love with," he said. Jacqueline looked as though she was about to comment, but didn't. Gwen glanced at me, and I shrugged; it wasn't a story I'd ever heard before. "I was nineteen," Elliot continued, leaning back in the chair and *still* not looking at Jacqueline, "and I had a pretty good memory myself: it came in useful. I was notorious, then, for keeping a harem; I could remember all of the names and most of the faces... only the bodies ever became numbers. I'm not proud of it, now... but looking back, I don't remember that I ever lied to anyone, or broke any promises... but I digress.

"It started with a game of chess, a tournament, at Trinity. I was defending my title as the King of Kings. I'd only made Rook in the Intercollegiates, the year before; the defending champion of Cambridge had come second for three years running, and was stuck with the title of Queen. I believe he now works for MI5." Gwen and I laughed; the others only looked puzzled.

"There were four males for every female in the university back then, and any alien being taking the chess club as a representative sample of humanity would derive some very strange theories about our reproductive processes. Of course, he would also drastically overestimate average human intelligence..." He coughed slightly. "It was rather startling to discover a girl sitting opposite me that I didn't recognise. I thought I'd gone through them all.

"She was pretty, though not quite beautiful, but her eyes... Eyes don't usually show very much, whatever the poets may say," and he stared across the room, straight into Jacqueline's; she held his gaze for a bad five seconds, then looked away. "No," he said, softly. "Not quite beautiful. They were dark—not the darkest I've ever seen, but they should have been. They were like..." He blinked, and then brightened. "Do you know how a pearl is created? Something sharp inside the shell hurts the oyster, and it coats it in a smooth, glossy material to hide the edges? And it grows a new layer every year... From the outside, it seems perfect; smooth, beautiful... And so were her eyes—when her guard was up. When it dropped, you saw a cross-section of the pearl; all the layers, all the years, and everything that had hurt her in the beginning."

He smiled slightly, or as near as I'd ever seen. "Actually, it was several minutes before I noticed her eyes, and days before I saw them that open; she didn't trust easily, and I can't blame her. The first thing I noticed was her voice; she was born in Colorado, raised in Boston, and spoke perfect English—better than mine, anyway—with an accent that was... unique, for all I know. Later, when I heard her speak other languages—she knew a dozen or more—the accent disappeared; by that time, I'd become quite fond of it."

He paused. "After the voice, of course, I noticed the sort of things I routinely noticed in those days. She was tall, about five ten, and thin, very thin. Lovely legs—hidden by jeans and the table, alas—but no figure; a fashion model, early-adolescent sort of body. Beautiful hands; you watch the hands, and I was almost staring at hers. Her hair was as short as mine, and dark. Her face..." His hands came up, gently sculpting curves in the air—I found myself thinking of the Durer print—and then fell back to the chessboard. He picked up the white queen, almost caressing it. "No. I don't have the words, or a photograph, and you don't have the mathematics. Never mind. She was pretty, and female, and she could play chess. The perfect woman; what more could I ask for?" He paused again, then said, wryly, "I *could've* asked her not to beat me.

"I didn't make any mistakes, I could swear to that... I didn't really mind that she'd won," he sounded convincing, if not convinced, "but she did it so *quickly*! She watched my moves, but she barely glanced at her own pieces. Her game was defensive, but *she* was all attack."

He glanced at Jacqueline, impassively, then stared into the fire. "Did she win?" asked the New Zealander. "The tournament, I mean?"

Elliot shook his head. "No. Bradley beat her—you remember Bradley, Geoff? He beat you, too, the next year."

I winced. "The maniac with the ponytail? Glasses like crystal balls?"

"Yeah, that was him. I went to console the girl, and ended up inviting her out to dinner, and she ended up accepting. She was in Cambridge alone, on holiday from the Sorbonne. She'd won a scholarship, studying French Lit—"

"Did she have a *name*?" asked Jacqueline, in her bitten-glass voice.

"Penelope," Elliot replied, "but she hated it. Call her Penny, and the room temperature would drop fifty degrees. I called her Sweetheart." He smiled, or maybe it was a grimace. "It was a trick I learnt from my sister: she was a teacher, and she had a lousy memory for names. If you can't remember someone's name, call them something flattering; it beats 'Hey, you!'. I'd let it become a habit.

"Dinner was okay, then we went to my room for another game of chess. She won again, then beat me at speed chess in less than seven minutes. I didn't think she was into wargames, or sex, so we played a friendly game of backgammon. That was the only win I had all night; I walked her home, and nothing but a kiss for my efforts—I *hate* walking—and a quick, superficial kiss at that. I remember thinking that she must have been the oldest virgin I'd ever met.

"I love a challenge; it was about the only type of love in my repertoire, then. I invited her out again, two nights later, and this time we talked; I mean, *really* talked. It took me nearly an hour to guess what she was trying to say; it was after midnight when she said it. Her father had been..." he stopped, and stared back into the fire. Then he shrugged. "She wouldn't say it either. I guess seven years of abuse does that to you. The Hell with that; call a rape, a rape. He'd been raping her since she was nine. She was sixteen before she realised that other fathers didn't do that."

Gwen gasped, very softly. Everyone else was silent, even Jacqueline. "She told her mother," Elliot continued, "and her mother refused to believe her, so she applied for a scholarship that would get her the Hell out of Boston... and here she was. One tough lady." He shook his head, looking less like a Michelangelo, more like an Edvard Munch. "Me? I was always ready to help myself to a damsel in distress; one of the best nights I ever had was with a girl whose parents had just broken up. Not that night. I held on to her until she cried herself to sleep, put her to bed and tried to work. No good; everything kept turning back in on itself..." He turned to me. "Maybe this would sound better if we put it to music. What's the saddest song you know?"

I took out my flute—I'm not the only Welshman in the world who can't sing, but I'm the only one *I* know who admits it—and played my own variation on Albioni's Adagio. Jacqueline put her book down, next to her cold cup of coffee. Elliot took the mental equivalent of a deep breath, and continued.

"She woke early, and I made breakfast—I'm quite good at it—and she left without saying anything but 'Thank you'.

"I gave her a few hours to sleep, and phoned her; she wasn't in. I tried again, a few minutes later; no reply. Eventually, I rushed out, grabbing a book without even looking at it, ran over there, and sat on her doorstep, trying to read, until she came home. She arrived at ten; she could at least have had the grace to look surprised, but no..." He stared into the fire. "No...

"She invited me in, shaking her head. The place was small, untidy; the only evidence that she was even passing through was a set of half-open suitcases and a travelling chess set. 'What *am* I going to do with you?' she asked. I didn't even dare offer a suggestion. 'I suppose you're about to tell me you're in love with me, right?'

"'How did you know?' I never knew what she was thinking.

"'I've heard it before—as I'm sure you have.' I nodded. 'Okay. Anything else you want to say?'

"'I *could* tell you that I've never said it before.'

"She looked at me, and obviously believed me—and why the Hell not? 'Anything else?'

"'You're the first girl who's ever trusted me with... I don't know. Your secrets. Your soul, maybe.'

"'My soul?' I thought, for a moment, that she was about to laugh hysterically. 'Souls, now. I'll bet that a week ago, you didn't believe in love *or* souls.'"

Elliot shrugged. "'I don't want to hurt you', I said.

"'I've been hurt by an expert,' she replied—flatly, no hint of a boast, or of self-pity. 'Do you know the worst of it? I can't forget any of it.' She turned and stared at me as though I were a new species of cobra. 'I'm serious. Read me a paragraph of that.'

"I started, remembered that I still had a book in my hand, and read her the Crab's speech from 'Crab Canon'. She quoted it back at me, word-perfect. I applauded her; she only shrugged. 'Party game. What would you like next? Blindfold chess? No...' Her voice was cold. 'No, I know what you'd like next.'

"'Only if...'

"'Only if I want it too, right?' She looked away from me, and down into her lap. 'Right. And I've heard that you're an expert lover—quite apart from being a Greek god.'

I saw Jacqueline's eyes widen, black pits within the jade. Elliot seemed to be blushing; maybe it was just the firelight.

"'Have you ever had a virgin?' she asked.

"'One.'

"'Did she enjoy it?'

"'Eventually. At least, she said she did.'

"'I'm not exactly a virgin,' she replied, 'but I've never... voluntarily...' The room was so quiet, it was murderous. Finally, she stood and said, 'Not tonight. Go home; I'll call you.'"

Elliot's voice had faded, nearly to the point of inaudibility; when I stopped playing, all I could hear was the wind under the door, and a nightingale which might have been miles away. "She rang at three thirty that morning. 'Do you think you can make me happy?' she asked. I was too tired to try to lie. 'Eventually,' I said. 'If you let me.'

"I suspect she smiled. 'Then you'd better come over here and get started.

"'Now?' She hung up."

Gwen shivered, and I realised that no-one had moved in nearly half an hour. I glanced at the dying fire, but Elliot shook his head, and I resumed playing. "The rest of this story is five days long." He closed his eyes. "I had, in my nineteen years, tried almost everything possible between a man and a woman—between a man and *two* women, for that matter. Except for deliberately hurting each other, of course—oh, sure, sometimes we left teethmarks. And scratches." Jacqueline quickly hid her nails, even though Elliot was facing away from her.

"Anyone insist on details? We kept the lights on—she said she wanted to see everything, remember everything—and started conventionally enough, exploring each other first with eyes, then with hands and mouths, always kissing, licking *something*, and... I'd expected to have to teach her, maybe play her the way you're playing that flute, but no, we played each other... more like a game of chess.

"Naked, she was almost beautiful, at least with her eyes closed, without her armour... She was wonderfully greedy for new experiences, new sensations; we tried more than a dozen positions, with whoever was least tired at the time going on top... We had anal sex twice, because she wanted to be *sure* she didn't like it... She loved having her nipples sucked; apparently, no-one had ever done that for her before..." I was glad it was becoming dark; even Danny and Jacqueline were starting to colour. "We scarcely left the bed; even when we did, we didn't let go of each other. It once took me an hour to get to the kitchen.

"By the fifth day, I could barely feel anything below my eyebrows. We once fell asleep during foreplay, or afterplay, or whatever it was by this time. We tried playing chess, but we kept losing the pieces, so Penelope suggested blindfold chess: she kept winning, but I was glad of the chance to shut my eyes."

"And when you opened them, she was gone," concluded Danny. Elliot shook his head, wearily.

"No, no... this was *her* room, remember? We just lay there, sometimes fantasizing aloud, playing word games, memory games... and in the morning, she threw me out. I was too tired to argue. When I rang her, the next day, she didn't answer; I didn't have the strength to sit on her doorstep again, and it was two days before it occurred to me that she might be gone.

"But that's not the end of the story.

"I told my tutors that I was going overseas, threatening to suffer a nervous breakdown if thwarted." He grimaced. "Suffer, Hell: I probably would've enjoyed it."

"Was she there?" the New Zealander asked.

"Yeah, in a grotty little closet in Saint-Germain-de-Pres. It only took me two days to find her. This time she *was* surprised to see me, but she wasn't pleased. 'I suppose you'd better come in.'

"'Thank you.'

"She smiled at that, and shook her head. 'No,' she said. 'No.' And she started unbuttoning her blouse. 'I thought you understood,' she said. 'How much do you know about the brain? Oh, of course, you know computers—but computers are stupid, aren't they? How do they compensate?'

"'They're fast.'

"'And?'

"'They never forget.'

"'Precisely. And neither do I.' She glanced at me, shook her head. 'Maybe I've never learnt how. You don't have an appendectomy scar—or any scars. Ever break a bone?'

"'Yes—my left leg, when I was fifteen. Skiing.'

"'Do you remember the pain?' She unzipped her jeans, dropped them. 'I don't mean the accident, or the hospital; the pain. The feeling.'

"I stared at the small scar just above her panties. 'No'.

"'No.' She looked down at her abdomen, then unfastened her bra. 'Luckily, I've never had a broken leg, but I can remember *that*—if I think about it. Physical pain isn't too bad; you have to concentrate, sort of. You don't wake up every morning seeing the *doctor* hovering above you.'

"'Your father...'

"'Yeah.' She grimaced. 'My fucking father. No, he didn't cause... this. I can remember being born, I can remember not being able to read... Maybe I'm some sort of mutant. It doesn't seem to have any survival value... Or maybe I'm wrong, maybe it *was* my father. Maybe some things, traumas, *can* take away the defence mechanisms, the ability to forget... shock, stress, fear, pain, hatred... bring back all your memories. Maybe love, too, but I wouldn't really know.' She stepped out of her panties, and lay down on the bed. 'You'd better sit down.' She stretched her arms out, cruciform. 'Look; no hands.' And she closed her eyes."

Elliot's voice was as dry as Egyptian dust; suddenly, he stood, stalked into the kitchen. We sat there in suspense until he returned with a glass of water. "And I sat there and watched her, damn me to Hell. She didn't so much as touch herself, but I watched her fingers trace along where my spine would have been; I watched them leave deep scratches in my back; I watched her nipples swell and harden, first the left, then the right... watched her lubricate and open, so wide open... watched her arch her back... watched... watched... For a long time, I wasn't even sure which was the real me; the one standing in the room, or the one who was with her, touching her, inside her... I heard someone screaming, screaming...

"She came six, seven times, and finally, she opened her eyes, black basketballs... no. Black holes. Everything fell in and nothing left, everything was trapped at the precise moment it reached her...

"And then she smiled. 'See? You *did* make me happy; very happy... Happier, I think, than you can actually imagine... Be happy for me, if you can.' She stood, a little unsteadily, and looked straight at me. 'I need a shower. Please go.'

"'I...'

"'I know,' she said, softly. 'I love you, too—that *is* what you were going to say?—and I will always love you, just as much as I do now... but I don't need you any more, and I don't want to hurt you. If I want to see you again, all I have to do is close my eyes.'"

Elliot was silent. It was at least a minute—it felt like an hour—before Danny asked, "*Did* you ever see her again?"

"No."

The German girl might have been crying: it was dark, and I can't be sure. Then Jacqueline stood. "At least she's never forgotten you," she said, and went to bed; her tone made it clear that she hadn't understood. The Germans said their *Guten Nachts* and followed, then Danny... The New Zealander seemed to be on the verge of saying something, but no words came; eventually, he too drifted off towards the dorms. Gwen, sitting near me, reached out for my hand and squeezed it, but I shook my head and she disappeared. Good night, ladies, good night, sweet ladies, good night, good night. Elliot stared into the fire, watching it die.

"Charles?"

"Yes?" He looked up. "Yes, it *was* a true story... except that her name wasn't Penelope."

"It seemed a little too appropriate."

"Then I'd best not tell you her *real* name. I knew a Penelope, once," he added. "First girl I slept with, in fact. We were faithful to each other for ten whole days."

"Are you okay?"

"Okay?" He shrugged, then with a 'May I?' gesture, took my flute and played the Adagio—a little slowly, but otherwise perfect. "I'm getting better," he said.

never seen by waking eyes

They say that we Photographers are a blind race at best; that we learn to look at even the prettiest faces as so much light and shade; that we seldom admire, and never love.

— Lewis Carroll, *A Photographer's Day Out*

The Reverend Charles Lutwidge Dodgson, the logician and photographer and lesser-known mirror image of Lewis Carroll, first met Alice Liddell when she was three. John Ruskin, a fellow lecturer at Oxford, was also smitten with young Alice, and later became obsessed with twelve year old Rose La Touche. Edgar Allan Poe married his thirteen year old cousin Virginia. Dante fell in love with Beatrice when she was eight and a half.

If you expect me to add my name to this list, you're out of your mind.

"He was terrified of the night," she said, softly. "Terrified of dreaming, I think. Even beds frightened him."

I nodded. I don't remember any night-time scenes at all in either of the *Alice* books, or *Snark*, or even *Sylvie and Bruno*, and the only mention of a bed to come to mind was '*summon to unwelcome bed/A melancholy maiden!/We are but elder children, dear,/Who fret to find our bedtime near.*' The hunters of the Snark 'hunted til darkness came on', with not a word of what happened afterwards, and *Sylvie and Bruno Concluded* ends (and not a moment too soon) with the stars appearing in a bright blue sky. True, 'The Walrus and the Carpenter' is set at midnight, and features an oyster-bed, but the sun stays up the whole time.

"How did you meet?"

Alice smiled prettily, without showing the tips of her teeth. "In London, outside a theatre—the Lyceum, I think. I'd seen him before, but I had no idea who he was. When I told him my name, he said, 'So you are another Alice. I'm very fond of Alices.'"

"When was this?"

"Winter. I don't remember the year, but he was about thirty, and he hadn't written *Wonderland* yet, and I think Prince Albert was still alive. 1860, maybe." I nodded. Dodgson was a compulsive diarist, but many of his diaries disappeared after his death, like his letters to Alice Liddell, and all of his photographs and sketches of naked little girls.

I suppose it started in the darkroom, at home: developing old, half-forgotten rolls of film is the safest form of time travel; you don't need a license, or even a seat belt. This roll had been in the Nikon for at least a year, and when I finally sat down with the proof sheet and a glass of Glenfiddich, I was ready to see anything. Forty minutes and two glasses later, I was still wondering why the Hell I'd taken five shots of Folly Bridge. Granted that it's where the famous rowing expedition and the story of *Wonderland* started, and that I don't get up to Oxford as often as I'd like, it's been photographed more often than Capa shot 'Death in the Afternoon'.

There was nothing mysterious about any of the other shots, at least to me. On the proof sheet, they all look harmless enough—a busy street in Bangkok, far enough from Patpong to be safe; a beach near Townsville; a park in Tokyo; the Poe Cottage in Philadelphia;

a slum in Brasilia or Rio. An extremely observant eye (such as Poe's) would notice a particularly beautiful little girl in almost every shot—never in the centre, but always perfectly in focus. She isn't the same girl. She's always the same girl. She always has dark hair, black or almost black; pale skin; large eyes. Small, slight, almost elfin. The girl in Townsville is probably no older than ten; the girl in Bangkok may be twelve or twenty or anywhere in between. She isn't the same girl. She's always the same girl. And her name is

I stared at the photographs of Folly Bridge; five shots, from slightly different perspectives, but all from the St Aldates side. Long shadows—evening, probably just before sunset. And no girl. Where the Hell did she go?

I slept badly, that night, but without disturbing anyone. My dreams were obscene; you don't need the details, except that the girl from Folly Bridge was... there.

She was smaller than the ideal, with the creamy pallor of the Londoner who can't afford to buy a tan. Her hair was short, but extremely untidy. Her eyes were too dark, impossibly dark, and her smile remained long after the dream had ended. It was not the smile of a little girl. It was the smile of something older, and wiser, and very hungry.

I woke shivering, expecting to find the sheets drenched with sweat or worse. Instead, they were completely dry, and cold, as though no-one had slept there at all.

Barbara is far and away the best secretary I've ever had. She's a law school drop-out, efficient, intelligent, computer literate, multilingual, empathic, diplomatic, moderately ambitious, extremely attractive, and devoutly gay; we've been having breakfast together for four years now, without ever misunderstanding each other (well, not seriously). Two of the juniors, both avid prosecutors, were sitting at a table near the door discussing the latest batch of ripper murders that were splattered across all the papers. A pot of coffee and a cherry danish were waiting for me in my booth, and so was Barbara.

"Rough night?" she murmured, as I sat down.

I nodded. "What have I got today?"

"Partners' meeting at eight, Druitt arriving at ten and the *Mirror*'s lawyers at eleven, political lunch," she grimaced slightly, "at the Savoy at two—"

"Oh, God, is that today?"

"I've left the afternoon free."

"Good. What about tomorrow morning? Am I in court?"

"No, not until Friday. You have two—"

"Postpone them."

She keyed something into her notebook without even blinking. "Where are you going?"

"Oxford."

Sullivan (okay, so that isn't his real name) was a numbers man for the Tories, known to his colleagues as the Lord High Executioner. If he ever invites you to lunch, hire a taster. I was still sitting down when he muttered, "I hear the *Mirror* settled."

He obviously had excellent hearing for a man his age; we'd signed the papers less than twenty minutes before. I merely grunted. "I hope it was expensive?" he probed.

"My client's reputation is worth a lot of money."

"So is yours, by now." He smiled. Like most of the people who run most of the world, Sullivan had managed to avoid the burden of a reputation; you probably still don't know who I'm talking about. A waiter appeared, and I ordered carpetbag steak and a good burgundy. Sullivan waited until he was gone, then asked, "Are you planning to stay in London long?"

"I go where the firm sends me," I replied, "but I think I'll be here for a few years yet. I'd certainly prefer to; it beats the Hell out of New York."

He smiled. "Good. I won't waste your time, or mine. Have you ever considered a career in politics?" I shrugged. "All right. What if I said there was going to be a safe seat vacant before the next election?"

"I'm not interested." I replied, without any hesitation.

"Think about it. This isn't America; you wouldn't have to quit your practice. I know what you're worth—believe me, I do—and all right, MPs' salaries are pitifully low: even the travel allowance isn't much of a compensation. But you wouldn't have to give any of it up. *I* haven't; you know that." I nodded; he'd been a client of ours for many years. "Hell, you already give away more money than most rock stars, more than most people can even dream about. All those kids you sponsor, all those donations to UNICEF and refuges—oh, don't look so bloody surprised. You really thought nobody knew? Welcome to the twentieth century, or what's left of it."

I said nothing. "I'm not going to bullshit you," he lied. "I don't know *why* you do it, what you get out of it, but I don't care, either, if it's what you want to do. But if you *really* want to help the street kids or starving Thais or whoever, you'll consider my offer very carefully."

"Why me?"

"Because I know you can win. You always do. You're the best libel lawyer in the business, you haven't lost a case in years; I've seen you convince juries that black is white and queer is straight. You're a born politician." He paused, leaning back in his chair. "And I'll be honest. I know the other parties haven't approached you yet, and I know they will, and I know we can double whatever they offer."

"You can relax," I assured him. "I'll tell them the same thing I told you. I'm not interested."

"Why not?"

"For one thing, I don't believe it'll be as easy as you make out. I'm single, and I've lived most of my life in the States. Secondly, it's not what I want to do. Thirdly, I've never intended to become a public figure; I prefer to keep my private life private."

Sullivan snorted. "Like I said, this isn't America; *we* don't expect politicians to be moral paragons. We've had too many kings, and far too many princes; nobody gives a damn if an MP's not married, or if he bonks his secretary occasionally. Besides, you were born here, your father was some sort of war hero, you grew up in Boston so you speak better English than half the BBC, and you're a Rhodes scholar to boot. As for your private life, all right, I know you can't give a lecture without bonking one of the students, but what does that matter? They're all *girls*, aren't they?"

I looked at him, and said nothing. He was probably right about English politicians' private lives; nobody's ever given *him* any shit about the curious resemblance between his twenty-seven year-old second wife and his fifteen year-old daughter. The wife's not brilliant, but I'm sure she's guessed which of them he really wants to fuck. "Yes, they're all girls."

"And all over sixteen." He waved his fat fingers dismissively, then shut up as the waiter returned with our lunch. "All right. At least consider it. I don't need an answer for another week."

I parked near the corner of Thames and St Aldates, and stared at Folly Bridge, wondering if it had ever deserved its name so thoroughly before. The urge to turn the Jag around and return to London was almost palpable. Instead, I took a deep breath, unbuckled my seat belt, opened the door, and stepped out into the thin October sunshine. Having come this far, the least I could do was visit some of the booksellers. Besides, it was a week before Michelmas term, and I could wander around the colleges again without hordes of undergraduates making me feel like a fossil.

It was past six and almost dark when I headed back to the carpark, footsore from the cobbles, with fresh catalogues from Waterfield's and Thorntons in my briefcase. There was a girl standing outside Alice's Shop, staring into the window, though the shop had been closed for over an hour. She turned when she heard me, and we stared at each other across the road.

I *knew*, even before I saw her face, that it was the little girl from my nightmare. She was small, maybe nine or ten years old, wearing ripped jeans, sneakers, and a very baggy sweatshirt; her shoulder-length dark hair might have been loosely curled or merely tangled. She leaned back against the window, her right hand cupped before her, in what must have been a deliberate imitation of Dodgson's photograph of Alice Liddell as a beggar-girl.

I stood there frozen for a moment, and then a tourist bus passed between us, blocking my view. Hastily, I turned and resumed walking south; when I looked back, over my shoulder, she was gone. I hurried along, not even wanting to wonder why.

She was five or six yards behind me when I reached the carpark, and she followed me all the way to the Jag. I fumbled for the remote and unlocked the door, almost expecting her to rush ahead of me and climb in. Instead, she disappeared while my back was turned, and I slid into the seat and locked myself in. I sat there for a moment, breathing heavily, then turned the headlights on. She was standing in front of the car, close enough that the lights illuminated the Oxford crest on her dirty sweatshirt but not her face. After a moment's hesitation, I reached across and unlocked the passenger side door, and waited. I heard the door close again, and she was on me; I felt her bite, and saw nothing.

The contents of my wallet were spread across the passenger seat when I opened my eyes again, but nothing seemed to be missing except the girl. I examined myself in the mirror; I looked bleary-eyed and slightly dishevelled, and maybe a little pale, but not injured. I peered at my watch; 7.56. If I hurried, I could be back in London by nine.

I decided to work late on Thursday, finishing a paper for the *Harvard Law Review*, but sent Barbara home in time for her karate class as a reward for not asking any embarrassing questions. The words I needed, exactly the *right* words, seemed to appear on the monitor as soon as I knew what I wanted to say; normally, when I write, there seems to be a block between my head and my hands, and everything I try to say clunks and screeches, and I spend hours facing the window rather than stare at the screen. This night, I became so absorbed in my work that it was well after midnight when I looked at my watch and realised why my coffee was so cold and the chambers had become so quiet; everyone else (even the Hatter, who still lives on Eastern Standard Time) had departed, leaving me utterly alone. I looked out the window again, and shivered, and reached for my overcoat and umbrella.

It was cold, and the rain had slowed to a drizzle, almost a mist. The whole city felt sombre and slimy and strange. The streets were deserted, and the only noise was the faint growl of the Jag and the occasional short hiss as something or someone appeared out of the gloom and I had to brake. The statue of Eros looked more like a vampire, and I thought I saw some shadows move beneath it as I passed, a huddle of junkies or a bag lady with a shopping trolley. Driving through London protected by tinted glass and electronic locks always feels *wrong*, somehow, even in filthy weather; on good days, I feel as though I'm cruising (or catacombing, as my Texan cousins call it); bad nights, I just feel like a voyeur.

As soon as I arrived home, I closed all the curtains and turned on all the lights, then chose a CD at random and turned the stereo up full blast. It wasn't enough to make the place feel like home (it's a company flat; even the paintings are investments), but at least it felt warm and relatively secure.

Most of the partners decorate their rooms with the inevitable Spy caricatures of judges; I prefer to leave the judges outside when I can, and my taste in art runs more to Brian Frouds and Patrick Woodroffes. My private library clashes with the rest of the leatherbound decor, but what the Hell. I collapsed on the couch, and reached for my much-thumbed copy of *Faeries*. The little girls scattered among the horrors and grotesquerie looked so clean, so innocent, so ethereal. A pretty elf looked back at me with almond-shaped night-shaded eyes, for all the world like

I dropped the book, which fell open to the sketch of Leanan-Sidhe. 'On the isle of Man,' the text read, 'she is a blood-sucking vampire and in Ireland the muse of poets. Those inspired by her live brilliant, though short, lives.'

There was a knock on the door.

I will drink your health, if only I can remember, and if you don't mind—but perhaps you object? You see, if I were to sit by you at breakfast, and to drink your tea, you wouldn't like that, would you? You would say "Boo! hoo! Here's Mr Dodgson drunk all my tea, and I haven't got any left!" So I am very much afraid, next time Sybil looks for you, she'll find you by the sad sea wave, and crying "Boo! hoo! Here's Mr Dodgson has drunk my health, and I haven't got any left!"

— Lewis Carroll, letter to Gertrude Chataway, 1875

I looked through the peephole. It was her, of course, still in the same dirty sweatshirt and tattered jeans. I drew a deep breath, and then opened the door slightly. She smiled.

"Can I come in?" She had a little girl's voice, a rather thin soprano, but it was well-modulated, almost polished: Marilyn Monroe with a hint of Oxford accent. Her tone was curious, rather than arrogant or imploring; her eyes merely watchful.

"Can I stop you?" I asked, only half joking. The building was supposed to be impregnable; even if she'd managed to sneak through the lobby while the doorkeeper was busy, there were cameras in every lift and corridor. "How did you get here?"

"By coach, and bus. Your address was in your wallet."

"Why?"

"Aren't you going to invite me in?"

"Who are you?"

"My name's Alice," she replied, as though that were an answer.

"*What* are you?"

She paused, smiling with her eyes as though she were trying to invent something. "What do I look like?" she asked, finally. "Aren't you going to invite me in?"

"What will you do if I don't?"

"Go away," she replied, "and not come back."

I stood there, trying to convince myself that it was stupid to be scared of a little girl, barely a metre high, no matter how dark her eyes were. I tried to imagine myself shutting the door, and going on with my life. And then I stepped back, and let her in.

"What do you want?" I asked, after she'd folded herself up on the chaise-longue, her arms around her knees.

"What do *you* want?" she replied, still looking around curiously.

"I asked first."

"A place to stay during the day," she replied. "Some new clothes. An alibi, occasionally. And maybe you could drive me somewhere, sometimes. I don't know how long I'll want to stay; probably a couple of weeks, maybe a month. Your turn."

"Is that all?"

"What else are you offering?"

"What are *you* offering?"

Her eyes lit up, suddenly; she'd noticed the open book on the couch, and the rest of the library. "You've got a lot of *Alice* books. How many?"

"Forty-two."

"Holy shit—oh, sorry. Why?"

"Different illustrators."

She nodded. "You must know a lot about Lewis Carroll."

"No, not really. There's a lot about him that no-one knows."

"I could tell you some of it. I knew him."

I sat down opposite her, and tried not to smile. "How old are you?"

"I don't really know. Eight or nine."

"He died in 1898," I said, gently.

She looked at me, impatiently. "I know. He got sick just after Christmas, and died a couple of weeks before his birthday. Or so I heard, after he didn't come back. I was still in Oxford; he could hardly take me with him to his sisters' home, could he?

"Don't look at me like that; you *know* I'm not making this up."

"Then you must be a hundred years old, at least."

She shook her head indignantly; I think she would have stamped her foot, if she'd been standing up. "I'm eight years old, and I'll *always* be eight years old. That was what he wanted. That's why he loved me.

"I knew him," she repeated, "and I know things about him that he didn't even tell his diary, things that no-one else remembers. I can tell you what I know, and I've told you what I want in return. Do we have a deal?"

"How do you know it's what I want?"

She laughed. It wasn't a child's laugh, but the way one laughs at a child. "I saw you when you came to Oxford last summer—June, was it?"

"July."

"I saw you looking in Alice's shop, and in Christ Church, saw you looking up at his rooms... And you took my photograph. You pretended you were just taking a picture of Folly Bridge. Have you printed that photo yet?"

"Yes."

"I wasn't in it, was I?"

"No."

She nodded. "*He* found that, when he brought me up to Oxford for some photographs. I didn't know; photographs were new and strange, then, almost magic, and *very* expensive. That's how he found out what I was. I'd never even seen myself in a looking-glass, and I didn't know that I never could; looking-glasses were for the rich, and clean water I could see myself in? In London, last century? Hah! I can't even remember seeing myself naked before—"

"You're a vampire..." I whispered.

She laughed, a little sadly. "'This must be the wood where things have no names,'" she quoted. "'I wonder what'll become of my name when I go in? I shouldn't like to lose it at all—because they'd have to give me another, and it would almost certainly be an ugly one.'" She looked at the mirror over the bar, and said, "You can call me a vampire, if you like. *I* always think of vampires as male. We usually call ourselves sidhe, or mara, or succubi, or even lamia. But don't worry; I promise not to bite."

"You bit me in Oxford."

She pouted. "Not *badly*; I didn't take any more than I needed. You'll be okay. We *do* live off the living, usually while they're asleep; they feel sick the next day, or depressed, but we don't leave any scars, and we try to give them time to recover. Nowadays, we mostly survive on suicides and roadkill and junkies who're going to die anyway; we leave before the ambulance arrives, and no-one notices if the bodies are missing a pint or two of blood... Maybe that's why they say suicides become vampires. Of course, they don't, or the world'd be full of them. Us.

"And there are the symbiotes, who know what we are—mostly artists or writers. They give us blood, and we give them dreams."

I slept badly that night. Knowing that there's a vampire in your guest room makes it difficult to relax, and I was terrified of what I might dream.

Why didn't I just throw her out? Maybe because I wasn't sure that I could, wasn't sure what she'd do to me if I tried. And she'd known Charles Dodgson for nearly forty years. Maybe she knew

I had no experience buying clothes for little girls, but I didn't want to tell anyone about Alice (not even Barbara), and I couldn't take her shopping until she had something better than her Oxford rags.

I stopped at a Marks & Sparks on the way home and bought a collection of garments that were roughly the right size. They looked wrong on her when she first tried them on, wrong as a gymslip on a page three girl, but she was a good enough actress to get away with it.

She spent the night telling me about her first encounter with Dodgson. "He asked if he could write to my mother, to get her permission. Anna, my teacher—another sidhe—was working at the theatre, so I told him she was my mother.

"His rooms were full of books—and toys, of course, but I remember the books better. Anna was teaching me to read, but she wasn't very good at it. When he saw how fascinated I was, he gave me a few books, to keep. I don't think it was meant as a bribe, though he always regarded Londoners as horribly commercial—he was a terrible snob.

"He photographed me in his rooms—this was before they let him build a studio on the roof—and let me watch as he developed the plates in a closet... I hadn't really known what to expect, and I think he was too surprised to be frightened. Every time I visited him, after that, he had more books on ghosts and things like that—*The Wonders of the Invisible World, The History of Apparitions, The Vampire*... most of it crap. They were easily gulled in those days. Arthur Conan Doyle even believed in *fairies*...

"I met the Liddell girls a few times. They were snobs, too, especially Alice, but angels compared to their mother. Alice *should've* been an absolute brat: she was beautiful and knew it, and *everyone* loved her; men, women, even a prince..."

"You?"

"I liked her. I didn't expect to, but I did."

"And Dodgson?"

She shrugged. "Dodgson loved all of them, like he loved most pretty girls who were willing to trust him—until they became teenagers, anyway. Ina was twelve or thirteen when I met her, and already seriously built; I think she scared him a lot worse than I did."

Saturday was a typical London spring day, bleak and damp and grey—though Alice warned me that we'd have to come home if the sun appeared; it wouldn't kill her quickly, but a few hours worth would hurt and could crack her skin. Driving down Gower Street, she glanced through the window at a bag lady, and sat up. "You know her?" I asked.

"Yes. She's... she's one of us, but she doesn't know it. She doesn't even know she's dead, she can't remember being alive, she doesn't even know why the sun hurts her; she just does her best to hide from it. She's probably been living on cats, rats, all sorts of garbage."

We turned into New Oxford Street, and I asked her to keep an eye out for a parking spot. "You said, last night, that you drank blood. Need it be human blood?"

She shook her head. "It has to be human, but it doesn't really *have* to be blood; sperm will do, but we need much more of it than one man can make. Hundred years ago, some of the sidhe could fuck or suck enough men a night to stay alive that way, but not now. It takes too long, and it's not worth the effort unless all the men come to you. There are still some vampires in the beats and the bath-houses—never trust the boys who don't ask you to use a condom, some things are a lot worse than AIDS—but even *they* need blood sometimes. I don't know why. None of us are scientists. But it has to be human, too, or you start losing your mind. Or your soul, maybe. You lose *you*, anyhow; you become stupid, you start thinking like an animal, hunting animals, and then you die. Anna said that's how the stories about vampires turning into wolves and rats began—that, and the way we used to catch rabies from them, and them from us. *There's* one."

I jumped, then realised she meant a parking spot, not a vampire. "Thanks."

The weekend passed much too quickly, and on Monday morning I returned reluctantly to chambers and the negative nineties. The Hatter and I were dissecting a lease and trying to bore a large hole in the boilerplate when the phone rang. It was Sullivan, wanting to cancel our lunch. I agreed, and hung up, and enjoyed the feeling of relief for nearly a minute before I realised that Sullivan and I hadn't *made* an appointment for lunch, and that he would simply have told his secretary to phone my secretary if we had. I asked the Hatter to excuse me, and slipped out of the room. Barbara was sitting at her desk, staring intently at the screenpeace as it created mazes and blundered through them. "I just spoke to Sullivan," I said, softly.

"Yes, I know."

"We weren't having lunch today, were we?"

"Not that I heard."

"What's happened? Is he sick?" He *had* sounded a little strange—almost emotional.

"I don't think so," she said, carefully. "I think it's his wife—and I think you'd better call him back."

I nodded, and ducked back into my room. The Hatter looked up from the photocopies he'd spread over my desk. He's a remarkably ugly man, with a distinct resemblance to a New College gargoyle—big hands and feet, big eyes, a huge nose, and frizzy ginger hair that no dye nor wig could conceal or control—as well as being a hopeless advocate, but he has an excellent memory for precedents and a fetish for minute detail. He started gathering up the papers as soon as he saw my expression, and quickly disappeared. I slumped into my chair, and reached for the phone.

Sullivan told me the story with remarkable economy, for a politician; Sylvia, his wife, had gone out on Saturday night, and not returned. He hadn't reported her as missing (the police won't act, or even listen very hard, until someone's been gone forty-eight hours), and wanted the whole affair kept as quiet as possible. There was something decidedly strange about the way he said 'affair', and I took a deep breath before asking, "What can I do?"

"If this gets out, I'm going to have to call a press conference. I'll need you there, just to make sure everybody minds their manners. Are you with me?"

If there was a threat in there, it was unusually quiet; he sounded more tired than anything else. If I'd said no, it probably wouldn't have cost me anything more than my job, maybe not even that. "I'll be there," I replied. "If necessary, that is. I'm sure she'll turn up before it comes to that."

He grunted. "Okay. Remember, if you get another offer, I'll beat it; that's a promise. I'll be in touch."

Alice was asleep when I returned home—or dead, maybe, but she *looked* asleep. She was lying on the bed in the guest room, curled up into a foetal ball, still wearing her jeans and anorak from the night before. Her eyes were closed, and her face had relaxed into a pretty, girlish pout. I stood in the doorway watching her for a few minutes, and then crept into the kitchen. I enjoy cooking, when I have the time, and I often suspect I make the best chilli in England. Alice appeared, wrinkling her nose, while I was chopping the garlic. "Sorry. Is this, ah..."

She shrugged. "Don't worry. It doesn't hurt me, it just fucks up my sense of smell. How was your day?"

"Pretty awful. I spent most of it helping a bank get away with knocking down an old building and replacing it with an office tower that looks uncannily like a giant refrigerator; the rest of the time, I helped a politician pretend to look for his wife. How about you?"

"Nothing exciting. Can you drive me down to Piccadilly, later?"

I nodded. She sat in the dining room and watched me cook, and chatted about some of Dodgson's other child-friends and models whom she'd met—Gertrude Chataway, Beatrice Hatch, Connie Gilchrist, Isa Bowman, Ina Watson, Xie Kitchin, others whose names she'd forgotten. He'd photographed all of them as near naked as they would allow, frequently with their mothers present; the child nude was a favourite subject of Victorian artists, and several of the girls had also modelled for Henry Holiday (then better known for his stained glass windows) or Harry Furniss. "I only saw most of them once or twice," she said. "He usually lost interest in them when they turned eleven or twelve—I remember he was particularly nasty to Connie, as though it were her fault that she was growing up—but he was still calling Gertrude 'dear child' when she was nearly thirty, and she let him; I guess she enjoyed it. I bumped into her when she visited in 1890-something, and she recognised me, and we had to pretend I was the daughter of the girl she'd met when she was eight." She laughed. "Of course, I didn't know any of them well; they were sunlight girls."

"He was lucky," I said, as I stirred the chilli. "Nowadays, parents can be arrested for photographing their own children naked, even in the bath. So much for progress."

She looked at me coolly. "Have you ever read any Victorian porn? A hell of a lot of it's about old men fucking girls of ten or eleven, and that wasn't just a fantasy; it was common practice. There's been *some* progress; women and kids are better off, even if the men aren't."

"Sorry. It was a stupid thing to say."

"Yeah. It was. And okay, it's a stupid law, but where do you draw the line?" She shrugged. "You want to know if he fucked them, don't you? That's what everyone else asks—or if they don't ask, it's what they wonder. Do you want me to tell you?"

I didn't answer. She sat there silently for nearly a minute, then, softly, "He didn't even want to.

"No, that's a lie. Sometimes, he *did* want to—he dreamed about it, even fantasized about it, though he did whatever he could to distract himself from these fantasies—writing letters, inventing mathematical problems... But I don't think he ever touched any of them, especially not when they were naked, and I think *that's* what matters.

"He never touched *me*, and I knew him for nearly forty years, and while I was physically as delicate and fragile and generally unsuitable for fucking as any of them, he knew I sure as shit wasn't innocent. He never let me touch him, either; and he hit me when I offered to fellate him. Knocked me across the room—he was a lot stronger than he looked—and apologized later. The thought really horrified him."

Which meant he'd probably had it before, I thought; a man confronted with a *new* idea, however horrific, has to think about it for a moment before he can react. But I didn't say anything.

"He wanted to be the White Knight, courteous and gentle and dreamy, and clumsy, and bad at his job... and he never removed his armour. I think what he *really* wanted was for sex not to matter. He wanted to be a boy again—no, a child. Even being a boy implied that sex existed."

"'I am fond of children'", I quoted, "'except boys.'"

She nodded. "He grew up surrounded by sisters and younger brothers, until they sent him off to school, which he hated. He wanted to return home; I think he spent the rest of his life wanting to return to that home. He was never really cut out to be an adult; he stuttered whenever he spoke to adults, he wasn't even interested in *money*, let alone sex. He just liked studying, and solving mathematical problems, and writing little satires and nonsense, and surrounding himself with toys and books and children—all the things he'd done as a child. He never 'put away childish things', as he once put it, and we loved him for it. Without him, *I* wouldn't have had a childhood at all."

I looked down at the skillet, and realised that I was burning my dinner. I rescued it as best I could, and asked, "Why didn't you make him a vampire?"

"I don't know how—Anna never taught me—and, anyway, he wouldn't have wanted it. It was too late; I couldn't make him a child again, couldn't give him back his innocence, and he wouldn't have wanted to be thirty or forty forever."

I nodded. There was something strange about the way she'd said 'innocence', but there wasn't time for a cross-examination before the news, and I had to know if Sylvia Sullivan's disappearance had been noticed yet. There were stories about increases in the jobless and homeless figures, a small shipment of crack intercepted in the Chunnel, and massacres in Peru, Kowloon, Johannesburg and Atlanta; I guess they were too busy to worry about a back-bencher's wife, however photogenic. "What's happening in Piccadilly?"

"You wouldn't like it."

"I wasn't expecting an invitation. Meeting more sidhe?" It was two days before Hallowe'en, which the British don't celebrate the way we do, but which might be 4th of July for vampires.

"Yes."

"Going out for a bite?"

She looked at me coldly. "Do you really want to know?"

One of the first things they teach lawyers is never to ask a question unless they already know the answer. "No, I guess not."

That night, I dreamed about my childhood—something I hadn't done in years. It was my tenth birthday, and everyone was there; it wasn't until I'd woken up, still feeling good, that I began wondering what was wrong with that. I'd had a tenth birthday party, yes, and

I *had* gotten my first real camera then, and my parents *were* still together and all my grandparents still alive, so what was...

Alice was in the en-suite, brushing her teeth. I'd stopped wondering how she was getting in and out; she'd had more than a century to study burglary. "Is that what you meant, when you said you give your victims dreams?"

"You're not one of my victims."

"Are you sure?"

She spat the toothpaste out of her mouth. Her eyes were blazing, and there was white froth on her chin; she looked horribly rabid. "You're a lawyer. I'm a vampire. There is such a thing as professional courtesy."

"I'm serious."

She shrugged, stuck the toothbrush back in her mouth, and glanced at the mirror; I could see my reflection, but not hers. Eventually, she said, "I didn't *give* you that dream; you dreamed it by yourself. I just helped you remember it. What's wrong?"

"Nothing."

"Bullshit. Nightmare?"

"No."

She smiled at the mirror. "Okay. So I screwed up. Sorry; you looked happier than you had in years, and I thought..."

"*Years?*"

"I remember when you were a student. You went to University College, right? Rooms on Logic Lane?"

I nodded. "Someone in admin must have had a twisted sense of humour... You mean you've been *watching me for twenty years?*"

"No. Just while you were at Oxford. I liked you; Hell, some of us even fall in love. And I remembered your face, the way you looked at me, and when I saw you again..."

"Did you bite me then? When I was a student?"

She looked away from me. "Not seriously."

"Seven years and six months!" Humpty Dumpty repeated thoughtfully. "An uncomfortable sort of age. Now if you'd asked my advice, I'd have said 'Leave off at seven'—but it's too late now."

"I never ask advice about growing." Alice said indignantly.

"Too proud?" the other enquired.

*Alice felt even more indignant at that suggestion. "I mean,"
she said, "that one can't help growing older."*

*"One can't, perhaps," said Humpty Dumpty; "but two can.
With proper assistance, you might have left off at seven."*

— Lewis Carroll, *Through the Looking-Glass and What Alice
Found There*

There was nothing about Sylvia Sullivan in the news that morning,
and, as soon as the partners' meeting was finished, I asked Barbara
to put a call through to Sullivan; it'd be just like the pompous prick
not to tell me if she'd come back. She hadn't.

A moment later, Barbara walked in without announcing herself.
I put down the brief that Midas had given me. "What's wrong?"

"You're looking for Sylvia Sullivan?"

I shrugged. As far as I knew, no-one was. "Do you know where
she is?"

"No..."

"But?"

She sat down, uncomfortably. "I've seen her around the bars
before..."

I blinked. "Gay bars?"

"Yeah. Not often—maybe once, twice a month. I think she's got
some boyfriends, too. Nothing steady. Do you know her?"

Obviously not. "No."

"I don't know her well, either... we've had a few drinks, and
talked, but never fucked or anything... I don't even know who *has*
fucked her. For all I know, she may be straight."

I had to think about that. It didn't help. "I don't understand."

"She was lonely. I don't think she was looking to get laid, but
she probably wouldn't have said no if that was the asking price.
She just wanted to be wanted; failing that, she got drunk, and took
a taxi home. Do you know the Elton John song 'All the Young
Girls Love Alice'? From *Goodbye Yellow Brick Road*?" I shook my
head. "Pity. Sylvia... she's a good looking woman, married to an

old bastard who never fucks her without fantasizing he's fucking someone else. Can you imagine what that's like?"

I tried. "Where do you think she is?"

"I don't know. I haven't seen her in weeks. There are lots of places she might have been that night."

"Can you give me a list?"

She thought about it for a moment, staring out the window. "Maybe. Promise me you won't just give it to Sullivan?"

"Why?"

"If you find her, that's one thing. She may be running away, hiding, whatever, from the old shit; she may not want to be found. If you look for her, find her, I can live with that—but I'm not handing her back to him on a platter. I don't know her well, and I never fucked her, but I owe her that much."

"If she was trying to get away, wouldn't she just divorce him?"

She snorted. "Divorce Sullivan? Where would she find a divorce lawyer who'd dare? Some kid straight out of school, if she was lucky. And he'd have the Hatter doing the research, and you or Ashcroft or Midas if it ever got to court... More likely the old bloodsucker'd get some shrink to have her committed—"

I shuddered, and stared out the window. London stared back at me, secure in her bulk, like a dinosaur that doesn't realise that it's being killed. "Could *you* go?"

"What?"

"Go to the clubs, or bars, or wherever. Take my card, and the Jag, and a photo, and ask if anyone's seen her. If they haven't, you don't even have to tell me where you went." I turned away from the window, and almost managed to look Barbara in the eye. "I'll pay you overtime, of course."

She hesitated, then nodded. "When shall I start?"

"Are they open this early?"

"A few of them..." I tossed her the car-keys, and she backed out of the room. I looked over at the window again, at the thick grey clouds and the thin grey sunlight. All the young girls love

Barbara returned at five, and I handed her a wad of taxi vouchers. I didn't need to ask whether she'd had any joy. Getting lost in

London is easy—you don't even have to try—and I had no good reason to believe that Sylvia was still in London. I'd tried to persuade Sullivan to report her as missing, and he said he'd think about it (Jesus, I hate being lied to, even if it's by a professional). At least he found her passport; her credit cards were still missing, but they hadn't been used since a visit to Harrods on Saturday morning, a fact that cheered him immensely.

I met Barbara for breakfast the next morning. Someone who *might* have been Sylvia Sullivan had been seen in a bar on Greek Street on Saturday night. She'd talked to, danced with, and accepted drinks from at least three men and one woman, but the barman hadn't noticed if she'd left with any of them. "What do you think?"

"I don't know what to think... but it doesn't sound as though she'd *arranged* to meet any of them."

I sipped at my coffee, forcing myself to wake up. "I agree."

"What now? The taxi drivers?"

I shook my head. "The old man can only cover up for so long; soon, someone's bound to notice that she's gone, and then it'll be the cops' baby. Or she might come back." I probably didn't sound very convincing.

I was ten years old again, looking through a viewfinder and waiting for the flash to recharge, and Irene was sitting on my bed reading, and someone touched my neck and shoulder

I lay there, wide-eyed in the darkness, feeling as though I were trapped in a bed that was smaller than I was. My feet seemed incredibly far away, and the ceiling much too close, and the red-lipped girl standing beside the bed was

"You were dreaming again," Alice said. "I thought I'd better wake you."

I sat up slowly, vaguely remembering that I was thirty-nine years old and six foot two. "Thanks... I think. What's the time?"

"About four."

I peered at her blearily, and tried to focus; my night vision isn't what it used to be (but then again, it never was). "Where've you been—no, forget I asked. Was it a nightmare?"

"Don't you remember?"

"I—" I blinked, and suddenly felt very cold. "I—no."

She stared at me, shook her head, and turned to walk out. "No. Please." I rubbed my eyes. "Look, I won't be able to get back to sleep, now. Tell me more about Dodgson."

She stopped, looked over her shoulder, said "No," and continued walking.

"Why not?"

"You're lying to me."

I sat there, numb, and watched her leave. Finally, I muttered, "I'm sorry."

A moment later, she reappeared in the doorway. "Tell *me* a story," she suggested.

"What?"

"You're obsessed with a children's fantasist who's been dead for nearly a hundred years—even more obsessed than you were when you were seventeen. *Why?*"

"I liked his books a lot when I was a kid. My mother used to read them to me; she still loved them, probably because they were so English. When I went to Oxford, everyone seemed more interested in Charles Dodgson the pedophile than Lewis Carroll the fantasist... and it pissed me off, hearing them turn someone who'd written books that made so many kids happy into some sort of monster. I mean, there wasn't any evidence, none of the kids or even the parents accused him, *you* know it wasn't true... I guess it became my first libel case, in a way. I did my damnedest to prove him innocent..."

Alice stared at me, darkly, and then nodded. It was nothing but the truth, though she must have guessed it wasn't the *whole* truth... "Okay." She walked back into the room, and sat on the foot of the bed.

"There's a Dodgson story I don't think anyone else knows," she said, quietly. "A few people may have guessed—shit, *I'm* guessing most of it, but I had about thirty years worth of hints.

"Dodgson was always so nostalgic about his childhood that I don't think anyone's even *wondered* if he was abused as a boy. They don't know, or they forget, how much he hated his schooldays at

Rugby. Maybe they know that he impressed the teachers, but they don't realise how much most of the boys hated him. They may have heard that he had a reputation for being able to defend himself, but they didn't hear him wishing that his school had given every boy a separate cubicle instead of putting all the beds in an open dorm...

"Maybe it was an older boy; more likely, it was a lot of them, more than he could fight off. But I'm only guessing..."

They found Sylvia Sullivan's Gucci handbag in a trashcan near Canary Wharf that morning. It gave them the clue they needed to identify the body they'd found between two of the half-empty office blocks on Sunday. The skull had been so shattered by the fall that even the dental records hadn't been enough.

No one knew how she'd gotten up to the roof without setting off a dozen alarms. I had a sneaking suspicion, but I didn't think the coroner would believe me.

> There are skeptical thoughts, which seem for the moment to uproot the firmest faith; there are blasphemous thoughts, which dart unbidden into the most reverent souls; there are unholy thoughts, which torture, with their hateful presence, the fancy that would fain be pure.
>
> — Lewis Carroll, Pillow Problems

I rushed home at lunchtime and opened all the curtains in the house, except for the guest room. It was raining, of course, but I couldn't wait for the sun to re-appear. Alice was asleep, or dead, and her clothes were scattered over the floor. I searched her pockets, finding nothing, and suddenly she rolled over and looked up.

I opened my wallet, removed a photograph of Sylvia, and flipped it at her. She caught it neatly, and flinched slightly.

"You do recognise her," I growled. "I'd hoped I was paranoid. Did you kill her?"

"What makes you—"

"I saw the photographs of the body. There was hardly any blood at all. The coroner's trying to convince himself it was washed away by the rain. I've been trying not to wonder where you've been feeding, but now I have to know. *Did you kill her?*"

She shrank back, then shook her head slowly. "Me? No. She was already dead."

"You found her in the alley?"

"No. There was a feast on the roof." She smiled bleakly. "I was guest of honour—the new kid in town, so to speak. I didn't know she was a friend of yours."

My knees buckled, and I pitched forward onto the bed, crying for someone I'd barely known.

"Kaarina found her," Alice continued. "She's good at spotting suicides before they jump. I don't know the whole story; she hangs around the bars and waits until she sees a jumper, usually has a few drinks with them, listens for a while, tells them that she's thinking of suicide too, suggests they both go along together... Most of them chicken out. Sometimes they take her home, but she leaves before they find out what she is. Some of them... say yes."

I managed to lift my head and look at her. "For Christ's sake—" My voice cracked, and I tried again. "What sort of a monster—"

"I'm a vampire," she replied. "You said so yourself. Or a sidhe. Or a boojum, maybe. I can't help what I am, what I need—"

"You can help what you *do*," I snarled. "You told me you can get the blood you need without killing anyone—"

"Sometimes. It's not always easy."

I rested my head on my hands, wearily. "Easy. How easy do you think it was for Dodgson? Hating boys, but never hurting them, just shutting them out of his universe? Loving little girls, but never touching them apart from the occasional kiss? Jesus, even *Sullivan*, who's as loathsome a human being as I've ever met... he wants to fuck his daughter, but he hasn't, and I bet he never will. It's not what you want, I'll forgive you that, we can't help what we want, even if it's wrong or obscene... but Jesus, what you *do!*"

We stayed there for what seemed like hours, me kneeling by her bed like a mourner, before she whispered, "What do *you* want?"

"I want the killing to stop."

"Is that all?"

I shrugged. Alice looked down at me, then reached out and touched my shoulder where it met my neck, and whispered, "Who's Irene?"

"What?"

"When you dream, you call out for 'Irene'. You did when you were at Oxford, too. Who is she?"

I looked at her. My eyes hurt like Hell from crying, something I hadn't done in nearly thirty years, and all I could see was the dark hair and darker eyes. I knew it wasn't Irene, but it might have been...

"Irene..." I began. "Irene was the first. The first girl I... She...

"She, uh, lived two houses away, when I was a kid. Year older than me. Beautiful girl, really beautiful... her mother died when she was, I don't know, seven or eight I guess, and she lived alone with her father. He was a... I can't remember. Doesn't matter."

I took a deep breath, and tried to start again. "She was the best friend I had, and the only one who lived nearby. Her father wouldn't let anyone visit the house, but she used to sneak over to mine before he came home in the evening. Mostly, she liked to borrow books—he wouldn't buy any, or give her any money—or just sit on my bed and read.

"When I turned ten—she was eleven and a half—I had a birthday party, and invited her, but her father wouldn't let her go. We kept hoping that he'd change his mind, or come home late, or whatever, so she was sort of guest of honour... but she didn't turn up. Jesus, I'd forgotten that party, until—anyway, my parents were splitting up, though I didn't know it then, and it was sort of my father's way of saying goodbye. He gave me a camera—a good one, a Nikon, with a zoom lens and flash... I'd used his camera before, I was better with it than he ever was...

"Irene came over the next afternoon. The rain was pissing down, I remember that... she was saying how sorry she was that she hadn't come to the party, and she hadn't been able to buy me a present. I showed her the camera, and she asked if I'd like to take some photographs of her. I took a few close-ups of her face, and then she started unbuttoning her blouse. She said it was okay, her father took photographs of her, like that, all the time...

"I can still remember what she looked like; dark hair, like yours, big dark eyes; she was a little taller than me, but skinny, very small breasts, little pink nipples...

"When I'd taken a few photographs, we..." I tried to talk, but there was a lump in my throat that I just couldn't swallow. Finally, I whispered, "did some of the other things she and her father did all the time...

"It was 1966, I was ten, sex education was... well, my parents hadn't told me anything, and my teachers sure as shit hadn't. Besides, she kept saying it was okay, and I... I really liked her."

"Did your parents catch you?"

"No; I wish to Hell they had. My father wasn't home yet, and my mother... I don't know. Irene dressed herself, and ran back home before her father got there. Of course, *he* knew what had happened, and when she told him that I'd taken photographs...

"He had a gun—it was supposed to be for scaring off burglars—and he went into the bathroom and shot himself in the head. But not before he shot her.

"I don't think we heard anything; if we did, we probably thought it was thunder. The rest of the story didn't come out for another few days. When it did...

"When it did, my mother took my camera, and ripped the film out, and burnt it. I don't remember what she did to me."

I took a deep breath, and threw up all over the bed.

Alice was waiting as I emerged from the shower. She'd closed the curtains, and the darkness was almost comforting, like a confessional. I suspect I still looked like Hell, but at least I felt human. Almost. I tied a robe around myself, and collapsed onto the couch. "You said she was the first," said Alice.

"Yeah. Well. I didn't have sex with *anyone* else until I'd nearly finished high school—my mother made sure of that. Just before graduation, a few of my friends and I drove down to the Combat Zone, but that was a disaster; she was older than me, with big floppy breasts and badly dyed hair and... I didn't even *try* again until I won my scholarship and came to England.

"Soho was a nightmare. I'd been told it was London's answer to the Zone, or Times Square, but I could hardly find a picture of a naked girl who wasn't being spanked, caned or whipped. It was like the London Dungeon —you know, the horror museum for kids—where it's okay to look at nudes, as long as they're being executed or tortured. Christ. Besides, most of the models looked old enough to be my mother.

"After that, it... became better. Easier. I met a few girls at Oxford who were still in their late teens... blondes were best, and redheads. They didn't look as much like Irene, I didn't have to worry about using the wrong name, and eventually I got used to them, but it was never as good as..."

Alice nodded. "But you never fucked any other little girls?"

"Once," I admitted. "In Bangkok. There was a child brothel that a client of ours knew about, out in the back streets, they had girls as young as seven. I picked one who looked about eleven; I don't know how old she really was." I shook my head. "I couldn't go through with it, and finally she gave up and I paid her and she said 'mai pen rai', never mind. I've sent thousands of pounds to Thailand since then, sponsoring kids, but it hasn't made me feel any better.

"And I bought some kiddie porn, once, by accident. Honest. There's a group in America, called the Lewis Carroll Collectors' Guild, and I sent them some money for an illustrated catalogue. I was expecting limited editions or something, not pictures of... anyway, I burnt it. Only time I've ever burnt a book. I guess that's when I started trying to clear the poor guy's name."

Alice nodded. "What do you *want?*" she repeated.

I thought about that, and finally replied, "Nothing I can have. I want Irene to have survived. Even *you* can't do that."

"No," she said. "I can't. Is there anything *else* you want?"

I stared into the darkness. I could barely see Alice, just a pair of eyes and a hint of sharp teeth. "Innocence. If not mine, then... I want there never to be another Irene. I don't want any more little girls hurt. I want the obscenity to *stop.*"

Long has paled that sunny sky:
Echoes fade and memories die
Autumn frosts have slain July.

Still she haunts me, phantomwise,
Alice moving under skies
Never seen by waking eyes.

— Lewis Carroll, *Through the Looking-Glass and What Alice Found There*

Sullivan survived his wife's demise—politically, I mean—but I think it's put his challenge for the party chairmanship back a few years. His daughter, I'm happy to say, has been sent away to a boarding school.

There was a postcard from Bangkok in my In Tray this morning. *Having a wonderful time; Alice.* It's good to know things are going well; it wasn't easy (or cheap), sending a dozen Sidhe to Thailand, finding flights that left and arrived at night, arranging passports for little girls who were born fifty, a hundred, or a hundred and fifty years ago.

I take another look at the article in the *Telegraph*, warning about tourists disappearing in Bangkok, and white male corpses being found in the back streets. *Bled* white. And then I fold the paper, and reach for the atlas, and wonder where I'm going to send them next.

a single shadow

It was November, which made it nearly two months since I'd arrived in Tokyo, and the local shows had been much funnier when I hadn't really understood them—but the apartment was tiny and my bed was also the Tanii family's sofa, so I sat there and tried to read. Maybe by the time I went home, I'd have learnt the domestic deafness which is the Japanese substitute for privacy—not that I'd need it back in Perth, but what the Hell. When Mrs Tanii ducked back to the kitchen, I turned to Hiroshi and said, as *sotto voce* as possible, "Saw you with Shimako today. Does this mean you're back together?"

Anyone who thinks the Japanese are inscrutable hasn't seen one jump the way Hiroshi did. He stared at me for a moment, then whispered back, "No! Not me! Haven't seen her in a week!" and hurried out of the room. Miyume, his sister, glanced at him over the edge of her magazine, and then disappeared behind it again.

"Was it something I said?" I muttered, in English.

Miyume looked warily at me, then shook her head. "You must have mistaken someone else for him, Dai-Oni-San," she replied, also in English.

"Please don't call me that." Less than a week after I'd begun teaching, I'd become known as Tony Dai-Oni, Tony the Great Goblin-Demon. I mean, it's hardly my fault I'm red-headed, green-eyed, and nearly two metres tall, neh? "And don't try to tell me you all look the same, either. I know Hiroshi when I see him. He was even wearing my *Cerebus* T-shirt."

"There's nearly twelve million people in Tokyo, Tony-san," said Miyume, patiently. "There must be more than one *Cerebus* T-shirt. And if it was Hiroshi you saw, then it was not Shimako you saw him with." I could have corrected her grammar, but didn't. "You do not know her as well as you do Hiroshi."

That was true, but while I'm generally pretty good at remembering faces, I'm *excellent* at remembering pretty ones, and Shimako, while too young for me, was nearly as stunning as Miyume (whose name, aptly enough, meant 'Beautiful Dream'). Okay, so I've fallen in love with one of my students everywhere I've taught—or so it always seemed at the time. Maybe one day, I'll find some way of knowing when I'm *really* in love, and settle down instead of hurrying to the next city. "Maybe," I conceded, just to see Miyume smile before she vanished behind her magazine again. I sighed silently, and returned to reading *Kwaidan*.

I've never been very good at researching the places I visit before I get there, and most of what I knew about Japan came from the *Lonely Planet* guidebook, a lot of Kurosawa movies, a crash course in the language, and the works of Lafcadio Hearn—a half-Irish half-Greek dishwasher, proof-reader and hack writer turned translator, teacher and folklorist (my sort of person, neh?). He'd written book after book of Japanese exotica ('Kwaidan' is Japanese for 'Weird Tales') a century ago, and written them so beautifully that no-one really cared whether the legends, poems and horror stories they contained were authentic. I lost myself for a few minutes in his story of the Rokuro-Kubi; when I looked up again, Miyume had gone, leaving the magazine on the floor open at the centrefold—a colour picture of a fairly pretty Japanese girl of about Miyume's age, naked except for a strategically placed octopus. Back home, it would have been considered pornographic, but this was a family magazine, with comics and a sports section.

One day, I thought, I might understand the Japanese language—but the Japanese themselves, never.

The next day, I saw Hiroshi and Shimako again—this time, at Shinjuku station. It looked as though he was following her, and she ignoring him, but that might have been some sort of courtship ritual. Suddenly, though, she ducked into the ladies' room, leaving him standing outside, looking foolish. He hesitated for a moment, then vanished into the crowd... or maybe into the toilets, or behind one of the vending machines; all I know is that he wasn't there when I looked again, a second later.

I didn't think of it again until I returned home, and found him watching a video of *Terminator 2*. "Done your English homework?" I asked, teasingly, as I sat down behind him. He reached down and handed me a sheet of paper. I looked at it, and then up at the TV screen when I heard Hiroshi chuckle. The *T2*, shape-changed into the brat's foster-mother, had just impaled the foster-father... which meant that the movie had been running for at least half an hour. The homework, even if it'd been done with maximum haste and minimal enthusiasm, would have taken another half-hour... "When did you get home?"

"About four-thirty. Why?"

I could've sworn I'd seen him on the other side of Tokyo at a quarter to five, at the earliest... and it was barely quarter past. "Any phone calls for me?"

"No," said Miyume, from the kitchen, before Hiroshi could answer.

"Thanks," I said, and started correcting Hiroshi's homework, wondering why he might bother lying to me. Maybe he thought it was none of my business—or none of *anyone's* business. He was only sixteen, after all, and Shimako already had quite a reputation as a heartbreaker: maybe the affair embarrassed him. But why was Miyume covering for him? Well, she was his sister, as well as a Psych major; she must have known him better than I did, and presumably had her reasons.

I finished correcting the homework, then reached into my day-pack for my battered copy of Hearn's *The Romance of the Milky Way* and turned to the chapter of 'Goblin Poetry'. It was weird, I thought, how many creatures in Japanese mythology were shapeshifters, routinely taking human form to deceive their victims—or maybe not *weird*, not in a country where gangsters openly wore the emblems of their syndicates on lapel pins, but certainly interesting. I didn't much mind that Hearn had decided not to translate the stories of the Three-Eyed Monk, the Acolyte with the Lantern, the Stone That Cries in the Night, the Goblin-Heron, or even the Faceless Babe, but I wished he'd been more impressed by the Long-Tongued Maiden and the Pillow-Mover. I also would have liked to have known more about how Goblin-Foxes turned old horse-bones into beautiful girls; it might come in useful—

"Still reading fairy-stories again, Tony-san?" I looked up, to see that Miyume was standing beside me, shaking her head. "Are you ever going to grow up?"

"Sit down and say that. Besides, this is anthropology."

"Anth—?"

I tried to think of the Japanese word for 'anthropology', without success. "Ah... you've heard of Margaret Mead?"

"Yes, of course: didn't she do that book about Samoa, after all of the native girls had lied to her?"

"*Touche.*"

"I suppose you think we turn into cats and foxes when your back is turned?"

I smiled. "Only some of you—you, for example. You're much too beautiful to be human, but you could be a cat, a flower, a tree—no, scratch that one, you're too short." I glanced at Hiroshi. "Maybe Shimako's the tree-spirit," I said, softly. Hiroshi ignored me, but Miyume covered her mouth and laughed.

"I assure you, I'm quite human," she said. "I don't doubt that Shimako is, too. And how many girls have you used *that* line on, before?"

"I think that one's an original."

"Thank you," she said, too politely. "What line did you use on your girlfriend in Taipei?"

"Mei? I tried writing her a poem, but my Chinese wasn't up to it, and her English..."

"And the one in Bangkok? Or Mexico City?"

"What are you trying to do, write my biography?"

"I'm trying to understand you, Tony-san. Isn't that what you're trying to do to us?" She leaned closer, and whispered, "Or do you just want to sleep with us?"

"Only you," I whispered back, without any hesitation; Mrs Tanii didn't understand English, and Hiroshi knew how and when to keep his mouth shut, "and only if it's what you want."

"Why only me?"

"Because it's only you I'm in love with. Don't Japanese ever fall in love without burning down Tokyo?" In the tiny park near the apartment, there was a memorial to O-shichi, a seventeen-year-old girl who'd been burnt at the stake in 1683 for torching her father's house in an ill-advised attempt to re-unite herself with her samurai lover.

Miyume laughed, loudly enough that Hiroshi turned around to look at us. She glanced at him, and he hastily returned his attention to the television. "Of course we do," she said, in more normal tones. "We haven't always regarded it as the most important thing in the universe, or everyone's inalienable right, but then, neither have Westerners... and we no longer think of it as the great dragon-demon, either. It's just something that happens."

I shrugged. I grew up on a farm, didn't even see a city until I went away to university, and I've long suspected that romantic love is like traffic jams and good bookshops, something you're much more likely to find in cities and the bigger the better. If you see a thousand women on the subway every morning, you can pick and choose, or at least *dream*: living in a small country town, you take what you can get. Me, I'd chosen to spend the five years since I graduated in some of the largest cities on Earth, cities so crowded you rarely saw your own shadow. "What about you, personally?"

"Me?"

"Have you ever been in love?"

She raised her eyebrows innocently, and smiled broadly. "Of course, Tony-san, but love is one thing, and sex another. Please remember, this is not Australia: rents are high here, privacy expensive, and most of us can not afford to leave home until we have been working for many years—often, not even then. Competition for places in the universities is much more intense—you must have heard of Examination Hell—so we have to spend more time studying." She pointedly didn't even glance at Hiroshi. "And our doctors will not prescribe the pills which your teenagers take for granted—perhaps because they believe them to be too dangerous, but possibly because they make too much money out of abortions. I know it's not romantic, but Japanese girls have learnt when and how to say 'no'; the meek little women who do everything men tell them are as mythical as your *kitsune*, *rikombyo* and *gaki*. In truth, we rule our men from birth; that's why they work so hard to keep what power they have, and why they never come home at night." Then she bent over, kissed me quickly on the tip of my nose, and ducked back into the kitchen.

I sat there, rubbing my nose absent-mindedly. *Kitsune* were goblin-foxes, and *gaki* were hungry ghosts, but what the Hell were *rikombyo*?

I found the answer in Hearn (where else?): a *rikombyo*, literally 'ghost-sickness', was a dopplegänger, an apparition created by unrequited love, or the love for someone now dead. In the poem Hearn quoted, the rikombyo stayed at home with the original, both yearning after the far-journeying husband, but Hearn also stated that 'one of these bodies would go to join the absent beloved, while the other remained at home'.

I looked over at Hiroshi, and shook my head. Sure, I loved ghost stories and old legends, but this was one of the most modern cities on Earth, it was like believing that there were vampires in Washington... well, you know what I mean. Besides, Hearn had written that rikombyo were 'of the gentler sex', whatever that meant in Japan...

I continued to stare, until the movie ended and Miyume began setting the table for dinner.

On Saturday night, Miyume took me to a party at Tokyo University to meet her Psych class. I was suspicious of her motives—Hiroshi had told me that she had at least three boyfriends at the university at any one time and was careful not to show favouritism to any of them, so this may have been just another psych experiment—but what the Hell, I would have followed Miyume into a leper colony or karaoke bar.

Once at the party, Miyume disappeared into the throng, presumably giving equal time to her troika (triad?), and leaving me to dance and converse with a group of students who knew even less about Australia than I did about Japan. It was exhausting, but amusing, and at least no-one asked me to sing; more importantly, it gave us a moment of real privacy on the way home, as we walked from the station to the apartment. Miyume had been teasing me about having drawn a crowd, and I was accusing her of the same. She denied it, and I asked, "So what were they? *Rikombyo?*"

She laughed unconvincingly, and said, "Of course not; there's no such thing. I told you that—"

I looked at her, and realised she was lying. She tried walking faster to get some distance between us, but it was a wasted effort; I could *hop* faster than she could run. "Then why do I keep seeing Hiroshi following Shimako when he's supposed to be somewhere else?"

"Then it couldn't have been him; you were mistaken…"

"No I wasn't. *Was* it a *rikombyo?*"

"I told you, there's no such thing; you saw someone who *looked* like Hiroshi…"

"Next time, I'll take a photograph."

"It won't work," she said, as we hurried through the park, and then stopped suddenly at the memorial to O-Shichi, her face white. We stared at each other for a moment, and then I asked, "You knew, didn't you?"

"Knew what?"

"About Hiroshi."

"No," she said, quietly. "I didn't know about Hiroshi until you told me."

"About *rikombyo*, then."

"Of course; I told *you* about them, if you remember…"

"They exist?"

"Yes, they exist," she said, heavily. "They're rare, and you can't duplicate them in a laboratory—it's been tried—but yes, they do exist."

We stood there in silence (apart from the passing traffic and the occasional plane from the nearby airport), and then I said, "Laboratory?"

"Psychologists have tried to create them, usually with hypnosis. It's worked sometimes, but not often enough for anyone to risk making a fool of himself by presenting a paper on it."

"Jesus."

"We still don't *really* know what causes them. What do psychologists know about love, anyway, right?" she said, with a twisted smile. "We know they're rare—but even if they were one in a million, there'd be twelve of them in Tokyo alone. They're real enough to fool anyone in most circumstances, but they don't cast shadows or show up on film. And we know they're sterile; we managed to get a sperm sample from one, and no, I'm not going to tell you how. There are old stories about men and women having sex with them; they're—said to be very good lovers, because they're eager to please and that's really all they exist for. Rather like butterflies."

"And do they die after a day, too?"

Miyume smiled. "You keep saying how often you've been in love, Tony-san; does *that* die after a day? However long the love lasts, unrequited and with that sort of intensity, *they* last. Usually, they just disappear. We've never found a body of one; I suspect a lot of suicide attempts are really *rikombyo*, but that's just a theory, I can't prove it."

I shuddered. "What'll happen to Hiroshi?"

"I don't know. Probably nothing; usually, they just get over it, find someone else who loves them back, fall sanely in love instead of madly."

The shock hadn't quite worn off by Monday, when the *rikombyo* followed Shimako into my English class—but Domeki-sensei was too polite to mention it, so what was a humble teaching assistant like myself supposed to do? A few of the girls giggled behind their hands, but nothing more; Shimako herself remained as poised as ever. I was sufficiently startled that it took me (me!) most of the lesson to recognise the telltale signs of a teenage girl who's just gotten laid and is trying not to be too visibly smug about it.

I stared at the *rikombyo* while earnestly trying to explain Australian Rules football to the class. He was as inscrutable as the Japanese are supposed to be. I babbled on, wondering if this was a tremendous hoax; perhaps there was no apparition, only an obsessive teenager who'd skipped a class to—

No. I knew the Japanese well enough to know that this being tolerated, especially this near Examination Hell, was much less likely than a ghost in a classroom. The lesson continued harmoniously enough until the siren sounded for the next class—the second-last of the day, I remembered with relief. A moment later, I remembered that Hiroshi was in that class... and he always rushed there, hoping to see Shimako before she left.

Shimako seemed to be taking forever to pack her bag and leave the room; she was only half-way to the door, with the *rikombyo* puppy-like at her heels, when Hiroshi walked in.

Back home, it would have been the prelude to a screaming match, maybe even a brawl... but Hiroshi merely looked from one face to the other for a few seconds, his expression horrified, then stared straight into the *rikombyo*'s eyes. It looked for all the world like one of those scenes from the Kurosawa films, the contest of wills between two samurai: for a moment, the apparition seemed to fade into the dingy painted wall—and then Shimako took a step forward, and then walked past Hiroshi without looking at him again. The *rikombyo* followed her out. Domeki-sensei turned to the blackboard, and began writing.

I was on my way to the station that evening, when I saw Shimako again. The *rikombyo* was still following her, but this time, he was wearing a *Cerebus* T-shirt again, with a new pair of Levi 501s and even newer Nikes—way beyond the Taniis' budget. He seemed taller, too, with clearer skin: in fact, I realised, though unmistakeably male, he looked more like Shimako than Hiroshi...

I scanned the crowd for the real Hiroshi, but there was no sign of him. I caught the next train to Shinagawa, and walked to the apartment. He wasn't in the living room, or his bedroom, but the place didn't feel empty. I tried listening, but the traffic noises from outside drowned out any recognisable sounds of movement. "Hiroshi?"

No answer...

I stood in the living room for a moment, and then noticed that Miyume's bedroom door was closed. I knocked on it softly, and there was a distinct gasp from within.

"Miyume?"

There was a sound inside that might have been scuffling, and then "What is it?"

"Can I come in?"

"No! Don't open the door!"

Despite myself, I smiled. "Okay... but I need to talk to you. Hiroshi... well, it's about your, uh, psych experiment. Look, I'll be waiting in the living room, okay?"

I collapsed onto the sofa, closed my eyes, and tried to think. Finally, I heard Miyume's door open, and then close again. I recounted the afternoon's events as concisely and dispassionately as I could, and concluded, "I guess the rikombyo's about equal parts Hiroshi's frustration and Shimako's narcissism, now. Is that common?"

"No."

"What'll happen now?"

"I don't know," she said, sitting beside me, smelling unmistakeably of dynamite sex. "It will probably disappear before very long."

"Or Hiroshi will... has he been home?"

"No."

I nodded, and opened my eyes. Despite her obvious worry, she was still glowing and looked even more beautiful than ever. "Your boyfriend—is he a psych student, too?"

"No."

"You might as well bring him out; he can't stay in there forever."

She smiled hesitantly, and something went click! in my brain. I rolled off the sofa, and hurtled down the corridor.

"Tony! NO!"

Opening her bedroom door would have been obscenely rude even in Australia; in Tokyo, it was probably a capital crime. But I had to know—

He was red-headed and nearly two metres tall; I couldn't see what colour his eyes were in the dim light, but I didn't need to.

I don't know how long we stared at each other, but suddenly Miyume was standing behind me. "You said you loved me," she whispered. "Isn't it good to know you were telling the truth?"

I turned around, and then walked out of the apartment without another word.

The youth hostel had a nine o'clock curfew, which was ridiculous for Tokyo, but it gave me time for a few drinks and a decision. I was on contract until the end of the school year, so I couldn't leave Tokyo... but if I stayed in a hostel and stuck to a vegetarian diet, I could save enough for an airline ticket. It only remained to choose somewhere to go.

The more Kirin beer I drank, the better Taipei looked. I could spend some time with Mei, maybe get my old job there back... I changed a few notes for coins, and headed for the phone.

The phone rang five times before being answered by a man with a faint Australian accent. It took me a moment to recognise my own voice, and then I hung up immediately. Then I went to the bar, had another drink, and my shadow and I went back to the hostel and to bed.

transit

I had just turned nine when Aisha walked into my classroom, stopping the conversation and stealing my heart in the same instant.

I think we all stared, and then, as Aisha looked back defiantly, we dropped our gazes back to our books as though we were suddenly interested in Stigrosc prime number theories. Pat, our teacher for the day, smiled a little thinly. "Class, this is Aisha, from al-Gohara."

A few of us looked up and muttered greetings, as Pat guided our new classmate to a seat near the doorway. A message from Morgan flowed across my book. *Pregnant*, e opined.

I glanced at Aisha's golden-pale profile out of the corner of my eye. *Don't think so*, I replied.

Must be. Look at the size of those boobs.

It was hard not to, despite Aisha's loose and very opaque sky-grey robe, but that would have been even more impolite than passing notes in class—and class was meant to teach us social skills: we would have learnt math much faster at home. *Can't be*, I protested. Aisha was taller even than Pat, at least two metres, but all the al-Goharans I'd seen were taller still, and Aisha probably wasn't much older than we were.

Morgan stared at er book for a moment, obviously gossiping to someone else. I stole a quick glance at Aisha's face, which was beautiful. Especially those eyes, rounder and darker and larger than any I'd seen outside of books. I love you, I thought, and was startled to see I'd written it on my book. I erased it hurriedly, relieved that I wasn't still passing my notes to Morgan, and went back to my math. A few of the kids were starting to talk again, but none of them spoke to—or about—Aisha.

Maybe they don't have contraplants on Al-Gohara, Morgan suggested, a moment later.

They must have, I replied.

Muslims aren't like us, Morgan countered, and then, *I bet they cut Aisha's thing off.*

What?

They do that. They used to, anyway. Ask my dad.

Why?

E couldn't answer that, and there was almost nothing about al-Gohara in my book or my ramplant, and I couldn't access the library during class without Pat noticing. All I could remember was that al-Goharans, being Muslims, liked to travel to Earth once in their lives, and their world was only one solstice jump from daVinci, with the worlds being in conjunction every six point something years (math isn't my forte, and I don't think anyone human *really* understands Stigrosc cosmography). From here, they went to Marlowe or Corby or Ammon, but that usually meant staying on daVinci for up to a year waiting for the next solstice. I was only three or four years old last time they'd visited, and the al-Goharans usually stayed near Startown, where they'd built a mosque, and didn't socialise much, but I'd never heard of them bringing their children here before. I wondered whether Aisha even spoke Amerish, and tried to imagine a voice that would match those eyes, that golden face, those breasts...

Aisha suddenly looked up, jacked out of er book, and then walked over to Pat's desk and whispered something. Pat looked startled for a moment, and then nodded. "Of course; I'm sorry, I didn't think of it. Will you be coming back today?"

Aisha smiled, whispered something else, and then walked out of the room. I remembered reading that Muslims had to pray so many times a day—though whether that was an Earth day, an al-

Goharan day, or a daVincian day, I had no idea. Maybe I could ask Aisha.

Aisha was standing in the shade under the trees at the edge of the basketball court, leaning against one of the old cedars with a book in er lap, but it was obvious from the way er eyes tracked that e was watching the game, or the players, or maybe their clothes: smoke and mirrors were back in fashion again, and modesty wasn't. I found myself watching Morgan's legs, as usual—e liked to wear the briefest, tightest shorts possible, to show them off—but kept wondering what Aisha's must look like.

I'd accessed the library as soon as class was over, and discovered that the gravity on al-Gohara was .82, the climate generally warmer but less humid, and the day nearly thirty standard hours; the ship, the *Arakne*, (Stigrosc don't give names to their ships, but they allow the human passengers to christen them if they wish to) had only arrived three days before, so e was probably still adjusting. I summoned forth all the courage I thought I might have and had never needed before, and walked over. "Hi," I said. "I'm Alex. I'm in your class." Aisha nodded, and we watched the game for a moment. "Do they play basketball on al-Gohara?" Another nod. I wondered what I was doing wrong, and realised that I was asking yes-no questions. "How do you like it here?"

The only reply to that one was a quick glance, and an expression I couldn't read through er shades. The solstice isn't for nearly a year, I thought; you're going to have to talk to someone sometime...

I saw Teri weave past Shane and slam-dunk the ball amid scattered applause, and Aisha muttered something; the words were unrecognisable, probably Arabic, but the tone said, clearly, 'Not bad'.

"Do you want to practice your Amerish?" I suggested.

Another glance, and then, quietly, "Don't you have any friends?"

"Sure," I replied, slightly nettled. "I'm just lousy at basketball, is all. If I were as big—I mean, *tall* as you, I'd probably be great. *You'll* probably be great, when you get used to the gravity; everyone will want you." At least I managed not to bite my tongue.

"The gravity isn't a problem," e replied, and muttered something that sounded like 'initially'. "It's less than Earth's, and we've been training for that. It's—"

"What?"

"Nothing. You just do things so differently here. I wanted to come to your school—it's been so boring on the ship, with no-one else my own age—and I had to pester my father to let me, but it's..."

I waited.

"Don't girls go to school on daVinci?"

"What?"

"I suppose I should have learnt more about the place before I came here. I'm sorry I didn't, but there wasn't very much about it in our library: we don't travel much, except the men, and that's usually only on Hajj... Do your girls decide not to come after they turn twenty-five, or is there some sort of law against it?"

I stared, calling up words from my ram and trying to understand what Aisha was saying, and hoping that I didn't look as stupid as I felt, if that were possible. "Or have they just sent me to a boy's school by mistake? I haven't even found a girls', uh, bathroom—"

A painful silence followed. "We don't have segregated schools," I began, "or segregated toilets, or segregated *anything*. We can't: we're all... we don't..." Oh, gods, I thought; this must be what Morgan meant when e said that Aisha's thing had been cut off. "I'm not a... I mean, I *am* a..." I took a deep breath. "Can I ask you a question?"

"I don't know. Can you?"

I tried to smile. "Do you know what 'monosex' means?"

It must have been Aisha's turn to stare at me. "What? No. What?"

"Or 'maf'—'hermaphrodite'?"

"You mean, like the Chuh'hom?"

"Yes. Monosex is the opposite; it means to be male or female, but not both..."

"But..." Aisha edged away from me slightly. "You mean *you're* a hermaphrodite?"

I nodded. "We all are."

"You mean, everyone in the school?"

"Everyone on the *planet*..." I replied, and then a thought hit me. "Well, except..."

Aisha slid slowly down the tree to sit with er arms wrapped around er legs, murmuring something in Arabic. I waited. "I've never met a hermaphrodite before," e said, weakly.

"I've never met a—girl," I replied, after a moment's thought.

A suspicious stare. "How come you know what the word means?"

I shrugged. "Old films and novels. Besides, we call our sports teams girls and boys—no-one wants to wear uniforms, so the ones with the shirts are girls. I don't know why; it's probably something that used to mean something once, like giving out gold and silver medals, or talking about 'going the whole nine yards'—" I glanced at the outline of Aisha's breasts, and suddenly guessed the origin of the custom. The feeling of knowing, discovering, *that* was more of a buzz, a jolt, than anything I could remember ever learning in class.

The game ended, and kids started drifting back into the classroom. I stood there silently, not wanting to leave Aisha.

When everyone else had disappeared, Aisha looked up, er golden face even more pale than usual. "This is too—" e looked around. "Do you think the toilets would be empty now?"

"Huh? I mean, yeah, sure."

"Great." I offered my hand, to help er up, but e ignored it and struggled to er feet without my help. We walked to the doorway, and Aisha stopped, until I offered to go inside and make sure there was no-one else there.

"Can you tell the teacher that I'll be back tomorrow, initially?" Aisha said, when e emerged.

"Sure," I said. "Will you be?"

Aisha hesitated, and then shrugged. "I don't know. I'll have to ask my father."

I nodded. It had never occurred to me before that monosexes had fathers, though it probably would have if I'd thought about it for a few seconds. "See you," I said, wondering if I'd ever see Aisha again, and knowing I had to.

I spent most of the afternoon accessing the library, to find out what I could about monosexes. There was a lot of stuff I'd never imagined, like needing separate pronouns for each gender—'he' and 'him' and 'his' for males, 'she' and 'her' and 'hers' for females. They seemed sort of redundant, but Amerish thrives on redundancy, and the female pronouns sounded exotic enough that I practiced using them whenever I thought of Aisha.

Monos were extremely rare away from Earth, except in some religious enclaves where no-one had maf chromosomes: otherwise, it required major surgery, which almost no-one bothered with. The first human mafs were born a few years post-contact, but the chromosomes were discovered by humans, not Stigrosc: Stigs don't believe in genetic engineering. Mafs remained a minority on Earth for more than a century, but many of them—us—travelled to habitable solstice worlds, where there was unrestricted birthright. Others became crew on the Stigrosc ships, or emigrated to the neutral worlds; Stigs can't tell one human from another, and the Nerifar say we all taste the same, but Chuh'hom and Tatsu find it much easier and safer to communicate with mafs. Meanwhile, on Earth, as gene surgery became easier and cheaper and more countries adopted 'one couple—one child' laws, mafs were seen by many governments as a way of avoiding serious gender imbalances in the population, and various incentives were offered to prospective parents—cheap health insurance, exemptions from combat service, places in the schools or the civil service or diplomatic corps reserved for mafs, that sort of thing. According to the library (which was at least seven years out of date), mafs made up sixty-eight percent of the population of Earth—and more than ninety-nine percent of the permanent populations of Marlowe and Avalon, where the al-Goharans would also have to stop en route.

There was nothing in the library—at least, nothing I could access—about how monosexes made love. I was wondering about that when school closed, and I guess I still looked pre-occupied when I went home: my mother, who is normally very careful not to invade our privacy, asked me what was on my mind.

"There was a new kid in class, today," I replied. "Off the *Arakne*. Her name's Aisha."

"Is that the one who's pregnant?" asked Rene, without jacking out of er eternal *Vaster than Empires* game. Sometimes I think that unrestricted birthrights are over-rated; I get on okay with Kris, but I think Mum and Dad should have stopped when they'd had one kid each. "She's not pregnant," I snapped. "She's..."

"She?" asked Kris.

Okay, *sometimes* we get on okay. "It's old English," Mum explained. "I didn't think the al-Goharans brought their kids with them..."

"They never have before," Dad agreed, without looking away from the holo. "How long is the trip? Two or three years each way? Hell of a time for a kid that age to be travelling—how old is e?"

That was Dad all over, making a judgement before e had any of the facts. "I don't know; she's tall, and her Amerish isn't too good, and she dresses like... I think she's about twenty-five or twenty-six," Kris stared, and almost dropped er book. "In al-Goharan years, which is—" My ram converted that into thirteen to thirteen point five standard. "Nine, roughly, so she'll be about twelve when she gets to Mecca."

"Great," said Dad. "Three years of er life wasted going to see a crater."

"Mecca's not a crater any more," I informed er. "Well, it is, sort of, but the radiation's down to a safe level, and they've built a new mosque and stuff. There was a load of new data for the library on the *Arakne*—stuff about Earth and a lot of other worlds, and only a few years old."

"Anything about how to get rid of razorvine?" e asked, sourly.

"Not that I noticed." As far as the library was concerned, razorvine was unique to daVinci (lucky us). It was probably a mutant strain of our terraforming fauna; it grew at about the same rate (much faster than the cyberfarms could process it into anything useful), and in everything from deserts to rivers, but was much harder to kill. Anything buried beneath it might be lost forever: it blocked infra-red and radar, and thrived on spotlights and X-rays. And it wasn't even attractive—the same monotonous tarnish colour as the solamat we use for major roads, with inedible seeds that you couldn't pick without the risk of losing a few fingers.

Dad's a builder, so e regards it as a personal enemy, but most kids play hide and seek among the thickets at least once—or as often as we can without our parents catching us—and there are the usual stories about secret tobacco farms hidden within razorvine jungles. "There *are* some new games and shows, from Musashi," I added, and Rene and Kris grinned, "and I don't know what else."

Dad grunted, and watched the holo for a few more minutes, then stretched. "Want to shoot a few hoops before dinner?"

"Sure, Mum?" said Kris, heading outside. Mum glanced at me, then folded er book. I was the last one outside. As usual.

"A Muslim monosex," Dad muttered, as e collapsed onto the bed. My parents' room was well sound-proofed, of course, but easy to bug on the rare occasions that I wanted to listen in. "Okay, e's nearly an adult, e's got er implants, you'd expect er to have crushes and fool around a little, but there are *dozens* of kids er own age here, why—"

"E'll only be here a year," replied Mum. "Besides, it may be good for Alex to get to know some off-worlders. You know e's good at xenology; e might even be a diplomat."

"Not if it needs math," said Dad.

Mum sighed. "E's better at languages than we ever were, and e enjoys them. I wouldn't be surprised if e learnt Arabic before this friend of ers flies away."

"What good will that be?"

"How many mathematicians do we need on a world this size? Biologists, builders, designers, artists, yes, but mathematicians? And what if e wants to go off-world?"

"Why would e?" retorted Dad. "What the Hell can e get off-world that e can't have here?"

Aisha arrived in class a few minutes later than the rest of us, clad in the same loose grey hooded robe or another exactly like it. Her dark eyes were slightly clouded, and I guessed she was having trouble adjusting to the shorter days. I thought of pointing out that she'd get more praying done this way, but I wasn't sure how she'd take it, and I couldn't think of anything else to say.

Our teacher for the day was Jai, an old fossil with a murmuring voice and an inexplicable enthusiasm for economics, both of which e used to try to explain the half-million years of human history pre-Contact. Most of us were already confused long before e came to the impact of third wave tech, and when e admitted that the whole thing had collapsed soon after the Stigrosc arrived anyway, most of us became irritated as well.

"This is irrelevant, isn't it?" asked Teri, while a few of us chuckled.

Jai bit er lip. "I rather hope so. You see, history is a wonderful labour-saving device; it saves us re-inventing and re-discovering so much. True, all these economic theories were based on the idea that resources were scarce and humans needed to work to survive. By the first century pre-Contact, of course, the scarcities were usually manufactured for commercial or political reasons—so that the rich could stay rich, or nations could control their populace by denying them food—and the work ethic had become a cancer. Many people worked at jobs they hated because they'd been convinced that there was no other way to survive; by the time the Stigrosc came to Earth, it would have been cheaper to simply feed, house, educate and entertain most of these people—but that would have violated the work ethic and destroyed the illusion of scarce resources. In this regard, capitalism and communism were almost indistinguishable—and when the Stigrosc arrived, and *gave* us cyberfacs and habitable planets, asking only for those ideas and data which were free to every human, both systems became, as you say, irrelevant. Our new economic system is, to a large degree, another gift from the Stigrosc—but, unlike all previous human economic systems, it is founded on the idea that human demand will never outstrip resource availability. If this happy state of affairs should change, then we will need a new system—and those of you who've been paying attention will have some idea which ones *not* to try." E drew a deep breath, and then—apparently for the first time—noticed Aisha. E glanced at the book open on er desk, and asked, "I gather things are the same on al-Gohara?" She was silent. "The cyberfacs and robots provide what is needed, and no-one is compelled to do work that they hate?"

Aisha shook her head violently. "No, of course not," she lied.

"Of course, there *are* some people who cling to the old ways," Jai continued, "simply because they are human ways—or, more importantly to many of them, *not* Stigrosc ways. Most of them are still on Earth, because they regard Earth as a human world, or because they *own* parts of Earth in a way they can never own part of any other world. What good this ownership does them now, I leave to you to imagine; if any of you succeed, please explain it to me. Aisha, it's nearly noon; do you want to go and pray? Now, are there any other questions?"

"Tell me about your world."

We were sitting under the old cedars by the basketball court again. Aisha glanced at me, and shrugged. "Why?" she asked. "You don't want to go there, do you?"

If all the girls there are like you, I thought, I might, but I didn't say that. "I won't know until you tell me," I replied.

She smiled slightly, beautifully. "It's warm, and much drier than it is here, and the sun's not quite as bright—"

"I know all that. Tell me about the people."

"People are people." She looked warily at me, daring me to challenge her.

"How much difference does having two sexes make?" I asked.

She looked even more wary. "I'm not going to discuss sex with—well, you're a *boy*."

"I'm also just as much a girl as you are," I replied, mildly.

She looked thunderstruck at that, then shook her head violently. "There's more to it than having a—besides, you don't have..." She looked puzzled for a moment.

"If you want to know what I *do* have—" I began.

"I don't—"

"You can access the library."

Aisha blinked, and then laughed. I waited until she'd finished, and added, "That's how I know what you've got. Sort of. I mean, I... unless you..." I sat there, trying to find the words.

"Have I been circumcised?" she asked, at last. "No. That was a primitive custom, much older than Islam and explicitly condemned in the Qur'an—you have heard of the Qur'an?—and while some Muslims on Earth did it, so did some Christians. By the time the Stigrosc arrived, it had been stamped out nearly everywhere, like foot-binding or breast implants. But there's more to being a woman than just the body."

"We can all get pregnant, if that's what you mean."

"No!" she said, shaking her head again. "More than that!"

"What, then?" I asked, but she stood and walked away. I tried following her, but she kept walking faster, and her legs were much longer than mine. I walked faster, and she began running. Finally, she ran out of the school and down the razorvine-edged road to Startown, and I didn't follow her.

The next day was Saturday, and I'd resigned myself to not seeing Aisha. Kris had slipped out early to play basketball and get out of gardening, which we both hated. Mum always maintained that if we did it often enough, we'd come to enjoy it as e and Dad did, but e let me go after an hour of cauterising the razorvine that was beginning to encroach on the watermelons. I spent the rest of the morning with a portrait program, trying to see if I could produce a fair likeness of Aisha, and maybe slot both of us into an old movie, a pre-Contact one with monosex characters: *The Princess Bride*, maybe, or *War for the Oaks*. That way, I could just superimpose her face on a female body, rather than have to try to imagine hers. Unfortunately, nearly all of the female bodies in the art history catalogue were of women from Earth gravity, while the few from the Martian Republic were *too* tall and slender. I'd always known that ideals of beauty varied between eras and ethnic groups, but seeing the demonstration flash before my eyes was startling. I'd never imagined that there were so many ways to mutilate living bodies.

I managed to devote three or four hours to Aisha's face, and another two to her figure, before succumbing to the temptation to access some pictures of female genitals. They looked incomplete, even deformed, with just this little bump where the penis should be, but apart from that, they looked just like mine or Morgan's. Males, I discovered, had external testes where the vulva should be, in what looked like an uncomfortable, if not hideously hazardous, position.

After forming a recognisable template of Aisha, I scanned us into *Forbidden Planet*; the eyelines gave me a little trouble, but once I'd fixed that, it looked wonderful, and it even made sense.

On Sunday, I made the mistake of reading a love poem by Andrew Marvell, 'To His Coy Mistress'—*Had we but world enough, and time*—and became determined to see Aisha again, or at least to *try*. The library told me that Sunday wasn't a religious holiday for Muslims—their Sabbath started Friday and finished Saturday—and there was nothing to stop me walking up Tranquillity Road to Startown; Aisha, a lightworlder, did it every day. Mum let me go with nothing more than the usual caution to be home before nightfall (razorvine is attracted by light, and can supposedly move fast enough to engulf anyone walking with a lantern), and I slipped out before Dad could object.

The streets of Startown were all but empty, but there was a soccer game in progress (if you can use soccer and progress in the same sentence) on Eagle Street two blocks from the mosque, and it had drawn quite a crowd—some of them in long-sleeved robes, some in jeans and shirts. I watched for a few minutes, scanning for Aisha, but though I noticed a few pale and beardless faces, I couldn't see any women present at all, or anyone under fifteen. I attracted some stares, not all of them friendly, but no-one questioned my right to be there.

A few minutes after the whistle blew for half-time, I heard the sound of a single, powerful voice booming from the direction of the mosque, and everyone turned and walked towards it. I followed until the last of them had disappeared inside the doors, and then headed back towards my home.

I'd reached the edge of Startown when, suddenly, it began raining. I heard doors open behind me, and laughter, and turned to see al-Goharans rushing out into the street, most of them staring at the sky and catching raindrops in their mouths as they laughed; a few even removed their skull-caps and let them fill with water before upending them over their heads. I turned about, but though I searched down every street, I couldn't see Aisha anywhere.

Eventually, after the rain stopped, I returned home, hearing the waterfed razorvine growing around me as I walked.

That evening, I began learning Arabic: the library had teaching programs for most languages, even ones that had been dead since before contact. It was a little easier than Chuh'hom Oratory, and it might even be useful.

"Why?" Aisha demanded.

"Why what?"

"Why are you learning Arabic? And why do you want me to help you?"

"Well, al-Goharans are going to be staying here after every solstice," I replied, reasonably enough. "We should have *someone* here who can speak to them without an interpreter."

"We all speak Amerish."

"Then why do you learn Arabic?"

"The Qur'an must be read in the original; all translations are invalid."

"What do you speak at home?"

"My mother used to call it Amerabic," she replied, and a beautiful smile suddenly appeared on her face. "Sometimes we'll start a sentence in one language and want to say something that's easier in the other language, so we switch. It's whatever language we think in—here, everyone speaks Amerish, so I think in Amerish."

I nodded. "I went to Startown yesterday, and everyone there was speaking Arabic."

"That's—you did *what?*"

"I went to Startown. I watched the soccer game for a while; then it started raining, and everyone seemed to get a big kick out of it."

"It doesn't rain very often on al-Gohara," she replied, looking at the cloudy sky with distinct approval. "I don't think I've ever seen it rain like *that* before."

"Then why weren't you out dancing in it like everyone else?"

"I—" She turned to stare at me; her beautiful face turned pale, and then pink. "That's none of your business. Anyway, I'm sure it'll rain again before I leave, initially."

I realised, suddenly, that all the times I thought she'd said 'initially', whether or not it made sense, she was really saying 'inshallah'—'if Allah wills it'. "Oh, sure," I replied. "Or maybe you can stop at New Seattle on your way back. Do you mind if I ask you a question?" She continued to stare, so I didn't wait for her to answer. "Are there any other girls—or women—in Startown?"

"No."

"Why not?"

"That's two questions..." She turned away from me, and watched the basketball game for a while. I was beginning to suspect that the reason she almost always headed for this clump of trees at lunchtime was that she *liked* talking to me, but wanted to make sure there were always plenty of witnesses, as though she was willing to regard me as a girl from the neck up. "Do you remember what Jai was saying last week about scarce resources and the Stigs?"

"The parts I stayed awake for."

"What she, he—what should I call him?"

"E," I replied, without hesitation. "We're all 'e', except you."

"Okay. What e said doesn't really apply on al-Gohara. There's one resource that's still scarce, and the Stigs control it: that's passage to Earth. The hajj, the pilgrimage to Mecca, is one of the five pillars of Islam, but there isn't enough room on the Stig ships for all adults to make the journey even once, so places are awarded randomly by a computer. At least, they are on al-Gohara; I don't know how it's done on other Muslim worlds."

I thought about this for a moment, and asked, "And women aren't allowed to go?"

"It's a little more complicated than that... women *are* allowed to go, but not without their husbands, so unless the husband has also won a place on the ship, the woman gives it to her husband. Or sometimes to her father, or an adult son, or she can trade it, inshallah. And there are some who think the computer may not be perfectly random—"

"Trade it? For what?"

Aisha shrugged. "Favours. Prestige. Luxuries that the facs don't make. A better marriage for her children, maybe, inshallah."

"Arranged marriages?"

She nodded. I refrained from whistling or swearing, but it was a near thing. "Some women complain about not going, but the men just blame the Stigs for not having bigger ships: some even say they're doing it to weaken our faith, because the Stigs won't even let us fill the ship, just in case someone wants to leave the worlds we visit en route, which no-one ever does. The imams and califas have tried petitioning the Stigs, but they don't seem to understand about religion, and almost no-one from," she hesitated for a moment, "other worlds, the non-Islamic worlds, ever wants to visit Earth. Anyway, if the Stigrosc cared enough to want to break our faith, they could leave all of us stranded on al-Gohara forever."

"Sounds like you're lucky to be here."

"Lucky?" She considered this, moving the tip of her tongue tantalisingly across her upper lip, as though tasting the air. "I'm lucky to be going on hajj, and glad I'll be an adult by the time I'm there, but I miss having other girls around. Men are boring."

I had to know. "How did you get a place when other women don't?"

"My father wouldn't leave me on al-Gohara alone."

"What about your mother?"

"She's dead," Aisha snapped. "Okay? Can *you* leave me alone, now?"

I walked to the other side of the playing field, so I could see her and pretend I was still watching the basketball game. The game ended a few minutes later, and I saw Morgan, wearing little more than a translucent helix of swirling silver light, glance at me meaningfully before walking off hand-in-hand with Teri.

Despite that setback, I finally *did* persuade Aisha to coach me in Arabic, after only four weeks of mispronouncing words and hideously mangling the grammar. In a moment of random curiosity, I learnt that she was named after Muhammad's third wife, and that her name was also Japanese for 'manipulating an overly sympathetic or soft-hearted person', a discovery that we both found hilarious.

Weeks passed, and though I became fairly good at reading and speaking Arabic, I couldn't write it or think in it. Aisha couldn't invite me to her home, nor come to mine, but occasionally she'd let me walk with her almost as far as Startown, on the condition that I stayed on the other side of the road. The only people who ever saw us were the razorvine clearing patrols, and they must have mentioned it to Dad, because one evening e said, with all the casualness of a sun going supernova, "Some al-Goharans volunteered for the clearing crews today, want MacLeod and me to teach them how to handle the lasers."

No-one spoke. I just stared at my dinner and kept chewing. MacLeod was Morgan's mother, and I wondered if e'd put them up to this.

"I don't know whether they were getting bored, or whether they just liked the idea of killing something," Dad continued, "but there was at least a dozen of them. There's nothing else happening at the moment, so we said yes."

"Maybe they want to thank us for our hospitality," replied Mum, mildly.

"Or maybe they don't want us coming any closer than we have to," said Dad. E seemed remarkably calm about the idea of armed al-Goharans: of course, the lasers have genescanners and safety switches built in, so you can't actually aim them at a human, and bouncing them off a mirror is much trickier than the thrillers make out. Dad wasn't setting me up to be murdered, but I wondered what e thought would happen to Aisha.

Kris looked from one to the other. "Why would they thank us for that? It's free. I mean, if we said no, the Stigs would stop coming here, right?"

Dad shrugged, and turned er attention back to er soup. Rene's eyes bugged. "No more Stigs? You mean no new games?"

"Relax," I told er. "It'll never happen. It's in the treaty the Stigs signed before they gave us Avalon and Terranova—that a ship would visit every human world every solstice, so we could always go back to Earth, or out to any new worlds..."

"Okay," said Dad. "What do you think would happen if, say, the al-Goharans landed and discovered that there was no mosque at Startown, or no food or water, or no cyberfac? Would the Stigs still keep coming?"

"The Stigs would," I replied, "but the al-Goharans might not..." My voice faded out, and we stared at each other in silence until Mum said, softly but pointedly, "None of us understand the Stigrosc well enough to know what they'd do. Or the al-Goharans, for that matter."

Aisha heard about the al-Goharan crews that same night, and the next day she asked me not to accompany her home again, in case her father heard about it and ordered her to stay away from the school altogether. On daVinci, that would be considered probable cause for a charge of child abuse, but I decided not to tell Aisha that: I was still wondering what I *should* say when she leapt up, and volunteered for the basketball game, on the sole condition that whatever team she was on would be the girls. I stayed on the sidelines and watched. Despite the gravity, she moved beautifully, like a gazelle with breasts.

To my irritation, this became a set routine for a few weeks: we'd be talking about something, when suddenly she'd stand up and join in one of the games. She wasn't quite as fast as Teri, and she had trouble allowing for the gravity when she had to throw the ball any distance, but she knew how to use her height and her reach, so she was always selected, while I usually had to sit back and watch. On days when it was too wet for basketball, she would sit in the classroom and watch the rain through the roof. "This is wonderful," she murmured. "Our buildings are made the same way as yours are—though the ceilings are higher—but they're designed to keep the sunlight out; I don't think this would ever have occurred to us. Even when it's not raining, I love watching your clouds, all the shapes, the way they move..."

I've never been that enthusiastic about rain myself, but I nodded. "You should see it in winter, when it thunders—but I guess you'll be gone before then..."

"Yes," she said, still beaming, and then, unexpectedly, "It's my birthday tomorrow."

"Happy birthday. How old will you be?"

"Twenty-seven: that's about, oh, nine and a half of your years."

I hesitated, then plunged in. "Of course, you could stay here."

She stared at me, and then shook her head sadly. "My father would never let me, Alex."

"So don't ask er." There was a shocked silence as I did the math. "In half a year, you'll legally be an adult—"

"Not on al-Gohara—"

"Right; you're *not* on al-Gohara. You're on daVinci, and subject to daVincian law—so you might as well enjoy its benefits. When're you considered an adult on al-Gohara, anyway?"

She looked away, as though she was fascinated by the way the rain trickled down the windows. "On my wedding night," she said, finally, very softly.

"*What?*"

"Of course, most women don't really treat you as an adult until you have a child of your own. Boys are legally considered men after puberty—do you know about puberty?"

I grimaced, and nodded, remembering my first and (so far) only period, before I had my contraplants inserted. "Sure," I croaked. "Is this part of your religion, or—"

"Some of it," she replied. "Some of it is tradition, I guess. Our ancestors weren't just Arabs; they came from every continent on Earth, and they brought a lot of different traditions with them." She shrugged. "My mother used to say it was intended to keep the birthrate up—we can't breed as fast as you can—but she may have been joking, I don't really know."

We sat there in silence for nearly a minute, before I asked, "Is this what you meant when you said that there was more to being a woman than... well, having female parts, being able to get pregnant..."

She nodded. "Well, it's also important *not* to have—male parts, or you'll never be trusted around the women. If you were to come to al-Gohara, the men wouldn't want to know you, and you'd be barred from places that were only for men *and* only for women, and you certainly wouldn't be able to marry. Men are permitted to marry non-Muslims, but women can't, so even if one wanted to... It'd be the worst of all possible worlds." She turned to look at me, and I noticed that she was on the verge of tears. "For you, that is. For us, it's—"

"Home?"

"More than that. It's... a world we created for ourselves." She looked down, and then scrambled to her feet and rushed out into the rain, looking at the sky, letting the rain run down her face. I just sat there and watched her, trying to think of the right thing to say, and finally I walked out behind her, stood within arms' reach but too scared to touch, saying nothing, nothing, nothing.

Weeks passed, and we spent them saying nothing, until Cori was giving us a lesson in xenology. Aisha was as fascinated as I was, possibly more so; unlike the rest of us, she'd actually *met* Stigrosc and Chuh'hom and Nerifar. Cori was becoming slightly bogged down in the details of Nerifar triads, thanks largely to Teri's love for asking unanswerable questions, when Morgan interrupted to ask, "Nerifar don't have any religions, do they?"

"No," replied Cori, er relief apparent. "They have a complicated ethical code, which is almost entirely concerned with sex and food, but because they don't believe in owning any more than they can actually carry—which isn't much—it's short enough for most of them to memorise."

"Like a hafiz," I interjected. Cori looked blank. "Someone who's memorised the complete Qur'an," I explained.

Morgan glanced at me, er expression unreadable, and then smiled back at Cori. "But they don't claim that this ethical code was handed down to them by any sort of deity?"

"No. It was originally composed as a series of songs—peace treaties from various wars, marriage vows, divorce decrees, medical treatises, lessons for children, proverbs and parables, that sort of thing. But because it's never been written down, there's no standard version; it's sung differently in different clans, new verses are always being added, and a few were changed or edited out when they were discovered not to be true, like the one about kidneys..."

"In fact," said Morgan, er smile becoming wider and er voice impossibly sweet, "none of the other species we've encountered— or that the Stigrosc have encountered and told us about—have anything we would call a religion, or a deity."

Cori considered this. "The Nerifar... don't, the Chuh'hom... don't, the Tatsu don't... We don't really understand enough about Stigrosc or Garuda culture to be sure; they often seem to regard the universe as a sentient being on a time scale beyond our comprehension, which I suppose you could consider a deity..."

"But they don't believe that it handed down a set of laws they had to obey?"

"Only mathematical laws—which for a Stig or a Garuda, is pretty important. But not their ethical codes."

"And none of them believe in a single ancestor for their entire species?"

"No."

"What about the Garuda egg?" asked Jo.

Cori nodded. "Well, the first Garuda presumably *did* hatch from the first Garuda egg, but the 'Garuda egg' in their histories contained *everything*, so it's probably a metaphor—or a poor translation—of the Big Bang. The Nerifar don't have any similar stories—the only mentions of eggs in their coda are instructions on how to care for them and when not to eat them—but the Nerifar didn't know the rest of the universe existed until the Stigrosc landed on their homeworld."

Morgan nodded. "Do any of them worship their ancestors?"

Cori considered this. "No. Chuh'hom worship the community; they believe in a form of reincarnation, but they're still arguing about whether souls can travel between planets, and if so, how fast." Chuh'hom love to argue, and their committee meetings should be avoided at all costs. "The Nerifar eat *their* ancestors, and never speak the names of the dead. Male tatsu worship their mothers, and no-one knows what the females think. Stigrosc revere their descendants, and if Garuda worship anything, it's the sky."

Morgan grinned, and sprang er trap. "Would you agree that only humans had religion because it was invented by human monosex males and enforced with violence, to compensate for the fact that they couldn't bear children, that their role in creating children was ridiculously small and for all they knew, might have been non-existent, performed by someone else—the same inadequacy that produced lunatic ideas like penis envy, sentient sperm, and women as mere incubators? That its mainspring was the idea that the *father* was the creator, not the mother; the father was omnipotent and omniscient, the father knew best—but not better than *er* father, or er father before er, and so on until the golden age before women fucked everything up?"

There was a brief silence while Morgan paused for breath. I glanced at Aisha; her face, normally pale, was the colour of dried bone. Cori began saying, "Well, I think that's a—", but Morgan was unstoppable. "And that becoming complete, becoming mafs, so that *everyone* could create children, could know that feeling, did even more to kill off the old religions than the bombing of Mecca and Rome?"

Cori—who was only eighteen or twenty, and had never been a mother—gulped, and began again. "I think that's an oversimplification; I don't think there's ever a single cause for anything as complicated as—" but I didn't hear the rest, because Aisha had run from the room, and I followed her.

She was running down Tranquillity Road, and I could *feel* her screaming, though she was saving her breath for the race. Her legs were much longer than mine, and she was nearly acclimatized to the gravity, and I didn't have a chance of catching her before she reached Startown unless she let me. She was at least halfway there before she began to collapse; fortunately, she slowed down enough that I could catch her before she hit the solamat. Holding on to her wasn't easy—standing up, my eyes were on the same level as her breasts—but I supported her as best I could while she cried onto the top of my head.

"It's okay," I murmured into her blouse. "E just doesn't understand, that's all."

She sniffed. "Do *you* understand?"

"No, but... I'm *trying* to understand. Besides, I..." I took a deep breath and said it very quickly, "I've been in love with you ever since I saw you and... well, Morgan and I used to..." I tried to remember an Arabic term for 'go steady', and couldn't think of one.

"What?"

"Well, I guess you could say we were... girlfriends, or something. Nothing serious, just kid stuff—kissing games, that sort of thing." She pulled away slightly and stared at me through her shades. "You don't play games like that on al-Gohara?" She shook her head

— 89 —

violently. "Well, I guess it's different for you. We all have the same sort of, uh, equipment, and we get to see each other naked in the change rooms, at the beach, places like that, or look in a mirror... but I think Morgan's a bit jealous." I shrugged. "I guess that's one thing we haven't gotten rid of."

Aisha raised an eyebrow at that, and then began crying again. "Thanks for coming after me... I'm glad we can say goodbye."

"It's—what?"

"I can't go back to school. Not after *that*."

I stared at her, suddenly weighed down by a horrible feeling of heaviness, of sinking. "Goodbye, Alex." She grabbed my head, kissed me quickly and violently, and then let go and turned away. I tried to yell something, but my mouth seemed to be stunned. I watched her walking, and then ran after her.

"And do what?" I panted. "Stay at home all day every day until *Olivia* arrives?" She kept walking. "Okay, you don't want to go back to school, you don't have to, neither do I, we can still see each other."

"No we can't."

"There's an empty house, way out of town, all on its own; it's a great place, completely private, and I have a key." She stopped, and looked curiously at me. "It belonged to Mad Cousin Yuri. It's a long story. Anyway, it's at the end of Barrows Road, you know, the turn-off we just passed..."

Aisha shook her head, and started walking faster.

"Send me a note if you change your mind," I called. No answer. "Or send me a note anyway, any time you want to talk. Please?"

She stopped, and turned. "Inshallah," she murmured.

"Is this why you call him Mad Cousin Yuri?" Aisha asked, staring at the half-finished artworks that lined the walls.

I nodded, wondering how Aisha had convinced her father to let her out unchaperoned. "E was my father's cousin, not mine: e wanted to be an artist, and e was pretty good at it, but e hated working." Aisha laughed. "E convinced erself that the only way e was going to finish anything was by removing erself from society altogether, so e petitioned for a house out here, no one around but the friendly neighbourhood razorvines. A lot of people tried talking er out of it, but e had the right to a house of er own, and the builders couldn't claim to be too busy or anything, so it got done; they cleared the land, built a road and the house, and moved er stuff out here. E stayed out here for three weeks." Aisha laughed. "E came back occasionally, staying for a week or two at a time—and usually with a model or two, rarely on er own. Dad never really let er live it down—it was the first house e'd ever built, which is how I got a key—but Yuri was too easy-going to get upset. E managed to finish a few small things—some portraits, a lot of sketches, a statue or two—but e was just too fond of the cafes and the bath-houses."

"Isn't there a bath here?" asked Aisha, a little nervously.

"Sure—down the hall, second right. You want to take a bath?"

"I'll need to wash before I pray..."

Stupid of me. "Yes, there's a bathroom—down the hall, there."

"Then why did e have to go to bathhouses?"

"Ah," I said, sitting down on a chair that was twice my age. "Well. We go to the bathhouses for sex—I mean, *I* don't, you have to be at least eleven, that's about thirty-one of your years—but that's what they're for. I think that's where my parents met, or at least—" I noticed that Aisha was looking disturbed, even slightly revolted, and shut up. I'd had to wait five weeks before she contacted me, and another four before she'd agreed to meet me here, which left only eleven weeks and three days before *Olivia* arrived—Time's winged chariot hurrying near, as Andrew Marvell would have said.

"We may be more different than I thought," she said, softly, staring at the picture that Yuri had been working on er final visit here. It was a sketch of er favourite model, Kai, the one e used to joke about being buried with. E was very pregnant, and topless—or bottomless, rather; Yuri hadn't drawn er below the waist, just a halo of curly hair, a beautiful round face, and beautiful round breasts with large nipples the colour of Aisha's eyes. "I mean, I shouldn't be lying to my father, I shouldn't even be here with you, especially not *alone*..."

I waited for her to say more, but she didn't. "Why not?" I asked. "I mean, we're not even *doing* anything—"

"But we *might* be!"

"—and what if we were? Whose business is that but ours?"

"You don't understand!"

"No! I don't!"

We glared at each other for a while, and then she shook her head. "What do you want?" she asked, softly.

"Where do I begin? I want to—I want us to be able to see each other whenever we want."

"I'm leaving in eighty days."

"You could stay here; you could be happy here—" She raised her eyebrows at that, and then blinked, as though the idea had never occurred to her before. "Anyway, we were talking about what I want. Next thing on my list is, I wish I knew what you wanted."

She continued to stare, and then shook her head. "So do I," she whispered. "Alex, you've been wonderful, you've been kinder to me than anyone since my mother..." She turned away, and I could tell she was about to cry; I reached up and out to touch her shoulders, comfort her, but stopped when my hands were only a few millimetres away. "My mother," she repeated, rather stiffly. "Was executed. For adultery. *Now* do you understand?"

I had the feeling that I was understanding less and less the longer I knew Aisha; I shook my head.

"My father brought me with him on this trip because he didn't trust my mother's family to watch me, he thought I might disgrace him—"

"That's—"

She turned and faced me, tears in her eyes and a crooked smile on her lips. "And how do you get on with *your* father?"

"That's not the point." I took a deep breath. "Okay, so maybe it is the point. But I know *my* father is wrong about you—and about a lot of other things. Is yours?"

"I'm here with you, aren't I?" She glared at me, then glanced briefly around at the windows, and then removed her scarf. As I stared, she shook her long hair free, pulled her jacket open, stepped out of her skirt, and then stood there wearing only a pair of pants and a strange harness-like garment covering her breasts. A moment later, that popped open, and then she removed her pants and sat down on a chair opposite me, legs slightly apart and one foot propped up on the seat. She was even more beautiful than I'd imagined.

"Now do you understand? On al-Gohara, I'll be my mother's daughter until I'm my husband's wife. Here, I'd be considered a freak, mutilated, incomplete—and that includes emotionally as well physically, sexually. We couldn't even have children naturally!"

I admit, I hadn't thought that far ahead—I couldn't legally switch off my contraplants until I was fourteen—and I was surprised that Aisha had. Of course, if 'naturally' meant 'without gene surgery', then she was right, but so what? Or was that against al-Goharan law, too? Suddenly, uncontrollably, I began laughing.

"What's up?"

I took a deep breath and leaned back in my chair. "I'm just glad I didn't fall in love with a Stigrosc; that would have made my life *really* complicated."

Aisha stared, her eyes bugging slightly—and then she, too, burst out laughing, which set me off again. I slid out of the chair and kneeled in front of her, close enough to almost taste her, close enough to hear her heartbeat. I reached out and stroked her hair, running my hand along the side of her face down to her lovely neck—and felt/heard the cry of the muezzin, transmitted through the bone from an complant, calling her to *zuhr*, noon prayer. She looked into my eyes sadly, then grabbed her clothes and ran to the bathroom, while I collapsed face-first onto her chair.

I heard the bathroom door slide shut, and then open, and she disappeared into Yuri's bedroom to pray (it's considered inappropriate to perform *salat* in a bathroom). When she re-appeared, fully clothed, I was sitting back in my own chair.

"When *Olivia* arrives..." I began, as she walked towards the front door. She stopped. "Just in case I don't see you before then," I said. "*Olivia* won't be able to wait for you; it'll only have an hour or two to rendezvous with the shuttles before going to the jump point. If you're not on the shuttle in time, your father will have to choose between you and waiting another six years for er hajj—six years *here*. Which do you think e'll pick?

"We can hide here," I continued, quickly. "Or, better still, we can hide in the razorvine; even if they can find us, they'll never be able to cut us out in time—"

"I can't stay here either," she said, "not in this house, not on this world..." and then she walked out. I stared at her back, waiting for her to turn around; then, when she disappeared behind the next hill, I grabbed one of the razorvines that was snaking around the house, feeling the thorns bite into my palm and my fingers, standing there silently, knowing that Aisha wasn't coming back, and understanding nothing.

The clouds were the same grey as Aisha's robes, and the razorvine rustled and groaned alarmingly as I biked down the road towards the starport. I'd crept out of the house as soon as the sun had risen, after the longest night I'd ever stayed awake through. I hadn't heard from Aisha since Ramadan began, five weeks before, and that had been just another goodbye. She hadn't even answered my mail; maybe her father had taken her book away. If e had, e'd know I was here, waiting; if not, she would.

I watched the first bus arrive as the shuttle hangar unfolded like a flower, then heard another bike behind me. I turned, and saw Morgan, dressed in jeans and a fine mesh jacket against the morning cold, dismount and walk towards me. "Saying goodbye?" e asked.

I didn't answer; I just turned my attention back to the shuttle. I couldn't see Aisha, but maybe she'd boarded while I'd looked away.

"I've been reading about monosexes," e said, sitting next to me. "Boys, girls... they were almost never friends. They didn't understand each other well enough, they were taught to want different things... It was really a scary idea, not being friends with your lover. I was really glad we'd gotten past that." I said nothing. "E's not going to stay, you know."

I saw a figure in grey, slightly shorter than the others, walking towards the ramp, and reached for my nocs. It was Aisha, and she looked around before sliding up the ramp and into the ship. "I thought we were friends," said Morgan. "We were friends for a long time, since we were kids. I thought we might even be lovers, one day. You know, you hurt me pretty badly, dumping me like that."

"I'm sorry," I said, quietly.

"Especially dumping me for er," e said, with some real bitterness in er voice. "A monosex. Someone who's not even *complete*. How do you think that made *me* feel, knowing I couldn't compete with half a person?"

"She's not half a person," I replied, dully.

Morgan shrugged, as the first bus pulled away and another crowd of al-Goharans filed into the shuttle. "Well, e'll be happier with er own people."

I opened my book: no new messages. Morgan opened er jacket as the sun broke through the clouds. "So, what happens now?"

I looked at er for the first time that day. "We're friends," I said, gently. "You're one of the best friends I ever had, and I'm sorry I hurt you."

E smiled, and shrugged. I leaned over and kissed er. "And I'm going to miss you," I said, and ran towards the shuttle, yelling "Wait!" at the top of my lungs.

The pilot was Jessi Vokes, Teri's mother, and e *knew* that I was still nearly twenty weeks short of turning ten—but e also knew that there wouldn't be another ship leaving for nearly four years. Faced with this dilemma and a strict schedule, e called my mother, who—to my astonishment—told er that I had er permission to leave, and woke Kris and Rene so we could say goodbye. Perhaps fortunately, fathers don't get a vote in these matters. We lifted off only a few seconds behind schedule, and docked with *Olivia* with time to spare.

The human crew here are doing their best to keep the mafs and the Muslims apart, so I haven't seen Aisha in a week—and, fortunately, her father hasn't seen me. But I have seen Nerifar, and Chuh'hom, and I hope to see some Stigrosc when they've finished shedding their skins. The ship's library is even better than the one on daVinci, and full of recent data about the planets we'll visit.

The atmosphere on Marlowe is rich in neon and the aurora look like waterfalls of blood, especially during the season they call Not-and-Live. Aisha and I will legally become adults there, long before *Isis* arrives. I think I could be happy staying on Marlowe, despite the weather, but if Aisha decides to continue on her hajj,

I'll follow. They say Avalon is as beautiful as Earth was between the Ice Ages, but if Aisha doesn't want to stay there, either... well, I've always wanted to see Earth. And after Earth, we have time. And worlds enough.

double action

The motel bed was only slightly smaller than Brian's cell had been. Brian stood on one side while the man in the suit, on the other side, hauled a suitcase up on to the bed. The case was as cheap and anonymous as the room, even though Brian knew that the man in the suit had money. His bail had been set at a quarter million, more money than he could imagine one man owning. The suit looked expensive, too; hell, the haircut and the shoes probably cost more than Brian's family had made in a week. The man reached into one of his pockets for a key-ring, and unlocked the small padlocks on the case.

Brian said nothing. The deal had been simple; his lawyer was waiting outside in the carpark, watching the door, but this meeting was strictly private. The man opened the case, and labouriously turned it around so that Brian could see inside. There were five guns, most of which he recognised from his father's magazine collection, and he began edging towards the door. If someone had bailed him just to have him executed...

"Relax," said the main in the suit. "This is a business deal." He picked up a small assault rifle, one-handed. "Ever seen one of these babies?"

"No."

"K2. Korean .223. This one's only semi-auto, but it has a 30-round clip. What about this?" He picked up a small handgun with his left hand, and tossed it onto the bed in front of Brian.

"Derringer." Without looking down, he picked up the handgun and examined it. ".357 Magnum." He managed not to whistle. The rifle remained pointed at the ceiling, even when Brian opened it to make sure it was loaded. It was.

"That's right. Good."

Brian glanced down into the case at the other guns still inside. "So what's the deal?" he asked, trying to sound tough.

The man smiled. His teeth looked expensive, too. "You've attracted a lot of media attention, Brian—do you mind if I call you Brian?"

Brian tried to smile back; the result looked more like a sneer, but the man didn't seem to mind. "For quarter of a million dollars, you can call me just about anything." His lawyer made a point of always calling him Brian, stressing his youth—he was still three weeks shy of sixteen—while the prosecution team called him Mr Bridger.

The man in the suit nodded. "Seven people killed in one morning. Nine wounded. And all with an old .30-30 Winchester and a 1911 Colt .45." Brian said nothing. "Not a record by any means, even for somebody your age, but you've made headlines around the state." He glanced into the case, and removed an oversized handgun with an enormous helical-feed magazine. "Ever seen one of these before, Brian?"

"Only pictures of one."

"9 millimetre, 50 shot magazine." He placed it, and the shotgun, on Brian's side of the bed. "Go on, they're yours. The others too."

Brian stared at him. "What's this all about?"

Another expensive smile. "Did you ever hear of Patrick Purdy?"

Brian hesitated. "I've heard of Purdy shotguns."

"No, different guy. Patrick fired into a schoolyard himself, a few years ago, in California. Killed five, wounded twenty-nine. But he used an AK-47 clone." Brian nodded warily. "Probably the most common assault rifle in the world; my father brought one back from Vietnam, preferred it to the M-16. They've probably sold better than Big Macs. But they never sold better in California than immediately after it got out that Purdy had used one. I remember seeing people standing three or four deep at the counters; a lot of shops sold out in less than a week. Of course, part of the credit for that has to go to the gun control lobby—people got scared that the AK would be banned, and so they rushed in to buy one. Or take the Glock. Used in the Killeen massacre—two pistols, twenty-two dead without needing to reload. Great advertising—do you know how many Glocks we sold after that? Not that they really needed it, they'd always been controversial, but *these* guns, on the other hand, just aren't selling the way they should. They're excellent guns, they're not even particularly expensive, it's just that people haven't heard of them."

Brian looked at him, puzzled. "Who are you working for?"

The smile twisted for a moment, as though Brian had made a joke in very poor taste. "I can't tell you that," he said, "that's part of the deal I made with your lawyer. For the record, your bail's been paid by a charity that's opposed to harsh sentences for minors, no affiliation to any manufacturer or business or any other organisation, and nobody's supposed to know where you got these guns from. If need be, we'll start a rumour that it was the gun control people, that usually works. People will always believe what they want to believe."

"What do you want me to do?" He took a few seconds to think of the right word. "Plug—I mean, endorse these guns? Like I was an athlete or something?"

"Exactly."

"You want to do an ad with me using these guns?"

The man's smile melted. "Not quite. I can see all sorts of legal problems getting ads like that onto the air—not to mention the fact that we couldn't pay you without the government confiscating any payment as the profits of crime. Of course, they can't stop news being reported, can they? Can't stop it getting out which guns were used? And so we can use the money to pay for good lawyers, instead, do plenty of research on the jurors before it gets to *voir dire...* we can probably get you out in a few years." Brian looked blank.

"Do you need me to spell it out? I know you took care of your parents and your ex-girlfriend, but what about the guy she left you for? Out of hospital already, and he's delivering the eulogy at her funeral this afternoon." He pushed the suitcase towards Brian—just a few inches, but enough to make him look down. "There's enough firepower in here to take out everyone you hate—they'll all be there—then turn yourself in. You'll make the headlines, and we'll do the rest. What do you say? Do we have a deal?"

Brian picked up the handgun and looked at it, then pointed it straight at the man's tie-pin, flicked off the safety switch, and squeezed the trigger. The first few rounds flattened themselves against the man's kevlar vest, but recoil jerked the gun upwards, sending bullets through his neck, mouth, and forehead. Blood, brain and bone fragments splattered against the wall and ceiling of the anonymous decor.

"Sounds good to me," said Brian. He stuck the Derringer in his pocket, then bundled the rest of the guns back into the suitcase and closed it. He picked up the case and, smiling broadly, walked to the cemetery.

Every news magazine in the country showed pictures of that smile, the next day. It was a very expensive smile.

amendment

"What's on now?"

"Lunch?"

Carol shrugged, leaned against the wall outside the hucksters' room to let a knot of people pass, and looked at her pocket program. "'The Future of Sf', 'Politics and Parallel Worlds', 'Jobs in Space', or *Moonraker*," she read. Lee grimaced. "Hey, it was filmed on location," Carol said, blandly.

"Yeah, with centrifugal force provided by Ian Fleming spinning in his grave," said Lee, who'd hated every Bond film since Connery had quit. "Who's doing the Parallel World panel? Heinlein?"

"No. H. Beam Piper, L. Neil Smith—"

"Give me Liberty, or give me lunch!" intoned Lee; both men were fervent Libertarians. "Personally, I'll take lunch. McDonalds?"

Carol returned the program to her pocket. "Okay, as long as you promise not to run around yelling 'It's a cookbook!' this time."

Lee grinned. "Promise." They headed for the door, but were intercepted halfway across the lobby by a teenaged gopher in a *Battlestar Galactica* jacket and flared jeans. "Lee," he panted. "The Day Manager wants to see you, she says it's urgent."

The grin twisted into a frown. "Did she say what it was about?"

"Something about the signing session for Heinlein," said the gopher, not quite going into a defensive crouch. "She says there's someone here from L.A. who might cause trouble."

"What sort of trouble?"

"I don't know. All I know is what she told me. Come *on*."

Lee glanced at his watch, a cheap digital. "Yeah, okay. I guess there's no such thing as a free lunch-break." He turned to Carol. "Are you free for dinner?"

She batted her eyelashes. "No, but I'm inexpensive."

The grin re-appeared. "Great. Be seeing you."

Penny, the day manager, was a solidly built woman with a *Property of Klingon Rollerball Team* button atop her huge right breast, opposite her name badge. "So this Preacher guy's a big fan of *Stranger in a Strange Land*," Lee repeated, to show he'd been listening. "So're a lot of people; I don't think it's a great book, but that doesn't mean he's crazy."

"It would if he liked *Number of the Beast*," muttered one of the *Illuminati* players behind him. Lee smiled; Penny glared.

"And he's bought a day membership because he wants to meet Heinlein," Lee continued. "So what? What's he done?"

"What *hasn't* he done?" said the day manager, heavily. "He's a doper and a thief and a pimp, and he's spent more time in jail than out, but I'm not worried about that, I'm worried about what he *might* do."

"What might he do?" asked Lee, patiently.

"Anything!" Penny drew a deep breath. "Look, Lee, you don't know this guy. He named one of his kids Valentine Michael. He was thrown out of a con in L.A. for supplying pot to minors, allegedly in exchange for sex. He used to be a Scientologist, and there are rumours he was a Satanist as well. He ran a nudist commune out in Death Valley, for Christ's sake!" Lee laughed, but turned it into a cough. "Three former members of his harem are in jail for murder!"

Lee raised an eyebrow at that. "Harem?"

She nodded, almost dislodging her glasses. "They stabbed and hacked three people to death and wrote lines from Beatles songs on the walls with their blood. The girls confessed; the D.A. tried to prove that Preacher was involved and they were protecting him, but there was no hard evidence and he couldn't make it stick, and Preacher just found himself some new women."

"When was this?"

"About ten years ago. '69 or '70. It was in all the papers—at least, it was in L.A.," she admitted. "But a lot of witnesses said he was heavily into knives and swords. Throwing them, too."

"Why do they call him Preacher?"

"It's what he calls himself. Sometimes. His women call him Charlie."

"Have you seen him here?"

"Not personally."

"Do you know if he's carrying a knife?"

"No, I *don't* know, but even if he's not, one of his women might be carrying it for him. I'm not expecting him to be violent, but he might... I don't know... ask Heinlein what human flesh tastes like, maybe offer to bring him some. Even if all he does is get his women to strip off in the signing session, or ask him to autograph their breasts, Heinlein's seventy-three, something like that could kill him." Lee, who'd lived in New Orleans for nearly half his life, and had briefly worked as a janitor and bouncer in a local burlesque club, swallowed a smile. "They say Preacher once met one of the Beach Boys, kissed his shoes, and ended up taking him for a hundred thousand dollars and some gold LPs," Penny continued. "I'm not asking you to frisk him or anything, just... keep an eye out for him. Okay?"

Lee shrugged. "Look, this is Texas; it's perfectly legal to carry a knife. And there's a stall in the hucksters' room selling everything from shuriken to bastard swords. But if you want me to shadow this Preacher for the rest of the day, I'll do my best, though you'll need another redshirt for the art show... What does he look like, anyway?"

She laughed. "That's easy. Very short, not much over five foot. Long hair, beard, and he still dresses like a hippie though he must be pushing fifty. There are two ways to find him; one is to stand downwind of him, and the other is to look for all the women. You can't miss 'em."

"Why not?"

"They're a sad fanboy's wet dream," said another of the *Illuminati* players, before Penny could answer. "None of them are exactly what you'd call good looking, but they'll fuck anyone he tells 'em to. Great if you can't afford to be fastidious."

"*And* your health insurance is paid up," said the first.

"Yeah, there is that. Come on, Orris, are you going to attack or not?"

"Okay," said the third player. "Survivalists, aided by the Society of Assassins, will attempt to control..." He looked at the cards before him—the CIA, Girlie Magazines, and the Secret Masters of Fandom—"the CIA" Play continued until Lee had walked out of the room, when the first player looked up and asked, "Was that necessary?"

Penny shrugged. "Kills two birds with one stone. I don't want him doing security at the art show; he can be too damn gung-ho, and he's got a temper. But he loves spy stuff, so this keeps him happy as well as busy."

"Unless this Preacher stabs him," Orris muttered.

"Better that than he stabs the Guest of Honour," she said. "Can one of you stop conquering the world for five minutes and put these room changes up?"

Lee found Preacher in the fan lounge, playing steel guitar and singing softly to the three shabbily-dressed (and scantily-clad for early December, even in Dallas) women clustered around his feet. He was heavily tanned, dressed in an ancient fringed buckskin jacket and much-patched jeans, and while his hair was long and wild and too dirty for Lee to do more than guess the colour, his beard was neatly trimmed into an iron-grey goatee.

Two fans were talking in one corner of the room, near the urn. Lee walked across the room, made himself a cup of coffee, and stood where he could watch Preacher while looking as though he were following the conversation; something about the coincidence that Aldous Huxley and C.S. Lewis had died on the same day. Preacher continued to softly wail about Devil's Canyon, but he looked straight at Lee and grinned as he sang. His dark eyes looked like something out of a Lovecraft story, and Lee reluctantly found himself turning away from his gaze. He forced himself to look back. Neither Preacher nor any of his women seemed to be armed, unless there were weapons in the guitar case. He watched as a young woman, a little older than his daughters and much prettier than any of the harem, walked around the cluster to get to the urn; Preacher stopped playing long enough to reach into a pocket and hand her a business card, which she glanced at, then dropped on the table next the sugar-bowl. Lee picked it up as she walked out with a cup of coffee, and pocketed it without reading it. He looked at Preacher, who grinned back.

"Crystal," Preacher said, without looking away from Lee, "go get me a banana smoothie." One of the women—Lee guessed her age at thirty—shot to her feet as though goosed and was out the door with a speed that Lee could only admire. "You a cop, man?"

"No," replied Lee, automatically. Preacher's grin widened a little more.

"Yeah, well, if you're after some dope, I'm not holding any, and if you're selling, I don't have any bread, either."

"You came all this way without any money?"

"Just enough for our memberships. The Lord will provide what we need," Preacher replied, and winked. "You from around here?"

Lee nodded. He suspected it would be safer to tell Preacher as little about himself as possible, and it wasn't exactly a lie; he'd lived in Dallas and Fort Worth for several years in the fifties and sixties, though he hadn't been back since his divorce. "You're supposed to wear your badges at all times," he said, feeling like an asshole. One of the women opened her mouth to speak, but Preacher reached into his pocket and removed four badges. Without reading them, he handed two to the women, and clipped a third to his jacket. "Anything to keep the peace, badge man."

Lee glanced at the badge he was wearing; it was yellow, indicating a one-day membership. The only name on it was 'Gypsy', while the women's badges—clipped to the waist-bands of their torn-off jeans, just above the crotches—read 'Preacher' and 'Crystal', but Lee knew that members were free to use any names they chose. "Long way to come for just one day," he said, mildly.

"Yeah, well, we just want to meet Mr Heinlein." One of the women giggled.

"So do a lot of people," said Lee, softly. "I'd like to meet him myself, but he doesn't have much time. He's not well enough to go to the room parties, or anything." He sat on a table near the group; he would have towered over Preacher even if he'd squatted on the floor, but from that height, it was like staring down into an abyss. "Did you bring a book to autograph, or anything?"

"I thought I might get one here," said Preacher.

"I thought you didn't have any money."

"No." He grinned. "Not right now, but sometimes good people give us money."

"You know he won't sign an autograph unless you can prove you've given blood in the past six months?" Preacher stared at him warily, trying to tell whether he was telling the truth. "He needed a lot of transfusions when he was sick, and he has a rare blood group; he thinks everybody should give blood as often as possible. It was in the progress reports," Lee added, trying not to smile, "and the program book. Look, it may not be too late to get down to the blood bank."

Preacher nodded. "Yeah, well, if Mr Heinlein wants blood, we got blood." He glanced at one of the women, who instantly sashayed out of the room. His smile said 'Your move'.

Lee managed not to swear. "Just thought you should know," he said, as blandly as he could manage. "Hate you to be disappointed after coming all this way."

Preacher grinned back at him. "Thank you. Anyway, badge man, it's nice talking to you and all, but I've got to go take a piss. You can stay and talk to Gypsy if you want." He stood, and Lee straightened up. The top of Preacher's head was level with his chin, but that didn't make him any less threatening; he was, Lee realised, taller than Attila the Hun, and about the same height as the Marquis de Sade. Preacher weaved past him and headed into the corridor, leaving Lee standing there flat-footed. He mumbled something to Gypsy, then ducked out of the room as she laughed. He watched as Preacher headed for the lift, then jogged down the stairs to the lobby, emerging in time to see the little man disappearing into the men's room. He walked past the door, and leaned against the wall on the far side, outside the hucksters' room where the signing sessions were being held. He reached into his pocket for his programme, and discovered Preacher's business card. 'Charles Manson,' it read. 'President, 3-Star-Enterprises, Nite Club, Radio and TV Productions.' No address or phone number. He shrugged, and pocketed it again.

According to the program, Heinlein wasn't going to be making any appearances before the signing at 1600, which was fine by Lee. His years in fandom had taught him that it was often a bad idea to meet people whose work you admired, and he'd liked a lot of the old man's earlier work, particularly the short stories. He stood there for a minute, watching the door, and noticed Carol walking out of the art show. "Hi, Lee. What did Penny Dreadful want?"

Lee waited until he was near enough to speak to without raising his voice, but was cut off by a shout of "Ozzie?" He turned around, and saw a balding, chunky man in cowboy boots, checked shirt and too-tight Levis waddling towards him brandishing a clipboard. Lee tried to smile, managing to show his teeth in a narrow grimace. "Hey, Shitbird!" the man called. "Long time no see! How're they hanging?"

"Hi, Dan." Lee had never made friends easily, especially during his days in the Marines, and didn't consider Dan as more than an acquaintance even after a dozen years of meeting at cons. Dan shoved the clipboard at him, peered at Carol's name badge—or stared at her breasts; Lee wasn't sure which—and introduced himself to her. "Anyway, Ozzie, I've got a petition here for you to sign."

Lee sighed inaudibly and took it. "What's it for?"

"Getting rid of some of the pain-in-the-butt red tape you have to go through just to buy or sell a gun, and a couple of other bullshit laws."

Lee laughed softly, and handed it back immediately. "You still flogging this horse?" Dan flushed. "Nah, I think the laws as they stand mostly make sense," Lee continued. "People living in cities don't need guns and most probably shouldn't have them. Look at me, for example."

"Yeah," spat Dan. "I did, and I thought that was a Marine Corps ring you're wearing. I must've been mistaken. Which side're you going to be on if the Russians invade, Oswaldskovich? You still reading Karl Marx?"

"Not lately," replied Lee, neutrally. "And the Russians aren't crazy enough to invade. *Nuke* us, yes, maybe, if Reagan doesn't clever up, but invade?" He shook his head. "Be seeing you, Dan."

Dan turned to Carol. "What about you? With the rising crime rate, women *need* guns, *especially* handguns, and *especially* in the cities."

She shrugged. "Maybe, but how would we stop men getting hold of them? No thanks."

Dan snorted. "Look, if you outlaw guns, only outlaws will carry guns. Prohibition's never worked for drugs, why would it work for weapons? Shit, there must be nearly half a million unregistered guns in the U.S., guns brought back from World War II or Korea, M-1s, M-2s, M-14s, Thompsons and God knows how many pistols..."

Carol shook her head, and watched him stomp off. Preacher walked out of the men's room an instant later, and Dan wheeled around and offered him the petition. "I take it you voted for King," said Carol, *sotto voce*.

Lee nodded. "Is that a problem?"

"No; so did I. I didn't expect him to win, but I thought it was time for a president who wasn't white. Why did that guy call you, uh..."

"Shitbird?" Lee smiled crookedly. "It was one of my nicknames when I was in the Marines, because I was such a god-awful shot. They also called me Oswaldskovich because I was reading *Das Kapital* and studying Russian. I wanted to get into Intelligence. Actually, I wanted to be Herb Philbrick."

"Who?"

"A spy, on a show called *I Led Three Lives*. It was my favourite TV show when I was a kid, probably before your time; it must have been cancelled in '55 or '56. Richard Carlson, you know, the guy from *It Came From Outer Space*, played him. I discovered James Bond a few years later. I even bought myself a little pistol, but the only person I ever shot with that was myself—by accident, of course. It got me busted down to private and three months of K.P. I am possibly the *last* person on Earth who should be trusted with a gun." He glanced at Preacher, as he signed the petition and walked down the corridor chatting to Dan. "One of the last, anyway. I used to be a real hothead. Sure, I was young, which is a pretty good excuse for being an idiot, but not for being an asshole. I used to pick a lot of fights, I even hit my first wife a few times, until she left me. After she and I were divorced, I had a nervous breakdown and ended up in hospital; God knows what I might have done if I'd had a gun *then*. The thought scares the shit out of me." He drew a deep breath. "But as I said, that was years ago. I like to think I'm a better person now."

She wrapped an arm around his waist. At thirty-five, an assistant librarian at the University of Texas and twice divorced herself, she'd lowered her expectations when it came to meeting men her own age. Lee lived too far away to have much potential as a partner, his sense of humour was unpredictable and she didn't share his enthusiasm for *The Prisoner*, but he didn't drink, was in good shape for a man of forty-one, and had been a pretty good friend for several years without ever trying to pressure her into sex. Maybe, she thought, it was time for *her* to make a move. "We all do stupid things when we're young. Jesus, some of the things I did in my student days... You still want dinner?"

"Sure, after the signing. Where shall we go?"

She shrugged. "I don't feel like getting dressed up. Why don't we try room service?"

Preacher and his women arrived at the hucksters' room a few minutes after four, by which time the slow-moving queue had already extended out the doors and down the corridor almost as far as the lobby. Preacher, Lee noticed, had a new-looking paperback of *Stranger in a Strange Land* in one hand, and the three women were giggling as at some secret joke. Lee stood behind them in the queue, trying to see what they had in their carry bags, and wishing that someone had given the committee an excuse to call the cops. The queue inched forward, and he realised that he was sweating. It took nearly twenty minutes for them to get inside the doors of the hucksters' room, and he was pleased to see another two redshirts flanking the table and that the sword merchant's stall was on the other side of the room from the queue. Without realising he was doing it, Lee began counting the people between Preacher and Heinlein, counting them off as the queue shortened. Twenty... nineteen... eighteen... Dan walked out past him, carrying copies of *Starship Troopers* and *Farnham's Freehold*. Fifteen...

Preacher was four or five yards from the table when Lee heard someone clear their throat from the doorway. He turned around, to see Penny standing there, her face red. "If I could have your attention, please," she began. A few people turned around; most—including Preacher—didn't. Eight...

"There was just a news flash on the radio," said Penny. "I checked with the other stations, in case it was a hoax. It isn't. John Lennon..."

Preacher turned around, and everyone fell silent. Lee saw the older man's eyes gleam as Penny continued, nervously but loudly. "John Lennon has just been stabbed outside his apartment building in New York. He was dead on arrival at the hospital."

There was a stunned silence that seemed to last for minutes. Lee stared at Preacher, softly, who had turned stark white. "Come on," said Lee, softly, kindly. "You look like you need to sit down."

"No..." whispered Preacher. He stared at Penny, his eyes seeming to become deeper and darker, and then a Buck knife appeared in his empty hand as though by magic. With a scream of rage, he launched himself at Penny. Lee stepped into his path to block him, and Preacher leapt up and slashed at his face. Lee recoiled, stumbling backwards, and Preacher weaved around him. Lee spun around to face him and make a grab for the knife, hoping his longer reach would give him an advantage, and felt another blade enter his back and grate against his bottom rib before being withdrawn. Preacher laughed, and Lee stumbled forwards and aimed a kick at his knife hand. Preacher merely dropped the book and caught the knife with his other hand, then leapt back out of Lee's reach. A student tackled him from behind, knocking him down, then two more rushed in to grab his arms. Lee turned around to face the woman who'd stabbed him, and saw all three standing there, knives drawn, looking as though they were waiting for orders. Preacher screamed wordlessly, and the women rushed at Lee, two with their knives held high, one aiming for his belly. They stabbed him fifteen times before he blacked out.

He half-woke two days later, seeing only whiteness, feeling as though he was floating. Only the stink of disinfectant and the dry dead taste in his mouth convinced him that he wasn't in heaven. He tried to focus, then to sit up. "Take it easy," said a voice from incredibly far away. "Give me a second to call the nurse."

"Where am I?"

"Parkland Hospital." The whiteness became a flat plane, a ceiling. "Don't try to move," said the voice. "You lost a lot of blood; I've seen a few people knifed in my time, but no-one with as many holes as you. You're lucky to be alive."

"Are you a doctor?"

A short laugh. "No, but I used to be a cop. Name's Tippit; people call me J.D."

"I'm Lee Oswald. What're you in for?"

"Heart bypass," said Tippit. "I was sitting at home on the weekend, watching the game, and next thing I know they're rushing me into the trauma room."

Lee managed to move his eyes enough to see vases of flowers on the nightstand. "You've had a lot of visitors," said Tippit. "Your lady friend's been here most of the time since you came out of surgery. But they've kept the photographers and reporters out. Everyone's calling you a hero."

Lee shook his head. "All I did was nearly get myself killed."

Tippit laughed. "Well, take it from me, you may's well make the most of it while it lasts. People don't remember heroes very long."

"Yeah," Lee replied, then grinned broadly. "You know," he said, mostly to himself, "I always wanted to be a hero."

the godfather paradox

It was a beautiful day for the beach, but terrible weather for a funeral, and Peter Daniels stood behind Hannah's family wishing he could faint, just to be away from there. The family glowered at him occasionally, maybe blaming him, maybe expecting him to throw himself into the grave à la Hamlet, or maybe wondering what he was doing there: for them, admitting that Hannah had had a boyfriend, especially a black boyfriend, would be nearly as bad as admitting that she'd OD'ed on hyper. Peter glanced at Melissa, wondering if the family had known all the details of *that* relationship. Probably not; Melissa had discovered the body and called the cops, which was enough to explain the hostile reception she'd received.

Melissa looked at the expensive coffin, the women's dresses, the old-fashioned three-piece suits, and the ancient memorials surrounding them. Burials were as twentieth-century as neckties—the rich were frozen, and everyone else cremated; she doubted that as many as a hundred people had been buried in New York (legally, anyway) since she'd been born. Hannah's family seemed like travellers from the 1980s, or maybe even the 1890s.

The two friends stood there until the service was over, then each took a few steps towards the family, which was folding up into itself like a fist clenching—or, Melissa thought, like a Roman garrison forming a shield wall bristling with spears. Melissa abruptly turned on her heel and strode towards the exit; Peter took another hesitant step towards the family, then sighed and followed her.

"I keep feeling like it's my fault," Melissa explained softly as he caught up to her, "and the last thing I need is a pack of sanctimonious leftovers from Edgar Allan Poe agreeing with me."

Peter nodded. "Well, they'd hardly blame themselves, would they?"

"Do you ever blame yourself?"

"No." He shrugged. "Okay, yes, a little, but nowhere near as much as I blame the slime who sold her the stuff, and I guess I'm glad I don't know who that was."

"What would you do if you did know?"

"I don't know... Probably nothing. I'm hardly the vigilante type; my ancestors went to a lot more lynchings than they would have liked. Besides, whoever it was, I don't think he wanted to kill her; he may have miscalculated the dose, or maybe she did, and she probably didn't tell him it was her first time, she hated admitting that, you know that."

"So you don't think it was anyone's fault?"

"You're the historian. Who killed the Kennedys?"

"What?"

"Who do you blame for the holocaust? Or the greenhouse effect? Or AIDS? Or the Hallowe'en War? No one person was responsible for any of them. Hannah shouldn't have taken the stuff. The slime who gave or sold it to her shouldn't have. The slime who sold it to the slime who gave or sold—and so on, *ad infinitum*. There's some blame left over for her parents, for telling her so much crap she felt the only way she could find out what was true was to try it herself... but I think the worst you can blame yourself for is not being in the right place at the time."

Melissa shook her head violently. "Everyone knows you can get drugs on campus, but no-one does anything about it, either because they don't care or because they're scared of the Mafia."

"People have been taking drugs for millenia, Hulkower," Peter said, softly. "It's as inevitable as the weather, and like the weather, everyone complains but no-one does anything about it, except maybe make it worse."

Melissa wasn't listening; she stopped suddenly, and stared at the tomb at the right of the exit. "Do you know who's buried there?" she asked.

"No."

"Frank Costello."

"The comedian?"

"The mobster—'Prime Minister of the Underworld', they called him."

Peter let her stare and cry for nearly a minute, then gently squeezed her shoulders. "He's dead, Hulkower. Hannah's dead. Everyone in this place is dead. If you try taking on the Mafia, you'll be dead. Let's get out of here, huh?"

He drove her back to her dorm, and spent the night in her room. He slept in her bed, holding her; they made love once before breakfast, and didn't see each other again for nearly two years.

The morning news shows devoted nearly half a minute to the experiment, including a few shots of the breadboard rig; none of them seemed sure how seriously to take it, but Daniels had expected that. He decided to devote the morning to marking test papers, a sure cure for over-excitement, and told the computer to record all calls unless they were from the Nobel Prize committee.

To his surprise, the phone rang at eleven. He glanced at the Caller ID; it was a four digit number, which indicated an internal call—and obviously someone who knew computers well enough to fool a Turing program, which ruled out most of his fellow physicists. "Daniels."

"Peter?"

The voice was vaguely familiar, but nothing more, and he wished that the university didn't regard videophones as an extravagance. "Yes?"

"It's Melissa Hulkower." There was a brief pause, then, "I hear you've invented a time machine."

"Well, sort of," he said. "I'm afraid it's no use to the history department—or any threat, for that matter. Anyway, how're you doing?"

"I'm okay," she replied. "What does the machine do?"

Daniels restrained a sigh. "What have you heard?"

"That you've used it to send small samples of radio-isotopes back a few weeks, and checked the rate of decay. Is that correct?"

"Basically. The results are in *Nature*."

"And you've found capsules that you don't have any record of sending, which have dates from several years in the future printed on them, that you assume someone is going to send."

"Yeah. That's caused the real stir. Of course, we've lost a few capsules as well, but that's hardly surprising—the damn machine can't send more than a few grams: the biggest sample, which is supposed to be from 2112, was just over 3.1 grams."

"What if you build a bigger machine?"

"We'd need a lot more power, for one thing—and it's exponential, not linear. Simone's worked it out mathematically, and she says the absolute limit's about forty-two grams and a hundred and seven years, even if you blow up the sun."

"Oh."

"Besides, the 2112 sample appeared in Price's office, two floors up from the lab, which seems to confirm that the further you send a sample, the harder it is to place it in a precise location. I forget how many of the bloody things we must have lost by now. Anyway, if you want to come and see it, you're welcome, but it really won't be any use to the history department..."

Melissa looked at the sprawl of equipment, nodding. "The glass case is the transmitter?"

"Uh-huh. It's a vacuum chamber—we can't afford to waste power sending air back into the past. And it's a receiver, too, when our future selves—or whoever—manage to hit it. There's always a burst of Cerenkov radiation when they miss, which is why we've put counters all around the building."

"And the capsules you send are radioactive, too?"

Peter nodded. "That's how we confirmed the mechanism. If you send an isotope back twenty-four hours, it arrives showing the same amount of decay as it would in twenty-four hours in, uh, normal time. The same sort of thing would happen if we sent something that was alive—assuming it could survive in the vacuum."

Melissa nodded. "Why all the security outside?"

Peter smiled. "A lot of the public think we can use it to hop back to the Cretaceous, or the Crucifixion, or whatever. A few have worked out what we could do—things like sending a list of stock market or sports results back to last year or whenever."

"Could you?"

"Yes. Of course, if you sent it back to last year, most people would just think it was a joke. The problem is going to be when people who've heard of this device start getting messages that're supposed to be from next year. We've been careful not to try anything like that, and none of the capsules we've received from the future have given us any hot tips. Maybe there's a cosmic censor out there that prevents messages like that getting through—I don't know.

"And, of course, the lawyers are worried about it being used for terrorism—it's not accurate enough to use for assassinations, you'd be lucky to hit something as small as a limo, much less a president— but in theory, they said, you could send biowar cultures into water supplies or air-conditioning ducts. We pointed out that (one) you could do that without the machine—a clipboard and a boiler suit can get you into almost anywhere, (two) the culture would have to survive the trip, and (three) the machine has a geographical range limit, too—about twenty-one miles—and isn't exactly portable, not with the power supply it needs, so anywhere outside New York is safe and even New York is still about as safe as it's ever been." He shook his head. "And for all we know, the past is immutable. If it wasn't, how would we know, anyway?"

Melissa stared at the device, thinking hard, and then smiled. "Thanks for showing it to me. Can I buy you a coffee?"

"Let's see if I've got this right," said Melissa, rolling over and propping herself up one elbow. "You can send two grams back a hundred and eight years to somewhere in New York City. Right?"

"Hmm?" Peter turned to face her and tried to focus (he always removed his contact lenses before sex; they tended to pop out when he was aroused). "Yeah... well, in theory. In practice, I'd say ninety years was the best we could do."

"1938," she murmured.

"Even then, you'd need a big target area, and you could miss the slot by a month or more..."

"How big?"

"Oh... something the size of a lecture theatre, but three or four floors high."

"A library or a large law firm..."

"Yeah, that should... what?"

She bobbed her head down and bit his nipple. "Never mind. Just an idea."

"You want me to what?"

Melissa counted to three silently. "Send this back to 1938. It'll survive the trip; I checked."

"What is it?"

"Photographic negatives. 35mm, black and white, just like they used back then, no-one will know where they came from. The originals were taken at about that time, or maybe a few years later... Four shots—well within the mass limit."

Peter put down his coffee cup carefully, and peered at the strip of celluloid. "These look like someone sucking a cock. Is that right?"

"Yes."

He peered again. "Either an ugly man or a damn ugly woman... Benito Mussolini?"

Melissa laughed. "Not exactly. It's J. Edgar Hoover. I copied them from the latest biography—the other two show him in drag."

"Hoover? The FBI man?"

"Yes."

"I thought these were supposed to be fakes—computer-generated."

"Maybe they are, but those photos *did* exist. Several people admitted to having seen them, including a few CIA agents. The Mafia used them to blackmail Hoover to get the FBI to leave them alone—which they did until the old man died, nearly forty years later."

Peter shook his head. "Jesus. Who was the other guy, a Russian spy or something?"

"No, just his boyfriend—the Assistant Director, actually. Look, you remember Hannah's parents. Most people in the western world last century had the same prejudices they do; sex was disgusting, gay sex revolting, and male gay sex was absolutely abominable and usually illegal. A lot of men committed suicide when they were discovered to be gay—Alan Turing, for one. Things didn't start to get better until the late sixties, and got worse again in some ways in the eighties; it wasn't until an AIDS cure was found that what we now consider sanity became the norm. But ninety years ago, photos like this could destroy a man's career—"

"And that's what you want to do to Hoover?"

"Yes. He used to do it to his political rivals, without any qualms. If we drop these into the offices of the *New York Times*—they weren't scared of Hoover, and he hated them for it—then his secret would be out. He might be able to keep his job—at least three presidents tried to fire him at various stages, but he blackmailed them into changing their minds, he had something on everyone—but it'd break the Mafia's hold on him. Or at least weaken it, which would weaken them... It might even keep them out of the narcotics business; that was always risky politically, and without him to protect them..."

So *that's* what this is about, Peter thought wearily. He passed the negatives back to Melissa, and rested his head on his hands. "We don't even know if we can change the past..."

"How else are you going to find out?"

He sighed. "There has to be a safer way than this. What if the past isn't immutable, and we changed it for the worse... What if the Ku Klux Klan or someone like that got hold of the photos?"

"Hoover," she said quietly, "left the Ku Klux Klan alone unless they claimed credit for a murder, but spent millions investigating and harassing black power groups and their supporters. He tried to blackmail Martin Luther King; he knew he was depressive, and tried to bully him into committing suicide. Some researchers even say that he hired the man who shot him—"

Peter held up his hands. "Okay, okay. I'll need time to think about this..."

"Sure," said Melissa. "Take all the time you need."

Cates was sweeping in the *Times'* morgue and fantasizing semi-platonically about the new cashier at Bookmart, when the sudden silent flash of blue light behind him startled him out of his reverie. For a moment, he stood and blinked, waiting for the black dots to disappear from his peripheral vision, thinking of lightning, flash-bulbs, police cars and welding torches and trying not to think of the Hindenburg explosion and Lovecraft's *The Colour Out of Space.* Wielding his broom like a warhammer, he advanced cautiously towards the source of the light. Seeing nothing out of the ordinary, he took a quiet step towards the door and opened it suddenly, looking up and down the corridor outside.

Nothing.

Cates stood there for a moment, shaking his head, then stepped back into the morgue. He stared at the ceiling, but all of the lights seemed to be working as normal. He sighed, looked at the floor, and noticed something small, dark and flat, with perforated edges. He knew there were thousands, maybe millions, of negatives filed away in the morgue, and pitied the person whose job it was to return this one to its proper place. He picked it up, looked at it to make sure it wasn't merely a piece of blank film, whistled sharply, and then leaned against the shelves and studied the pictures closely. The negatives might have come from the *Times's* archives, he decided, but the photographs had certainly never appeared in its pages, or those of any other newspaper. He also suspected that the subject had not consented to the shots being taken—and while he didn't recognise the face from the negatives, it was ugly enough to be someone of some importance.

Cates looked around the room anxiously, and then carefully wrapped the negative in his handkerchief and pocketed it.

"Meyer, can you do me a favour?"

"Sure. How much?"

"It isn't money," replied Cates, and then lowered his voice further. "I need a couple of prints, and I don't want anyone else to see 'em. Can you do it?"

"I'm pretty busy... can't you take 'em to Kodak?"

"No."

"No?" Meyer Berger stared at the younger man with exaggerated astonishment and genuine curiosity. "What have you been up to, Chris? I wouldn't have thought you had time, what with *two* jobs."

Cates squirmed slightly. He'd come to New York a week before the Wall Street Crash, sixteen years old and hoping for work as an actor. A friend had gotten him a job as a copy boy at the *Times* in time to prevent him starving; he still worked there as a janitor three mornings a week. "I found these. I don't know who the guy is, but I thought you might..." He handed the negatives to Berger, who peered at them, then did the best double-take Chris had ever seen.

"You look as though you haven't slept yet." Chris shook his head. "Go and get yourself some breakfast; I'll meet you in the diner on the corner in an hour."

Cates was dozing in a corner booth when Berger walked into the diner with a newspaper under his arm. The journalist slid in opposite him and said, softly, "I'm glad you're sitting with your back to the wall. It's a good habit."

Cates opened his eyes. "Who was it?"

Berger regarded him sadly, then withdrew an envelope from the newspaper and handed it to him. "There's two sets of prints in there, a proof sheet, and the negatives. What you do with them is up to you, but I haven't seen them."

"Huh?"

"And if I had seen them," added Berger, "I would have hidden another set of prints in a safe deposit box, with orders that they were to be opened in the event of my death. Do you understand?"

"No," replied Cates, hesitantly. "Who is he?"

"J. Edgar Hoover."

Cates half-stood, and blurted out "Jesus! J. Edgar Hoover is a—" and then sat down again, hurriedly.

"So it would seem," replied Berger.

"You could get another Pulitzer nomination out of this one..."

"Posthumously, perhaps," said Berger, drily. "Chris, I don't know where these came from. I know there are homosexuals in your profession; I assume one of them gave them to you." Cates shook his head. "That's as may be. Unfortunately, the *Times* cannot print these photographs, for obvious reasons, and without them there isn't a story—we have no dates, no places, nothing but the pictures themselves, which might be faked.

"And then there's the question of who would want us to know this and publicise it, and why. Hoover's made a lot of enemies, and most of them aren't the sort of people you'd want to aid and abet. What's worse is the photos themselves. If they're fakes, they're brilliant. If not, then Hoover must have been set up—a camera behind a one-way mirror, maybe, in his hotel while he was on vacation. I had to wonder, who could do that? Even the smartest mobsters in the country would find it difficult... and then I wondered, what about the communists?"

"Communists?" said Cates, dubiously. "The Communist Party's a joke."

Berger shook his head. "Not the local party. The Russians— the OGPU, or NKVD, or whatever it's called now. They could have done it, and they might want Hoover replaced with an FBI Director who's soft on communism...

"But that isn't the main reason I'm queasy about this. What do you think would happen if these photos were published? Hoover's not the sort to resign, so Roosevelt would either have to fire him... or not fire him. Now, even if the photos are real and Hoover's as queer as a three-dollar bill, does that mean he should lose his job? I'm not sure that it does—he does it well enough, and that should be the only issue that matters." He smiled thinly. "On the other hand, if Hoover isn't fired, whoever prints those photos will have made an enemy of the most powerful man in the United States. Are you sure you want to do that?"

"Well..."

"Think about it. Take your time."

Cates nodded. "I will. Thanks, Meyer."

"My pleasure."

Hoover returned to his office from lunch at the Mayflower in a jovial mood; less than a minute later, he was fighting not to vomit over his mahogany desk. He slammed the phone down, drew a deep breath, and made two calls—the first to his secretary, asking her to hold all calls, and the second summoning the assistant director, Clyde Tolson.

He was still red-faced and sweating freely when Tolson arrived and closed the door behind him. His expression, as usual, was solemn. "What is it, Eddie?"

"I've just had a call from an informant at the *New York Times*," said Hoover, heavily, without looking at him. "He says Meyer Berger has copies of some photographs of you and me."

Tolson narrowed his eyes. "Is that all?" He stared at his boss for a moment, and then blanched. "Oh god not *those* photographs..."

Hoover continued to stare silently through the window.

"How? Where did he get them?"

Hoover shrugged. "Berger has a lot of sources, most of them scum. I'm more concerned about his plans."

"So we bring him in and ask him. What's the problem?"

"Who do we get to bring him in? What do we tell them?" Tolson gaped at him, then swore under his breath. "Never mind, Junior," the director continued, almost kindly. "It was my first thought, too."

"I could go."

Hoover pursed his lips, thinking hard. "That's possible. You might be recognised, but it would be better than sending an agent..."

"Okay."

"No... not yet. If we go up to New York on Saturday and drop in at the Stork Club, it won't look as though you've made the trip just to see Berger."

"What if he prints the photos before Saturday?"

Hoover shook his head, ponderously. "If he tries that, I'll know before anybody else does."

Pittsburgh Phil Strauss—Murder Incorporated's most prolific hitter and the Beau Brummel of the underworld—slouched in the back seat of a Lincoln Zephyr and watched the passers-by from under the brim of a pearl-grey fedora, careful to keep his guns out of sight. He'd been parked on Broadway for nearly twenty minutes, and Strauss (whose real name was Harry, and who'd never been to Pittsburgh in his thirty years) was beginning to suspect that the bum wasn't going to show. This really wasn't his sort of job; he didn't like having to make a hit out on a public street, even this late in the morning, and he didn't like knowing his victim's name. But he knew it was urgent—word was that the contract had come straight from Anastasia himself, and they hadn't even had time to find out the bum's address, he had to be hit before he got to work—and it was going to be remembered, especially if they hit him right outside the *New York Times* like the bosses wanted.

"Is dat him, Phil?" came a voice from the front seat.

Strauss glanced at the rear-view mirror. Vito 'Chicken Head' Gurino wasn't particularly bright, but he had excellent eyesight. The man leaving the subway matched the description they'd been given—late twenties, 5'11", 150 pounds, dark wavy hair, thin moustache, handsome in a Rudolph Valentino sort of way, cheap clothes—and he was hurrying in the right direction. "Could be... but don't say nothing till I say okay, okay?"

"Okay."

Strauss waited until the man was close enough for him to see his profile, then muttered, "Okay."

Gurino stuck his head through the window and bawled, "Hey, Cates!" The man turned and looked at the car, and Strauss raised the Thompson and pulled the trigger.

Cates hit the ground as soon as he saw the gun and, panicking, rolled towards the Zephyr and into the gutter. Strauss, half-blinded by the muzzle flash and deafened by the roar of the gun inside the confined space of the car, peered through the smoke, baffled. "Where did the bum go?"

Gurino, also partially deafened, didn't reply. Cates stared up at the gun; part of his mind was yelling at him to get out of there, to crawl along the gutter away from the car, but his body refused to obey.

Strauss removed the gun from the window, and cautiously stuck his head out. Cates inhaled and slid further under the car. "I think we better get out of here, Phil," said Gurino. "Heat'll be here soon."

Strauss swore. It didn't matter that this was only the second contract he'd failed to hit (the other bum had escaped because it had taken Strauss too long to steal a fire axe); this was the hit that would make his reputation, one way or the other. He dropped the Thompson and reached for his briefcase. "You go," he snarled. "I'm going to find this bum."

He stepped out of the Zephyr just as Cates slid out from under the other side and ran across the road towards the subway entrance, not glancing back until he reached the sidewalk. "Dere he is!" yelled Gurino, reaching for his revolver. Strauss spun around, and began chasing the actor, inadvertently placing himself between Cates and Gurino before the other gangster could aim. Gurino watched the two disappear down the stairs, swore, and then holstered his pistol and drove back to Brooklyn.

Cates leapt the turnstile gracefully, shedding his overcoat as he ran and slowing down only slightly to drop the wadded coat into a trashcan. A few seconds later he was studying the subway map, taking care not to breathe too heavily, and concentrating on appearing stooped and old and inconspicuous. A moment later he saw Strauss charge past him, look about furiously, and disappear into the men's room. Cates stared, and allowed himself a slight smile.

Bette Lang was dreaming that she was playing Lady Macbeth clad only in her showgirl costume, to the sound of enthusiastic, almost frenzied applause—a staccato rapping that continued after the rest of the dream faded into embarrassment. She opened her eyes, and realised that the rapping was real. She sat up, arms crossed over her large breasts, and looked around. The sound seemed to be coming from the window; it took her a moment to remember that there was a fire escape outside. Cautiously, she clambered out of bed, grabbed her glasses and a robe, then tiptoed over to the window and raised the blind. It took her several seconds to recognise Cates; she stared at him, and then raised the sash. "What're you doing out there?"

"I need your help," he said, sliding in, then quickly shutting the window behind himself and lowering the blind.

"If you think I'm too sleepy to say no at—what time is it, anyway?"

"Four a.m., I think," he replied, "and it's not that. The FBI is trying to kill me."

"Huh? I mean—"

"They were waiting for me outside the *Times*, with a tommy-gun." He sat down on the floor near the window, and reached into his pocket for the negatives, and told the story from the beginning, leaving out the blue flash, as Bette sat on the bed and listened.

"You're sure it was a fed?" she asked, when he'd finished. "He sounds more like the guys we get at the club."

Cates shrugged. "He looked like one—tall, clean-cut, good suit... he even carried a briefcase."

"How did you shake him?"

"I dumped the coat, acted like I was someone else, and dropped my lighter outside the little girls' room; the guy's probably still there, screwing up the courage to go in. Then I caught the first train out of there—it went to Harlem, so he couldn't exactly blend into the crowds, and I don't think the FBI has any black agents. Then I tried to think of someone I could still trust—and I came here."

"Are you hurt?"

He raised his right arm, showing the tear in his shirt and the graze underneath it. "Only this—he only got one good shot at me before I hit the dirt, and I guess my coat made me look bigger than I am."

"Lucky you couldn't afford one that fits," she replied. "So, what do you need me to do—apart from darning your shirt?"

"They're probably watching my place," said Cates. "I can't go back there, and I need some stuff—clothes, a suitcase, some more prints of those photos, maybe some sort of disguise. I've got to get out of town, become invisible..." He stared at her poster of *Othello*, and a smile spread slowly across his face. "Can you get me some make-up, too?"

"Invisible? Like Claude Rains?"

The smile broadened into a grin. "More like the Shadow, I guess. By the way, do you know any communists?"

"Mr Berger? I'm Clyde Tolson; could we talk for a moment, please?"

Berger looked up from his desk neutrally. "Sure. Talk."

Tolson attempted a smile. "Your editor's lent us his office for a few minutes."

Berger shrugged, and stood. He knew that Tolson, despite his stereotypical G-man looks and his nickname 'Killer', had never served as an agent, and had less experience of violence than Berger himself. Tolson led the way into the office, and sat down on the corner of the cluttered desk. "Shut the door. I won't keep you: I'm sure you're working to a deadline. I hear you gave some negatives to one of your darkroom people the other day."

"What negatives?"

"Did you?"

"I may have done," replied Berger. "I don't take photographs myself, but there are times when a picture—well, you've heard the saying. Could you describe the picture?"

Tolson turned pale. "Listen, Berger, I can have you arrested—"

"On what charge?"

"Or I can shoot you now and think of something later—"

"Maybe," replied Berger, with a nervous glance through the glass walls of the office, "but I don't think anyone will believe it was self-defense." He smiled thinly. "Maybe one of my colleagues out there knows about these photographs. Maybe they all know. Shall we ask them?" He leaned against the wall, scared that his legs were going to give way despite his brave front.

Tolson snarled. "Where did you get these negatives?"

Berger sighed. "I do have the right not to reveal my sources."

"Do you have the negatives?"

"No; nor do I know where they are."

"Can you find them?"

"Why should I want to do that?"

Tolson stared at him, and then tried another tack. "We can do a lot for your career; we can give you exclusives—"

The journalist shook his head. "No. I advised my source—who is also a friend—not to try to publish those photographs, in part because I believed that your boss's taste in lovers didn't reflect on his ability to do his job. The longer you remain here, the more I start to wonder. This might be a good time for you to leave."

Tolson flushed, and strode out, slamming the door. Berger watched him go, and then slid to the floor, his legs no longer able to bear his weight.

The sign in the barber's shop said 'Closed', but Frank Costello knocked on the door and was admitted without question. He stood for a moment, biting the end off a Havana cigar and watching the barber sliding a razor along Hoover's throat. Lot of people would like that job, he reflected, and smiled. "Good morning, John."

Hoover opened his eyes and stared into the mirror. "What's good about it?" he growled.

"I heard you were having some problems."

"What sort of problems?"

Costello smiled. "Shall we say, an image problem?"

"Somebody shot up Times Square the night before last," said Tolson, who was sitting near the door. "Did you have anything to do with that?"

"*Mea culpa, mea culpa, mea maxima culpa,*" replied Costello, removing the cigar from his mouth and bowing his head.

"What?"

Costello looked up again, his expression serious. "I told them to get him, not hit him, but I guess they misunderstood me."

"Get who?"

The mobster opened his mouth to answer, and then closed it again. "The guy with the negatives... what's his name again?"

"You mean Berger?" asked Tolson, before Hoover could speak. The Director swallowed a groan and rolled his eyes.

"Nah," replied Costello, lighting the cigar. "Any lunkhead knows not to go after a reporter."

"Where is he now?" asked Hoover, blandly, keeping an eye on the mobster's hands. Costello had one of the best poker faces in the country, but his hands were much more expressive.

"I don't know. He disappeared into the subway, could have taken any one of a dozen lines. He hasn't been home since, or to either of his jobs: the photos weren't in his room, either. He could've gone anyplace."

"You lost him?" said Tolson.

"Hey, you never even *found* him," said Costello, yawning, and sat in the chair next to Hoover's. "And now you want me to tell you his name? What's in it for me?"

"Neither of us wants those photos made public," snapped Hoover. "Who do you think Roosevelt will get to replace me?" Costello's hands shook slightly. "And imagine what the scandal would do to his re-election chances. Do you want Dewey as your next President? He made his reputation putting—" Costello raised an eyebrow, and Hoover faltered. "—uh, some associates of yours, in jail... Do you want to risk that?" His tone changed to a wheedling whisper. "We can help each other. We can find him for you. Just tell me his name."

It was nearing midnight when Melvin Purvis, once the FBI's most famous agent, strode along the corridor to Hoover's office (known to agents as the Bridge of Sighs) for the first time since resigning three years before. He handed his revolver to Helen Gandy, Hoover's long-serving secretary, and chatted with her for a few minutes before being ushered into the great octagonal office. His carefully neutral expression soured when he noticed Tolson sitting beside the mahogany desk. "Hello, Mel," said Hoover. "How're the memoirs coming along?"

"Fine."

"And the Melvin Purvis Junior G-Man Corps?"

Purvis rolled his eyes. "You didn't bring me all the way here in the dead of night to talk about a breakfast cereal gimmick. What do you want?"

"We're looking for a man named Christopher Cates."

"I've never heard of him."

"He has some confidential information that could greatly embarrass the Bureau," said Hoover, spitting the words out with obvious disgust. "He's disappeared; we need to find him, and you were always good at that. We can put you back on a SAC's salary—"

"Hold on a minute," said Purvis, looking intently at Hoover's neck. "It's about you, isn't it?"

"What?"

Purvis glanced at the stony-faced Tolson, and smiled. "He's picked up some dirt on you, and you don't want it to get out. Right?"

Hoover glowered silently. "Do you want the job?"

"Work for you again? After the stories you've been spreading about me? If someone's blackmailing you, you son of a bitch, then maybe there *is* some justice in the world—"

"Do you want to sell cereal for the rest of your life?" asked Hoover.

"Hell, no." Purvis leaned across the enormous desk until he was close enough to Hoover to smell his perfume and the whiskey on his breath. "I want an endorsement from you—I'll write it, you just have to sign it."

Hoover pursed his lips. "Is that all?"

"No. I want to make sure you can't have me blacklisted without risking your own neck: I want to know what this Cates has on you." Tolson stumbled to his feet, his face ashen; Purvis ignored him. "I'll have to know about it if I'm going to find him—Jayee."

The two men glared at each other for nearly a minute, and then Hoover asked, "Is *that* all?"

"That, and the freedom to work without either you or Beady-eyes over there breathing down my neck."

"Can you start tomorrow?"

"Fine." Neither man offered to shake hands. Purvis walked out of the room, retrieved his gun, and escorted Helen Gandy back along the Bridge of Sighs to the outside world. A janitor watched them leave together, filed the fact for future reference, and then returned to work.

A year passed. Pittsburgh Phil made the hit that would eventually send him to the electric chair, Orson Welles panicked thousands of Americans with his broadcast of *War of the Worlds*, hundreds of synagogues were burnt in Germany, Franco captured Madrid, and Hoover ordered his staff to begin compiling a Custodial Detention

List of both Communist and Nazi sympathisers. Bette Lang went to Hollywood for a screen test, landed a role as a gangster's moll, and became a regular in Republic serials—usually wearing a low-cut dress and a lot of rope. And Melvin Purvis and a small cadre of agents tapped phones, intercepted mail, and interrogated more than a dozen people without finding Christopher Cates.

"He was somewhere in Washington last December," he told Hoover, as Tolson sneered. "He sent Christmas cards to his family—no return address, of course, but postmarked Washington. He's probably still writing to his zoftig girlfriend, but she's getting so much fan mail nowadays that I had to give up reading it, and my secretary embarasses too easily. He always types the envelopes, using a lot of different typewriters. He hasn't asked anyone for money, and we know he's worked as a waiter, a dishwasher, and a janitor at various times, so he could probably find a job almost anywhere. My guess is that he pushes a broom in some offices somewhere and uses their typewriters when no-one's listening."

"What about the photos?" growled Hoover.

"Same problem. It's too easy to hide photos, especially in a newspaper office. It's a lot like 'The Purloined Letter'; the best place to hide a letter is in a sack of mail." He noticed the puzzlement on Hoover and Tolson's faces, and rolled his eyes. "Didn't you guys ever read any Edgar Allan Poe? Never mind. I'll bet Cates did. He may even be working for another newspaper, thinking that's the last place we'd look..."

"Have you looked?" asked Tolson.

"Sure. No-one remembers anyone who matches his description, but Hell, he's an actor; he could've changed his appearance so much his mother wouldn't recognise him. He might even be passing himself off as a woman," he added blandly. "It's a pity we don't have any female agents; a lot of people will tell a woman things they'd never tell a man."

"Women aren't strong enough to shoot straight," fumed Hoover. There had been three female agents in the Bureau when he'd become director in '24; he'd fired all of them.

Purvis didn't comment. He was tired of Washington, tired of after-dark meetings, tired of an investigation that was slowly leading nowhere, and overwhelmingly tired of Tolson and Hoover. He excused himself, walked out of Hoover's office, sat down at Helen Gandy's desk, and began writing his resignation. He had torn up two drafts before he noticed that the typeface was familiar. He stared at the typewriter, an incredible idea slowly blossoming in the back of his mind, then hurtled down the Bridge of Sighs and ricocheted from office to office, examining every typewriter he saw.

The idea was pounding now, threatening to split his skull from within. He rushed back to Hoover's office, but the Director had already left. He swore, then grabbed Helen Gandy's phone and called Hoover's home number.

"Listen," he said, as soon as the phone stopped ringing. "This is urgent. What time do the janitors leave the building?"

"What? I don't know—"

"Get some agents in here and stop them leaving. One of them is Cates."

There was a moment's stunned silence, and then Hoover exploded, "That's ridiculous! All our janitors are niggers!"

The four men sat in a room at the Mayflower—Hoover and Tolson natty and tense, Purvis reclining on the bed with his eyes half-closed and his .357 Magnum close to his hand, and the dungaree-clad Cates handcuffed to a chair. "Where are the negatives?" asked Hoover.

"I told you; I gave them to a friend for safekeeping."

"Meyer Berger?" asked Tolson.

"Meyer might or might not have a copy; he doesn't have the negatives."

"Bette Lang?"

"Bette hasn't even seen the damn things." Cates shook his head; sweat was running down his face, streaking his brown make-up. "And if you go near her, I'll make sure everyone sees that damn picture if I have to carve it into Mount Rushmore myself. For the twenty-seventh goddamn time, I'm not going to tell you who has the negatives. I didn't ask to find them in the first place; since I did, I've been shot at, I've had to give up my friends, my family, my job, I've had to work like a slave and live in houses that you wouldn't keep your dog in. If you hadn't sent one of your goons to shoot me, I might have—"

"We didn't send him," said Hoover. Cates glanced at Purvis, who shrugged. "We wouldn't have risked killing you—"

"Until you had the negatives and knew there weren't any more copies?" asked Cates. Hoover flushed. "So who was it?"

"I can't answer that."

"Okay, so maybe it wasn't you then, and you haven't tried to kill me today—yet—but the bottom line is *I don't trust you*. So, if I don't get back home by Monday morning, my friend will start sending copies of those photos out to politicians and newspapers here and overseas. Even *you* won't be able to intercept them all." Cates smiled: he'd never had a captive audience listen to him so intently before. "Okay. I've had enough of being black; I've made some friends and had some good times, but the pay is lousy, the housing stinks, I hate being called 'boy', and I'm sick to death of having to make love with the lights out. Give me a thousand bucks to live on till I find a job, and I'll catch the first bus to L.A. If I outlive you, you've got nothing to worry about."

Hoover looked thoughtful. "He's lying," snapped Tolson. "Sending out that many photos would cost a fortune, and we could trace them back to their source: no-one would dare do it. Shoot the son of a bitch and that'll be the end of it."

Purvis shook his head. "There are people who could and might do it—or it might be a company. Berger works for the *New York Times*, the Lang girl sends out hundreds of signed photos in a week..."

"They wouldn't dare; they'd be fired in a—"

"Some people aren't as scared of losing their jobs as you are, Clyde," replied Purvis, softly. "I know some of them hate your boss enough to risk it."

Hoover looked at all of them in turn, uncertainty in his eyes. "He's right," said Cates. "My friend's a member of the YCL."

Hoover and Tolson stared, and then Hoover began to chuckle. "The Young Communist League?"

"That's right."

A grin spread across the director's face. "We have dossiers on every member of the YCL, Cates, every red sympathiser and every subscriber to the *Daily Worker* and *New Masses*. We have agents in every communist front there is: we have so many agents in some of them, our membership dues are their main source of income."

Cates looked away from him, and glanced at Purvis's revolver. From six feet away, the muzzle seemed big enough to crawl into. "I had wondered about that," he said, softly. "That's why I gave it to one of their women."

The chuckles stopped suddenly, followed by a stunned silence that filled the room. Then Purvis began to giggle.

"Well, they do most of the office work," explained Cates. "They run the mimeograph machines, stuff the envelopes, that sort of thing. And I knew she couldn't be a Fed..."

Purvis was rolling on the bed by this time, laughing uncontrollably—but when Tolson reached into his jacket, he sat up and drew a bead between the assistant director's eyes as though everyone else was in slow motion. "Don't be stupid, Junior," said Hoover wearily, getting up and walking out. "Give the rat his money, and let him go."

"You wanted to see me, Edgar?" FDR smiled encouragingly; he had never seen the FBI Director so obviously distressed. He hoped it wasn't just another rumour about his wife.

"Yes, Mr President." Hoover sat down, leaned back, squirmed slightly, and then grabbed the arms of the chair and leaned forward. "It concerns, uh... national security and... civil rights... and, uh, the morals laws." Roosevelt raised an eyebrow. "To be specific, the laws against sodomy."

Oh God, thought Roosevelt, who is it this time? "Yes?"

"For reasons of national security," Hoover continued in a staccato monotone, "at a time when war seems not only likely but inevitable..." FDR nodded; Hitler and Mussolini had signed their 'pact of steel' a week earlier, and England had just re-introduced conscription. "You are aware that the number of espionage cases the Bureau now handles has more than quadrupled in the past two years... It is well known that homosexuals in important positions

are very often subjected to blackmail by agents of foreign powers...
and because we cannot afford this to continue... I believe that our
laws against, uh, sodomy, should be, uh... repealed."

Roosevelt gaped. He'd heard rumours about Edgar before, but
this was the last thing he'd expected. "Repealed?"

"Furthermore," Hoover continued, "I believe that a Federal act
should be passed making it illegal to discriminate against homosexuals
in questions of employment, including military conscription and
other government service. And, uh, immigration. Apart from closing
an escape hatch for able-bodied men wishing to avoid military service,
it will enable the FBI to concentrate on far more important matters."

Roosevelt stared at him, then blinked. "Is that all?"

"Mr President?"

"Not that I'm disagreeing with you," the President assured
him hastily, "but even if you could get an act like that through
both houses, well, you can change the law, but what about public
opinion? It might inspire a worse witch-hunt than the one you're
trying to avoid; lynchings, bombings, especially if we're seen as
turning this country into a haven for homosexuals and—"

"I think," said Hoover, with a slightly crooked smile, "that
we both know the worth of a good public relations staff. Most
importantly, if we can present the public with some suitable, uh,
role-models, some homosexuals who are also *already* public heroes
and heroines, that it will do much to overcome prejudice of this
sort. There may be some backlash at first, but given time..."

Roosevelt considered this. "Did you have anyone in mind?"

It was a beautiful day for the beach, but terrible weather for a
funeral, and Peter Daniels stood behind Hannah's family wishing
he could faint, just to be away from there. The family glowered
at him occasionally, maybe blaming him, maybe expecting him
to throw himself into the grave a la Hamlet, or maybe wondering
what he was doing there: for them, admitting that Hannah had
had a boyfriend, especially a black boyfriend, would be nearly as
bad as admitting that she'd had an illegal brain-boost.

Melissa looked at the expensive coffin, the women's dresses,
the old-fashioned three-piece suits, and the ancient memorials

surrounding them. Burials were as twentieth-century as neckties—the rich were cyborged, and everyone else cremated; she doubted that as many as a hundred people had been buried in New York (legally, anyway) since she'd been born. Hannah's family seemed like travellers from the 1930s, or maybe even the 1390s.

The two friends stood there until the service was over, then each took a few steps towards the family, which was folding up into itself like a fist clenching—or, Melissa thought, like a Roman garrison forming a shield wall bristling with spears. Melissa abruptly turned on her heel and strode towards the exit; Peter took another hesitant step towards the family, then sighed and followed her.

"I keep feeling like it's my fault," Melissa explained softly as he caught up to her, "and the last thing I need is a pack of sanctimonious leftovers from Edgar Allan Poe agreeing with me."

Peter nodded. "Well, they'd hardly blame themselves, would they?"

"Do you ever blame yourself?"

"No." He shrugged. "Okay, yes, a little, but nowhere near as much as I blame the slime who sold her a counterfeit brain-boost, and I guess I'm glad I don't know who that was."

"What would you do if you did know?"

"I don't know... Probably nothing. I'm hardly the vigilante type; my ancestors went to a lot more lynchings than they would have liked. Besides, whoever it was, I don't think he wanted to hurt her; he may not even have known he was selling shoddy goods."

"So you don't think it was anyone's fault?"

"You're the historian. Who killed the Rockefellers?"

"What?"

"Who do you blame for the holocaust? Or the greenhouse effect? Or Apollo 34? No one person was responsible for any of them. Hannah shouldn't have had the boost. The slime who sold a counterfeit to her as a genuine Apple shouldn't have. The counterfeiter shouldn't—and so on. There's some blame left over for her parents, for telling her so much crap she felt the only way she could find out what was true was to try it herself... but I think the worst you can blame yourself for is not being in the right place at the time."

Melissa shook her head violently. "Everyone knows you can get cheap brain-boosts on campus, and they know the Mafia is selling counterfeit cyberware, so they know there's a risk, but no-one does anything about it, either because they don't care or because they're scared of—"

"Cyberware's big business, Hulkower," Peter said, softly. "It was inevitable that the Mafia would muscle in on it."

Melissa wasn't listening; she stopped suddenly, and stared at the tomb at the right of the exit. "Do you know who's buried there?" she asked.

"No."

"Alan Turing."

"*The* Alan Turing? The cybernetician?"

She nodded. Peter let her stare and sob for nearly a minute, then gently squeezed her shoulders. "He's dead, Hulkower. Hannah's dead. Everyone in this place is dead. If you try taking on Silicon Valley, you'll be dead. Let's get out of here, huh?"

salvation

The sign on the door read

MUSEUM
ADULTS ONLY
MON-SAT 1.00 P.M. TO 11 P.M.
ADMISSION: $10.00

It was competently hand-lettered, but I guess in a place like Mercury you'd have plenty of time to practise calligraphy. I'd been surprised not to see any satellite dishes outside, until I saw the rack of videos—a third of them R-rated—in the roadhouse. I guess that answered any questions I might have had about what people did for entertainment around here.

Heidi had started making strange noises late that afternoon when I was heading back to the highway; I'd hastily grabbed a map to see if there was any place closer than Salvation, and discovered Mercury. The guy at the garage had promised to look at her and see if he could patch her up well enough to get me to a town where they might have some replacement parts for a '69 Kombi, but this threatened to take all night and he recommended I stay at the motel. The Mercury Motel proved to be an old mining company pre-fab hut behind the roadhouse, but I suspected that if I didn't hire a room, I'd find the $60 added to my bill at the garage. Besides, the showers were free to hotel guests, against five bucks for transients, so I paid up. The room was spartan, its paint job reminiscent of a hospital, and the bed no better than the mattress in Heidi; no TV, no phone or phone jack (there was a solar-powered phone booth outside, but no-one was expecting me for at least a month and I couldn't think of anyone who'd be particularly happy to hear from me), no fridge, no bar, no plumbing, no towels or soap, but it had a noisy air-conditioner, cleanish sheets, a bolt on the door, a chair and table, and that courtesy common in English and Australian hotels and so often missing from their American counterparts, a kettle and the makings for tea and coffee. I plugged the laptop in to recharge, and looked through my haul of the last few days. Apart from an opalised ammonite, a beautiful *Dactylioceros* about 5 cm across, there was nothing to become excited about, and this showed in my notes for the article I was supposed to be writing. Wondering if there was anything interesting in the museum, I headed for the shower to make myself a little more presentable.

The water was so hard that I could barely even get the shampoo to lather, and it took me nearly half an hour to wash enough of the dust out of my hair and beard so that I looked like a blond instead of a redhead. Then I shaved and, wearing my cleanest jeans and T-shirt, walked back through the dust to the roadhouse.

There was a pretty blond girl behind the counter, almost certainly the daughter of the woman who'd taken my money for the room. She looked to be about seventeen, with eyes of dark blue flecked with green, eyes that a jeweller would have paid a fortune for. She was nodding to the sound from the cassette player, a C&W version of 'Green Green Grass of Home', probably someone's idea of a joke. The only green for miles was the paint on the roof, though maybe that changed in the rainy season. "Hi. Can I help you?"

"Museum open?"

"Sure. Ten bucks, and you get ten bucks off if you decide to buy anything."

"Okay." I fished two fives out of my wallet. She rang it up on the old cash register, then handed me a key she took from the drawer. I unlocked the door, hit the light switch, and then stared around the small, windowless room.

It was furnished like a bedroom, and once I'd gotten past the shock of the pictures on the wall, I guessed it'd been a girl's bedroom. Most of the pictures, however, were stills and covers from blue movies. I was reading one of the covers when the television behind me came on, showing a conventionally pretty redhead with augmented breasts performing a hasty striptease. I stared at this for a few seconds, then turned my attention back to the video cover. *Red Scorpio*, it screamed in imitation Cyrillic. *A Heavenly Body with a Stinger in her Tail*, starring Natalia, Cinnabar, Tianna, Ona Zee, Tony Tedeschi, T. T. Boy. The redhead on the cover might have been the redhead on the TV screen, but I wouldn't have sworn to it. The next title, *The Gods Must Be Horny*, boasted Domonique Simone, Janet Jacme, Nina Hartley, Cinnabar, Marc Wallice, and Julian St Jox. Cinnabar was the only common element (pun unintended) in *Bust in Space*, *Deep Down Under* and *Night of the Loving Redhead*. If I'd been left in any doubt, the two covers furthest from the door were for *The Sins of Cinnabar* and *A Taste of Cinnabar*.

Interspersed among the porn were amateur shots of the same girl pre-surgery—in a ballgown; in a leotard; in a bikini; in a gymslip; in the uniform of a popular fast-food chain; in a t-shirt and broad-brimmed hat accessorised with a bolt-action rifle; topless behind a bar; between another two pretty girls outside a King's Cross strip joint. I glanced around the room, and saw a bolt-action rifle—the same model, if not the same gun—and ballgown on display in a locked glass case amid an exhibition of bras, panties, corsets, suspender belts, high-heeled pumps and boots. The TV screen now showed the top half of Cinnabar's face; the video had been cut down for an R rating. I leaned against the door, and shook my head.

I've seen a lot of tourist traps, from Graceland to the London Dungeon, and I'm not easily appalled, but Mercury was starting to make my flesh creep. I kept glancing over my shoulder, half-expecting to see the Candid Camera team. Why a monument to a porno starlet here, in the middle of the outback? Even the probability that she'd been born here and named herself after the place (Cinnabar is a sulphide of mercury, approximately the same colour as her hair) didn't justify it.

Or maybe it did; maybe this reflected glory was Mercury's greatest claim to fame. Local girl makes it into movies, even if you can't see the bottom half of her face.

I took one last look, then walked back out. Before I could speak, the girl behind the counter handed me a catalogue. I looked at her, noticing the family resemblance for the first time; she looked almost nothing like the Cinnabar of the videos, but a lot like the girl in the ballgown and the bikini. The catalogue gave prices for different videos, magazines, and underwear. "The videos are uncut," she said, quietly.

"No, thanks," I said, and smiled weakly. "I don't have a VCR."

She looked at me more closely. "Is that where you're from? California?"

"Huh?" I looked down at my T-shirt; it showed a dinosaur eating a city, with the caption 'Let's Do Lunch in California'. "No, the shirt's from San Francisco; I'm from Sydney."

"What's it like?"

"Sydney? A lot like San Francisco, but warmer. They're my two favourite cities, but don't ask me to choose between them."

"Don't they scare you?"

"What? No. Why?"

"They'd scare me," she said, a little wistfully, and then looked me in the eye. "You're staying the night, aren't you?"

"Looks that way."

"Will you want dinner?"

"So, what brings you out this way?"

By eight o'clock, I was fairly sure I'd met the entire human population of Mercury. Sharon cooked and cleaned and worked in the shop, the mechanic was her brother, and her mother managed the place and kept the bar when there were any customers. There were none that night, so she was sitting opposite me at my unsteady table while I chewed at my microwaved cheeseburger.

"I look for rocks," I said. "Fossils, meteorites, that sort of thing."

"Why?"

I laughed. "It's what I like doing. I'm a geologist by training, and a bum by nature."

"You can't get a job as a geologist?"

I considered telling her that I could, if I was willing to work for my father, but she didn't inspire that degree of trust. "I probably could, but picking fruit pays better."

She grunted. "Sharon says you've been to America."

"A few times; my mother has family there."

"You been to Santa Monica?"

"Yes."

"My daughter used to live there. Cindy."

"It's a big place," I said. "Los Angeles... nearly as many people there as there are in all of Australia."

"I didn't think you'd know her," she said. "Just she's the only person from Mercury ever became famous. Town started drying up ever since they shut down the railway, we're too far from the highway, nobody comes here any more, the roadhouse is all that's left—that, and some ruins around the place. Roo-shooters used to come here, but there hasn't been a cull in a couple of years. Even our regulars are moving out, or going to Salvation for a drink, or dying. Where's your home?"

"Parked in the garage next door."

She stared at me, obviously trying to decide whether I was joking. "That's all you've got? That old van? Seems to me you could do better than that. No job, no home... what does your family do?"

"Work for a mining company; that's how I became interested in geology." Actually, they *own* the company, but I don't like telling anyone that.

"Are they disappointed in you?"

"Dad is. Mum... I don't know. Her parents were beatniks, big Kerouac fans." She looked at me blankly. "I used to spend holidays with them, and they'd drive me around the country, didn't much matter where we went."

She shook her head. "Strange people." I don't think she meant it as a compliment, but I let it pass.

Sharon hammered on my door the next morning, waking me. "Sorry about this, but Tom says he can't fix your fuel pump without getting some parts flown in. He needs to know right away so he can get them put on the plane."

"Plane?"

"There's an airstrip at Salvation, and they can put it on a truck through to here, but it'll cost—maybe more than the car is worth, according to Tom."

I nodded. "Can you give me five minutes to get dressed?"

Tom, the mechanic, was leaning in the shade of the verandah, half-way between the garage and the phone. The cost of having the parts flown to Salvation was steep but it wouldn't break me, and quite apart from Heidi's sentimental value, I didn't see any other way out of Mercury in a hurry. "They should be here by sunset," Tom muttered. "Have you out of here tomorrow."

"Thanks."

He grunted. "Look, we're having a party here tonight. As long as you're staying, you want to come?"

I glanced at Sharon, who was looking at me with something like hope. "Yeah. Sure. What's the party for?"

"It's a surprise. You'll see."

The truck arrived at quarter to six, and the driver was carrying two parcels; Tom took one, and wandered back to the garage, and his mother grabbed the other and disappeared into her room. I expected the truckie to leave, but after filling the tank and grabbing a Pepsi, he also wandered into the garage. Less than an hour later, an old Land Rover pulled up outside, and by seven thirty, there were eight vehicles in the carpark, and another eleven men in the bar.

At quarter past eight, when everyone had a beer, our landlady looked around the tavern with mingled excitement and disappointment, obviously resigned to the fact that no-one else was turning up. "Okay," she bellowed, "the moment you've all been waiting for." There was a loud cheer from Tom and the truckie, quieter approval from the others. I looked at her nervously; she was standing beneath a blow-up of the picture of Cinnabar topless in the bar, and I wondered what was coming next. Was she about to strip, or would it be Sharon? Then I remembered the package, and relaxed slightly; it was probably just another video, Cinnabar's latest opus. "The newest additions to the museum have arrived," she announced. "For the next hour only, admission is free!"

The truckie led the procession out of the bar, past Sharon, and into the room next to the rack of videos. I didn't notice anything different at first, but I followed Tom to the display case. There, on a small table, were a small revolver and an urn full of ashes.

"Some people say she was murdered," trumpeted her mother from the doorway. "Some say she shot herself. Whichever story is true, the important thing is that she's finally home!"

"Took a lot of red tape," Tom muttered, "but they got here at last. Reckon this'll bring a lot more people in, huh?"

I don't know what I said, but I slipped out of the crowd as quickly as I could without drawing attention to myself, walked a few hundred metres into the desert, and threw up.

"Are you going to be coming back?" asked Sharon, as I hauled the backpack into Heidi.

"No, I don't think so." Tom emerged from the gloom of the garage to hand me my receipt, then disappeared again to nurse his hangover. "But let me know if you're ever coming to Sydney."

"I can't," she said. "Mum needs me here. She's tried getting other people in to cook since Cindy left, but they keep leaving; besides, we can't afford to pay them any more. And this is our place, this is where we've always lived."

I looked at her, wanting to drag her into the van and drive away with her, just drive; instead, I grabbed my collector's bag and removed a small partly pyritized ammonite, a *Clymenia*. "I found this near here," I said. "They lived here when this place was under the Inland Sea. This species died out about 400 million years ago. Keep it."

She looked puzzled, then brightened. "Thank you. Have a good trip."

"Sure. Can I have another look in the museum before I go?"

"Yeah, no worries." I reached for my wallet, but she put her hand on my arm. "It's okay, no charge."

"Thanks." I took the key, walked in, shut the door behind me, then took a deep breath. The TV came on, showing Cinnabar straddling a ponytailed man in the back seat of a Land Rover. Forcing the lock on the display case was easy, and I emptied the urn into a ziplock bag, which I sealed and stuffed back into my kit. Then I replaced the empty urn, closed the display case, walked back to Heidi, and headed for Salvation.

It was a bleak grey April day when I returned to Sydney, and the beach was all but empty when I poured Cinnabar's ashes into the ocean and stared out to sea as the sun set behind me. I didn't know you, girl, I thought, but I think I know how you feel. There are some places no-one should ever have to go home to.

founding fathers

Phil Carmichael was playing Kelly pool against three of his deputies and Bennett, the Dean of Genetics, when his secretary (a subroutine of the city computer), speaking through his wristcom, told him about the message from offworld. He swore mildly—his duties as a censor occupied more of his time than intervening in domestic disputes—before potting the three, putting himself out of the game. "Duty calls," he apologised to the other players, and opened the mike on his wristcom. "Where's the signal from?"

"The source identifies itself as the spaceship *Altair*."

"A ship?" Carmichael had reached his office—only five paces from the pool table—by now. "What's the message?"

"'Greetings to the people of the Free State of Ivory. This is the spaceship *Altair*, requesting clearance to land a shuttle. Estimated time of arrival one hundred and seventy five Terran hours. Have wonderful news.'"

"One…" Carmichael lowered his bear-like bulk into a chair hurriedly. "That's less than three days."

"Two point eight nine," nitpicked the computer.

"And there's been no previous contact with this ship?"

"No."

Carmichael shook his head. "That's bullshit. No sign of it at all?"

"No."

"Do you have a fix on it?"

"Yes," replied the computer. "Two point oh four billion miles distant, a little over three light-hours." A holo appeared above Carmichael's cloned oak desk, showing the ship's position relative to the planets orbiting 70 Ophiuchi A. Carmichael, no astronomer, stared at it for a moment and did the math on his wristcom. A journey of three light-hours taking nearly three days, that was less than five percent of the speed of light... but they wanted to land a shuttle, so they'd have to be decelerating.

"Hold on a second," he said, rubbing his chin. "Do you have any reading on how fast this ship's moving now? Or how big it is?"

There was a moment's silence. "Not at present. I have summoned the Dean of Astronomy."

"I don't like this," Carmichael growled. "A ship shouldn't just be able to sneak into a system like that with no warning. Could it be a probe some joker's sent up from here?" He looked at the clock hanging next to the picture of his wife, to see if it was April first on Earth. It wasn't.

"Insufficient data."

If you mean you don't know, say so, he thought. "What's the maximum size it *could* be and not give you a clear reading?" he asked, wondering whether it was worth the risk of disturbing the mayor for what might still prove to be a hoax. He rather liked his job, and knew that he was unlikely to be re-elected without Burgess's endorsement.

"The object is clearly less than two miles in diameter with a mass of no more than ten trillion tons."

So, maybe a fifth the size of the *Forrest*, or maybe much smaller. It could still be a starship, he thought; maybe one with a more efficient drive, or just a smaller crew. Of course, a probe could be as small as two feet diameter and weigh less than ten pounds. "Do we have any record of a starship named the *Altair*?"

"No."

"Nothing of that name being built before we left? No other radio transmissions?"

"No."

"Shit," he muttered. "Where is van Neukirk? At the observatory?"

"Yes."

"Call him, tell him I'm on my way."

At this distance, the planet was invisible against the orange sun, but Natsuki picked up the radio signals within seconds of the wormhole closing behind them. "That answers *that* question," he said.

"It's inhabited?" asked Paratene.

"I think so. I'm getting music, voices in Amerish... doesn't sound like a probot. It's coming from near the edge of the ecosphere, which fits; I can't be sure until we're closer, but it's almost certainly the second planet, the one *Pathfinder* reported."

Paratene nodded. "What do we know about it?"

"One point oh two gravities, atmosphere seventy-two percent nitrogen, nineteen percent oxygen, five percent carbon dioxide, two percent argon," said Melendez, the planetologist. "Consistent with aquatic life. Surface water sixty-eight percent. The probots didn't find any life on land except for plant formations on the coastal plains, and all we really know about those is the colour; blue-green shading to indigo the further you go from the equator. One moon, about four hundred klicks diameter. Axial tilt is about thirty-three degrees, so seasonal effects shouldn't be too bad, and the probots didn't pick up any major windstorms; the tropics, at least, should be habitable."

"And the settlers?"

"One ship," said Toure. "The *Forrest*. Left Earth thirty years ago, so they would have been here five, six years at most."

Paratene nodded again, as her headware did the math. Twenty four years trip time as measured on Earth, seventeen point one as measured on board, but still a hell of a long time to spend on a colony ship, even with eighty to ninety percent in coldsleep at any one time. "Population?"

"4320. It was built for five thousand." Toure shrugged. "The record suggests they left before any more decided to opt out."

"What do you know about them?"

Toure stared into the images conjured up by her headware memory. Paratene and Melendez were more than a century her junior, even if you combined their ages; they'd never been to Earth, and she wasn't sure how much of its history they'd been taught. How to explain white supremacists to people who'd only heard of the Ku Klux Klan in a Sherlock Holmes story, or the National Front to people who had no experience of nations? "They're genetic purists of a sort you wouldn't be familiar with," she said. "They believe that the genes for certain physical characteristics—pigmentation, mostly—were linked to those for intelligence and some behavioural traits. It's been a common delusion on Earth—" She shrugged, her expression wry. "And it probably still is, but only a minority of the believers became militant enough to form groups and arm themselves against what they saw as a menace. Most of the groups were disarmed—some slowly, some suddenly and with force—and many of them merged until the names became meaningless.

"A few thousand of those militants built and manned the *Forrest*; their intention was to create a world for pale-skinned people of north-western European ancestry. It's an old idea—it was called segregation, *apartheid*, or *lebensraum*, depending on where you were from—and often a poisonous one, though it's had most of its teeth pulled over the past few centuries." One of the greatest blows to white supremacists had been the cloning of *Homo neandertalensis* and pleistocene *Homo sapiens* from fossil DNA, in the early 22nd century; the Neanderthals had proven to be fair-complexioned and blue-eyed, with hair shading from platinum to reddish blond (with a tendency to early male-pattern baldness), while the Cro-Magnons were olive-skinned with dark eyes and curly hair. "But you know how difficult it was to find people with the necessary skills who were willing to leave Earth without any hope of ever returning. Most migrants were fanatics of one stripe or another." This was greeted with a stony silence; Toure was, after all, talking about Melendez's parents and Paratene's grandparents. Athene and Tvashtri had been settled by curious scientists and adventurers, but the last three space arks sent to more distant worlds had been populated by lesbian separatists, the solar system's last communists, and finally white supremacists. None of these groups had been content with small, enclosed communities on the planets or asteroids of the solar system; all were looking for somewhere *completely* isolated from whoever they saw as their oppressors or enemies. Toure wondered idly who would have been given the next world if wormhole navigation hadn't been discovered.

"Will it be safe to land?"

Toure shrugged. "Ask me after we've spoken to them. We don't *need* the planet; there's always the option of building a waystation on one of the larger moons in the system. The big gas giant has one with nearly half a gravity, far enough away for radiation not to be a problem. The Martians would be happier there, anyway."

"I know," said Paratene.

"And they *chose* to isolate themselves from Earth," said Natsuki. "Do they have weapons, Rahal?"

Toure looked through the data, and nodded. "They had mammoth embryos in their gene bank, and took cyberfac specs for sidearms powerful enough to kill mammoth, as well as scatterguns for hunting and tasers for police work. And some of the groups had a tradition of weapons training, even for their children. How *many* guns they have, I guess we'll have to wait to find out."

Pieter van Neukirk, the Dean of Astronomy, had a job even cushier than Carmichael's, though he'd been busy enough on the voyage and had spent almost no time in coldsleep en route. At seventy-six Terran years, he was the second oldest man on the planet, and had been thinking of retiring before he was called on to teach high school. He listened to the message from the *Altair* nervously, privately agreeing with Carmichael; it *should* have been impossible for a starship to enter the system without him detecting it, and he was worried that he might have screwed up royally. "Whatever it is, it's on the night side," he explained. "We won't be able to determine its size until after sunset; it's just lucky we have a comsat there."

"Do you think it's a hoax? Some clown sending up a probe with a recording or a simple computer—"

van Neukirk shook his head, as the instrument readouts reflected on his shiny scalp. "Not without either of us knowing about it. Besides, everybody here's either too old or too young for that sort of practical joke. Give it another, uh, ten years," he predicted gloomily.

"So what do you think it is? They sent another ship to settle the other side of the planet, or something?"

"They shouldn't have done, not without clearing it with us... but..."

"What?"

"Maybe they thought there weren't enough of us to survive. Remember when somebody, uh, destroyed all the human embryos in the gene bank?"

"I'm not likely to forget it," said Carmichael, drily. It was the only serious unsolved crime they'd had since leaving Earth—the destruction of ten thousand human foetuses, frozen at a week old ready for implantation into host mothers or the *Forrest's* artificial wombs. Few people were happy with the official explanation that the security guard on duty at the time, who had suicided a few days later, had been responsible. Both of Carmichael's predecessors had tried to unravel the crime, and he suspected that their failure had something to do with their failure to be re-elected.

van Neukirk apologised. "Of course not. But maybe this is an unmanned ship loaded with replacement embryos. It wouldn't need a crew, just somewhere to drop the cargo..."

"Wouldn't somebody have told us? Shit, Piet, building a starship just for stork duty wouldn't be cheap, and it's not like we still have a lot of supporters back on Earth."

The astronomer nodded. "You're probably right. But if you're scared that this is, uh, an invasion force, I think you can stop worrying. Nobody would bother."

"You're sure?"

"Yeah. They would've just sent an AM-bomb to take out the ship while we were decelerating. *Much* cheaper. Of course, that thing *could* still be some sort of bomb, but the probability's not more than... uh, say one in six." He grinned.

Despite van Neukirk's warning that the ship would be invisible to a naked eye, nearly half of New Virginia's seven thousand people were standing out in the snow at sunset, staring up at the sky. Jessie Randolph, arguably the most influential woman on the planet now that her children were old enough to be left in a creche, was among the crowd with a camera and microphone perched on her shoulder like a parrot, while her male colleagues waited in the observatory or outside the mayor's office. On Earth, Jessie's blonde good looks had gotten her a job as a weather girl on an Idaho flatscreen channel, which made her Ivory's second-best qualified journalist. Perhaps more importantly, she was the wife of chief medtech John Randolph, the descendent of Grand Dragons and Imperial Wizards, and the daughter of Harry Poulsen, the settlement's Chief Justice, official historian, former Attorney-General, and oldest male citizen.

"Why do you think they've come here?"

Jessie knew Aline Bennett's voice too well to need to turn around, though the settlement's only female lawyer wasn't a particularly close friend. "I don't know. van Neukirk says its too small for a colony ship; we don't even know if it's manned at all."

"A new *Pathfinder* or something?" asked Aline, leaning against a wall. She was seven months pregnant, and her feet hurt like hell. "Then why would it need clearance to land a shuttle?"

"Maybe it has cargo for us, something we can't manufacture ourselves."

The lawyer nodded. "van Neukirk suggested embryos, to replace the ones destroyed by the saboteur."

"What does Ben think?"

"He said something about Greeks bearing gifts; how're we supposed to be sure their genes are all white? A sort of one-two punch; the saboteur kills the babies we brought with us, an accomplice on Earth sends us enough genetic trash to form a majority. Before you know it, we have a load of mongrels running around, after all the precautions we took." She shook her head. "But I guess we'll have to wait and see."

Jessie suppressed a shudder. "No-one would do that. They must know we're not dumb enough to fall for a trick that obvious. It'd only take us a few weeks to scan all of the foetuses..." She shook her head. "If they wanted to destroy us, it would've been a lot cheaper and easier to have put a bomb in the ship. Chances are that nobody would have found the wreckage, even if they'd looked; the pieces would've gone in a million different directions and travelled forever."

Aline shrugged. "Maybe they were just too damn soft to kill us outright. Anyway, it's only a theory. Bet you wish you were at the observatory."

"Yes."

Another shrug. "I know how you feel. Every time I go into court, I wonder if I'm doing my client more harm than good just by being a woman."

"Any conclusions?"

She smiled sourly. "Only that a lot depends on the jury, which you can't predict, and sometimes on whether my client is in the right or not."

"Why do you stick with it?"

"I don't know. I'd take Phil up on his offer of a female deputy's position, but not while I'm pregnant; I don't want to waste my time stuck behind a desk. Besides, the judges aren't going to live forever, so there may be a vacancy on the bench for me someday. Any help you can give is appreciated, of course."

"Sorry," Jessie replied. "Dad and I have our differences, but I'm not going to kill him just to get you a promotion."

"That wasn't what I meant, and you know it."

"Sorry. Besides, if they make you a judge, it'll be more than twenty years before we have another female lawyer... unless there's one on that ship, of course."

van Neukirk stared at the instruments, and nodded. "At a first estimate, it's a little more than half a mile long, maybe three hundred yards at its widest point. Moving at about thirteen thousand miles per second, and decelerating. Radiation consistent with a conventional anti-matter drive. I suppose it *could* be manned, but if it is, then either the crew is damn small or they like cramped quarters. The messages they've sent give the impression that it *is* manned, but I'll want to see some people in the flesh before I take that on faith." He managed to keep the fury out of his voice; there was no explanation he could give for a ship that large entering the system undetected, and it looked as though he might have to retire even earlier than he'd expected. He hated farming almost as much as he hated the thought of being shut out from the observatory; the only consolation was that they wouldn't make him teach.

Burgess, the mayor, nodded sagely, then turned to Carmichael. "Any more word about the purpose of their visit?"

"A little. It seems that someone on Athene has invented a faster stardrive, fast enough for crews to make return trips between here and Earth—or any other inhabited system. This one ship has already travelled from Athene to Earth, to Tvashtri, and now here. They haven't said anything about the size of their crew, but they seem to be explorers rather than colonists."

"Why do they want to land?"

"I'm not sure. They haven't answered many of our questions; turnaround time for a message is still nearly six hours." He glanced at van Neukirk, who seemed to be absorbed in his headware. "If I may make a suggestion, your honour..."

van Neukirk suddenly sat bolt upright, almost falling from his stool. "A faster stardrive!"

"What?"

"How much faster could it be? We were travelling at point seven c for most of the voyage—seventy percent of lightspeed," he explained, for Burgess's benefit. "At most, it could be about forty percent faster—ninety-nine percent lightspeed. The trip here would still take more than seventeen standard years objectively, about three months shipboard time. Now, that may make return trips between systems practical, though I'd doubt it; a round trip from Earth to here is still nearly thirty-five years, and Earth can change a lot in that sort of time. *But—*" He drew a deep breath. "Athene to Earth to here is twenty one point four standard years, even at that speed, so the ship would have had to be built at least that long ago. Right?"

The others—Carmichael, Burgess, Poulsen, Bennett, and Keys— looked at him blankly. "So?" asked Burgess.

"Radio," said Carmichael, after a moment's thought. "It's still slower than radio, so news would get here first... but it didn't." He blinked. "You think it can travel faster than light? I thought that was impossible."

"It was, and maybe it still is, but, uh, it *would* explain why we didn't detect it until it was only a few days away."

"So would some new sort of stealth technology," suggested Keys, the Attorney General. "Which do you think is more likely?"

Burgess glanced at Carmichael, who shrugged. "What do you suggest?" the mayor asked.

"We still have a few days to learn their intentions before needing to make a decision," said Carmichael. "At present, I'm in favour of letting them land a safe distance from town and meeting them there... but ask me again tomorrow, and I may say something completely different."

"Piet?"

"He's right. I know *I* have plenty of questions I want to ask." He chuckled. "I gather the same is true of the rest of you? I say we write any questions down, you and Phil can assign them a priority, and we just keep talking until the time-lag gets down to, uh, a more manageable level. Unless anyone else has any better ideas?"

Choosing a landing party took Paratene and Toure two standard days. After listening in to communications with the settlement on Ivory, Toure insisted on restricting the choice to fair-skinned males of western European ancestry who were raised in one gravity. "It's just a hunch, but I don't think they recognise women as being in authority either," she said. "Everyone we've spoken to is male; I haven't seen any evidence that there are any women *alive* down there."

"The records say there were 2109 women on the *Forrest*," replied Paratene.

"That was decades ago! The men may not have bothered waking them out of coldsleep; they might just be raising embryos in the artificial wombs."

"They only have ten of those, and I thought racists tended to homophobia."

"They took plenty of sheep embryos, too."

Paratene laughed, despite herself. "You really dislike these people, don't you?"

Toure looked at her, wondering if the concept of hatred had made the journey to Athene. "I dislike the type, and yes, I admit that's a prejudice. I have a problem with societies that will class me as inferior on first sight—and I grew up in one, so I know of what I speak. But I still think we'd be better off with a man leading the party, at least."

"How large a party do we need?"

"I'd recommend two—a pilot for the shuttle, and someone who can serve as a diplomat. You shouldn't need more than two, and I'd advise against taking fewer."

Paratene nodded. "What about Jean Bailly and David Everett?"

"Everett's a good choice," replied Toure, after a glance at his file. The medtech and psychist-apprentice was younger than she would have liked, only twenty-seven standard years old, but he stood nearly two metres tall, with the handsome looks and athletic build common on Athene. His hair was a rusty brown, his eyes blue-green, and he tended to freckle. "But the Ivorians probably don't like hermaphrodites, either. Do you have another pilot?"

"Alyssa Catania or Madelon Schaefer."

Toure shrugged. "Either would be okay; Everett can choose, if you prefer. He's going to have to *look* as though he's in charge, at least."

"Okay. How long do you need for the briefing?"

"As long as we have. The more history I can teach them, the better they'll understand the Ivorians, and the less likely they are to make any dangerous mistakes."

Despite Keys's protests about leaving the town inadequately defended against a sneak attack, the welcome party—Burgess, Carmichael, Bennett, van Neukirk, and four deputies—left New Virginia six standard days later, while Krueger, the settlement's planetologist, headed back from his surveying expedition on Ivory's far side. Krueger had chosen a landing site on a floodplain where tough terraforming lichens had begun the work of turning rock to soil, and was far enough from town to satisfy Carmichael and Keys.

van Neukirk stared down at the landscape as the tilter flew over it, and shook his head as though he still wasn't used to seeing planets this close up. Much of Ivory was too cold to be habitable, especially during the thirty-hour winter nights; New Virginia straddled the equator, and while the weather there was pleasant enough by his standards, he doubted that they would ever build any towns outside the tropics. He wondered how much population the planet could support. The terraforming plants were doing their work on schedule; there was already enough grass around the town for their sheep and cattle, and in a few years, there would be a habitat large enough for the animals now kept in the zoo—deer, antelope, mammoth, short-faced bears, lions, wolves, passenger pigeons. Only the human population growth would be slower than planned, despite the best efforts of the settlement's men to keep their wives pregnant for the rest of their safe child-bearing years.

"What's wrong?"

van Neukirk looked around, to see Carmichael sitting on his left. "Wrong?"

"You looked worried."

The astronomer shrugged. "I have this strange feeling of *déjà vu*. My father hated cities, kept moving as far from them as his work allowed—that's probably how I became an astronomer; less light pollution, easier to see the stars. But the cities kept expanding and catching up with us, no matter how often we moved." He stared at the native vegetation on the shore, a vast mat of vascular plants similar to terrestrial *Cooksonia*, but more blue than green. "We all chose to isolate ourselves from, uh, the bulk of humanity, and now it's caught up with us."

"They say they'll build their waystation on Terre'Blanche if we don't want them building one here. Not that I understand why they need waystations..."

"They travel by wormhole," said the astronomer, "and the wormholes only form at certain times—don't ask me to explain that, I can't, yet. Most of their travel time is actually spent travelling from wormhole to planet, or just waiting around for the wormhole to form, so the ships aren't built for, uh, long-term occupancy. They've even said there'll be less radio noise to worry about—mail will be so much faster than radio, and cheaper—which will make both of our jobs easier. But I'm wondering how, uh, many of us are going to choose to remain isolated. It won't be difficult to stop people we don't want coming here, but how do we stop the ones we *do* want from leaving? And, uh, do we have that right?"

"You think people will *want* to leave?" asked Burgess. His Australian accent, normally subdued, was strong, a sure sign of anger. van Neukirk glanced at him, then shrugged again. "Some will. We were all prepared to, uh, tough it out when we thought we had no choice, but now that we *do* have a choice..."

"So we don't give them a choice," snapped Burgess.

"I don't know," said Carmichael. "It might be better to have a safety valve. The shortage of single women over the age of five is already causing problems; this might help us do something about the ratio."

"That wasn't my fault," grumped Burgess. "I wanted to restrict emigration to couples, but if we hadn't included single males, we would've gone under the four thousand and they would've taken the planet away from us."

van Neukirk looked at him without much sympathy; he was single himself, being twice divorced, and had been glad to see an exception made. He'd never been particularly political, but he'd been passed over for earlier crews and there hadn't been any competition for the astronomer's position on the *Forrest*, where his qualifications and his Boer ancestry had been considered more important than his social skills. "We're not blaming you," he said. "I'm just wondering what'll happen if enough, uh, people leave that Earth decides that we're no longer viable. Are they going to insist on immigration, maybe giving part of the planet to, uh..."

"Non-whites," muttered Burgess. He reached for the radio. "Jesus, if I could get my hands on the asshole who flushed those... Ben? We need your opinion on something."

David Everett managed to look at the party who stepped out of the tilters without cracking a smile. Five men in khaki, all with huge pistols on their hips; two in high-collared black suits, which might have been formal wear or military uniforms without insignia; and one in a long black robe and a heavy gold chain. Toure, watching through his headware communicator, tentatively identified them as the mayor, security staff, and two advisers, probably scientists. Everett suggested to Madelon that she remain on the shuttle, and walked down the ramp, hands obviously empty. "Welcome to Ivory," said Burgess, flatly.

"Thank you." He resisted the temptation to say either 'We come in peace' or 'Take me to your leader', settling for, "It's good to be on a planet again. I'm David Everett, Executive Officer of the *Altair*." It sounded good, for a totally meaningless title.

"Stick close to them," Toure whispered into his com. "Those are rocket pistols, probably with explosive heads; they're not lethal at point-blank range, and they won't have time to home in on you."

Burgess introduced his team; Everett shook hands with all of them, wondering if he was supposed to be giving the countersign to a secret handshake. "Forgive the informality," said Burgess. "We weren't expecting any visitors."

"That's fine," said Everett, smiling. "This isn't an official visit; I'm just here to make sure everyone's okay, and see if there's anything if you need."

"Did you come alone?"

Everett hesitated. "Tell them the truth," urged Paratene. "We may learn a lot more if Madelon can speak to the women."

"No," he said. "My pilot's in the shuttle. She can fly back to the ship if you prefer, but I'd rather she came with me."

Burgess glanced at van Neukirk and Carmichael, both of whom looked up at the sky. Heavy clouds were gathering above them. "There's room in the tilters for another two," said Burgess, trying not to growl as a drop of rain splattered on his balding pate. "I guess it's up to you."

–II–

Madelon looked at the young mammoths in their pen, which seemed far too flimsy to hold adults. "We won't be releasing them until there are enough trees to feed them all," said Jessie, "and apart from the wolves, we won't be breeding any of the carnivores until then, either. The ecologists on Earth made us take some sabertooth embryos as well, said we'd need them to keep the mammoth numbers in control, but there's no plans to raise them, unless we decide to keep a pair for the zoo. If we need to control the mammoth population, we have guns for the job. Besides, sabertooths are too dumb to learn not to attack humans, and as far as we're concerned, that's too dumb to live. Biodiversity is one thing, but do we have to preserve obvious mistakes?" She shrugged. "Of course, the wombs aren't being used for much, anyway."

Madelon looked at the young animals, and nodded. "David's asked our historian, Dr Toure, to look back at your records to see if she can help your sheriff find out who was responsible for that."

"What can she do?"

"I'm not sure; possibly find something that your people missed at the time."

Jessie shook her head. "People've been trying to solve that one for nearly ten years now, we publish a new theory every year or two, and the best hypothesis is still that Wallace, the security guard who committed suicide, was responsible."

"Toure doesn't think it was one person; she says the job's just too big."

"Everyone thinks that; I suspect it's just that the consequences are too big for the blame to fit on one person. Like political assassinations; most people are unhappy with the idea that one man with a gun can bring down a man with that much power. They'd rather believe in conspiracies. How much longer will you and David be staying?"

"The wormhole won't form for another five standard days, so we'll be gone by then, but David's still negotiating with your council."

"What about? I thought we'd all agreed that you weren't going to be building a base here?"

Madelon nodded. Paratene had agreed with Burgess that all of the Ivorians had chosen to isolate themselves from any other human worlds, and that creating a waystation there in case anyone decided to leave was contrary to the will of the community, though

Toure had tried to insist on a vote. "We've suggested a moratorium of ten standard years. Shortly after that, however, some of your children here will be legally adults under Earth law, and the political climate may have changed." She turned up the heating circuit in her jacket; even spring days on Ivory were much colder than she was accustomed to, and after seventy hours planetside, she was longing to return to the *Altair*. "I suppose we'll have to wait and see."

"A lot of people won't like it," warned Jessie.

"Maybe. I suppose that depends on how they're told about it, doesn't it?"

"What do you mean?"

"Well, forgive me if I've misunderstood the way things are done on this world," said Madelon, "but all of the political jobs seem to be held by men—unless you regard yours as a political job, of course."

Jessie silently walked to the next enclosure, which contained a short-faced bear who looked uncannily like Bert Lahr's Cowardly Lion. "What makes you think that men and women here are going to disagree on this issue? Or any other big issue, for that matter?"

Madelon blinked. "Well, on other worlds..."

"This isn't 'other worlds'," replied Jessie, sharply. "We all agreed on our reason for coming here, and we'll raise our children as they should they be raised, do you understand?" Numbly, Madelon nodded. "I don't know if you think our men can't or don't care about their children, but if you do, you're wrong. They're our bloodline, our future; that's why we gave them a world of their own. You can ask us again in ten years, or ten thousand, and that will still be our answer. What're you going to do then?"

"This is ridiculous," said Toure, as she read through the sheriff's files on the sabotage, which Everett had uploaded from the settlement's computer. "If these people *want* this crime solved, why didn't they keep any records of their interviews?"

"I asked Carmichael that," said Everett, lying on the murderously uncomfortable bed which had been hastily constructed from children's cots. "He says that since everyone who was interviewed was cleared, there was no point in keeping the records. At least, that's what his predecessor told him."

"That's bullshit. If their records are correct, there were only 481 people out of coldsleep. Now, I know that's a lot of interviews for one sheriff and three deputies, but Hell, this was the only serious crime they had to deal with in the entire voyage."

"The sheriff is elected," Everett replied. "I don't know what he needs in the way of qualifications. And he appoints his own deputies."

"Then whoever was sheriff at the time—Fleischer?—must either have been an absolute incompetent, or have had reasons of his own for a cover-up. Even *elected* officials aren't usually that stupid. Look, under their law, abortion is murder, isn't it?"

"Yes."

"So we're talking *ten thousand murders*, supposedly performed by one person overnight—not that I believe that part either—and fewer than 500 suspects. That may sound like a large number, but he knows that at least *one* of them has to be guilty. And it's easy for a computer to scan someone and tell when they're probably lying; listening for changes to heartbeat and respiration, tremors in the voice, watching eye movement, infra-red to detect blush response..."

"His notes say he interviewed everyone who wasn't on duty, and had the computer collate the alibis. Those whose alibis didn't pan out, he interviewed again. No-one confessed, and he didn't find any forensic evidence, so..."

"So he gave up, and his successor—Earl?—not only adds nothing to what little is known, but scrubs the interview records of everyone he thinks must have been innocent. Have you spoken to these idiots?"

"Fleischer is dead—heart attack, about a month after the *Forrest* landed. Earl, who was one of his deputies, ran for re-election, was beaten by Carmichael, and is with a survey team mapping farside." Everett shrugged. "We still have the duty roster, if that helps. It clears another twenty people, including the chief medtech."

Toure sighed. "Let's hope he doesn't erase more than he finds this time around. Have you looked around the gene bank?"

"Yes."

"You're a medtech; you must have some training with that sort of equipment." Everett nodded. "How long do you think it'd take one person to circumvent the security system, remove ten thousand embryos from the freezer, and—what was done with them?"

"There's a matter recycler in the lab. According to the computer, and Fleischer's records, it must have been running hot; it disposed of 230 pounds—that's about 105 kilos—of matter in less than an hour. It would have been much easier to let the embryos thaw, but that would have destroyed the animals too."

"105 kilos? That's two adult corpses worth! Didn't that trigger any alarms?"

"The security guard wasn't at his post."

Toure whistled. "So that's why the dog didn't bark."

"What?"

"Sherlock Holmes. Never mind. Where was he?"

"He wouldn't say. Fleischer's notes say he suspected he was with a woman, but he wouldn't name her. As there weren't any single women out of coldsleep at the time, that meant adultery, which is considered about as serious as dereliction of duty—worse, even; they might accept mitigating circumstances for deserting a post, but adultery tends to be fatal for both parties. Lynch law. The guard, Wallace, hanged himself in his cell—it seems Fleischer forgot to confiscate his belt—apparently to protect the woman."

"Uh-huh. That strikes me as suspicious, too; even if his getting laid were a regular occurrence, it's a pretty remarkable coincidence that this was done while no-one was looking after security for that section. What other security was there on the gene bank?"

"Locks, alarms, and scanners, but the individual got past them all, which meant they probably had to either work for security or the gene lab... or had access to their security codes, anyway."

"Cameras?"

"They fooled the infra-red by increasing the heat in the room to forty degrees. The holo camera did a scan of the room every fifteen minutes, but someone unplugged it between 1418 and 1433 hours ship-time and plugged it in between 1503 and 1518, while the guard..."

"Was having his brains fucked out, yeah. Could one person do all that in forty-five minutes?"

Everett thought about it. "I don't think *I* could, even if I knew exactly what I was doing with the security system. I think it'd take two people. Three would be even faster."

"And a third or fourth to keep the guard occupied. Let me guess; all of the security and genetics lab staff had alibis, so Earl wiped the record of their interviews?"

"It looks that way."

"How much of this has Carmichael noticed? How bright is he?"

"I don't think he wants to criticise a former superior, but he seems genuinely pissed that all the interviews were erased. Most of the people here believe there's been some sort of cover-up, even if it's only of the sheriffs' ineptitude after the fact."

"Which sounds—just a second." Toure looked up from the monitor; a window had appeared on the screen, showing Paratene outside her door. "Yes?"

"Can I come in? I have to talk to you about the treaty."

"Just a second." She turned her attention back to Everett. "Good work. I'll call you back. Okay, come in."

Paratene walked in. Unlike her own cabin, which was decorated with copies of Maori art and holos of a New Zealand her ancestors had known but which she'd never seen, Toure's showed nothing of her origin except for a holo of her family tree growing ivy-like from the desk. The floor and one wall were blank, and the ceiling and other walls showed the planet below and the surrounding starscape. Paratene sat down on the bed, the only item of furniture apart from the desk and chair, and looked at the image of the planet. "We've finished drafting the agreement with the Ivorians. Do you want to read it?"

'We', Toure knew, meant Paratene and the computer, the nearest they had to a lawyer on board. "Yes. Thanks."

"I'm sorry for not giving you more of a voice in the negotiations." Toure nodded stiffly. "You and Burgess would never have agreed, and if we'd stayed and waited for a vote... I doubt it would have made any real difference. Has anyone approached Everett or Schaefer, asking to be taken offworld?"

"No," replied Toure, sourly.

"I guess we're never going to agree either."

Toure raised an eyebrow. "Agree on what?"

"On this." Paratene shifted uncomfortably on the bed. "On the Ivorians and their children. Okay, we agree on their right to leave when they become adults, but you obviously don't believe the adults have the right to censor what their children read."

"When you put it that way, I'm surprised *you* can defend it."

Paratene shrugged. "I didn't want to quibble over wording. But look at it from the Ivorians point of view. All they want is to preserve their genes. What's wrong with that? Why do you think we're seeding the planets with species that are extinct on Earth? Mammoths, dodos, passenger pigeons, wolves, tigers, blue whales... How long was spent reconstructing enough Neanderthal DNA to clone Neanderthals? Why should we be so determined to stop them?"

"If it were just their genes," said Toure, slowly, "I'd agree with you. But they want to preserve a way of thinking, too, and that way of thinking is poisonous. At the core of it is more than their right to survive; they believe they have the god-given right to dominate humanity, and to exterminate what they can't subjugate, and their heroes are men who've killed for this right."

"Most societies have killers for heroes," Paratene reminded her, gently.

"Really? Who are the heroes of Athene? Or Tvashtri? Or Sappho? Or Mars?" Paratene opened her mouth to speak, but Toure hadn't finished. "Of course, if you mean most societies on *Earth*, you may be right. How many 'societies' are there on Athene? Do the physicists sit around and reminisce about how their ancestors nuked the geneticists? Is anyone ready to fight to the death for the superiority of the haiku over the sestina?"

"Rahal, this isn't a joke..."

"Have your cricket teams ever shot it out? Or fans of your soccer clubs ever beaten the living crap out of each other? Has a major riot ever broken out because of the accent of an actor chosen to play Macbeth? *That's* happened on Earth."

"Last millenium," said Paratene, waving her hand as though the nineteenth and twentieth centuries were merely a bad smell.

"No, of course nothing like that's happened on Athene; even if one of them could get a gun, there aren't enough cricketers to play a match if anyone's injured."

"I gather they haven't passed the enthusiasm onto their children?"

"No; most of them get bored with it and stop playing when they hit adolescence..." She noticed the smile on Toure's face. "What?"

"You included?"

"Yes. So?"

"I know that at least some of your ancestors came from New Zealand. You don't feel you have to preserve cricket as one of the traditions of your nation?"

"Cricket's a tradition of the British Empire, which has been dead for centuries... I know, you're about to say the same for white supremacy, aren't you? I don't think it's all that good an analogy."

Toure shrugged. "Maybe not—as long as your cricketing society defends the right of people *not* to play cricket or to be bored comatose watching the bloody game. I don't think the Ivorians are that benevolent. If there's anyone they hate more than non-whites, it's white nigger-lovers."

"Nigger?"

"Black. From 'negro'. Nigger-lovers are whites who associate with people like you and me. That's why I've agreed to the ten-year embargo; I don't think the planet will be safe for visitors until the current population are safely dead. Maybe the society could have remained stable without any outside influence, but I doubt it; these people need an underclass to feel superior to, and I have a sneaking suspicion that role will fall on the women. I just hope their children aren't past redemption."

"*All* new settlements tend to keep the women pregnant and sheltered for the first few years," said Paratene, heavily. "Do you want to separate all the children from their parents? That strikes me as violating the rights of the children *and* the parents. What rights do you think the Ivorians *are* entitled to?"

"No, I don't want to break up the families," snapped Toure. "That's not only a violation of rights, it's an obscenity. I will defend the human rights of every human on that planet. The *society*, however, has no rights, except those of the individuals who make it up."

"That's a bit extreme," said Paratene, cautiously, after thinking for a moment. "As you said, some of my ancestors were Maoris, and without the tribe..." Her voice trailed off.

"Yes, I know," said Toure. "You divided the world into your tribe and the *pakeha*, those not of your tribe. My 'tribe' was a small Muslim enclave in the south-west of Australia. They practised female circumcision as part of their religious tradition."

"What's circumcision?"

"In men and hermaphrodites, removal of the foreskin; it's still performed in medical emergencies. In women, it's removal of part or all of the clit hood, sometimes the clit itself, sometimes the labia minora as well." She looked at Paratene, who had turned pale. "If a man had done that to a child, back when I was young, he would have been imprisoned as a monster, and probably beaten to death by his fellow inmates, whatever excuse he'd given... but because it was the practise of a *society*, the Australian government didn't dare interfere. Freedom of religion meant the freedom to mutilate children—as long as they're your own children, of course, and after all, it's not as though they were doing anything to the *boys*." She grimaced reassuringly. "Don't worry. I had a new body cloned for myself when I was twenty-seven—this is my third—and as far as I know, I'm the last survivor of that community and female circumcision hasn't been practised in decades, even on Earth. But what if we'd given *them* their own planet?"

"Damn, you're good," muttered Carmichael, as Everett potted the black.

Everett grinned. "It's the only sport we have room for on the ship, unless we want to do laps of the spa."

"Uh-huh. We had a stadium with a baseball diamond, a football field... everything except golf, which is no way for a grown man to spend his time anyhow." He racked the balls. "So, how much room you got on that ship of yours for passengers?"

"Why?" asked Everett, still grinning. "You're not thinking of leaving here, are you?"

"Shit, no," replied Carmichael, grinning back. "Just wondering if anybody else was."

"I can't tell you that," said Everett, instantly serious.

"Guess it doesn't matter. Just figured that after all the fine work you done on the sabotage, it'd be funny if the saboteur used your ship to escape on."

"Why would they do that?"

"What would happen to them if they did? Is killing babies a crime where you're from?"

Everett stood there, quietly chalking his cue. "In this case, it'd be treated as sabotage. It wouldn't attract the death penalty, which I gather would be the punishment here?"

"At the least."

"It'd be a mess," said Everett, after a moment's thought. "The wormhole drive is fast enough that extradition becomes possible; the question is whether anyone would return suspects here if they knew the probability existed that they'd be executed." He narrowly avoided saying 'lynched'. "You think the guilty parties are likely to try escaping?"

"I don't see why not. They obviously don't agree with our way of life—unless they want to stick around and do some more harm."

"Or are already dead."

"Yeah, that's possible. I'd still like to know for sure, though."

"How many deaths have there been since the incident?"

"114. Mostly natural causes or accidents; only twelve suicides and seven murder or manslaughter, all solved. It's your break."

"What? Oh, thanks." A few seconds later, staring at the constellation of balls on the table, he asked, "Have you told anyone else about the investigation?"

"Only Keys and Burgess; I don't know who they've told. Why?"

"Not important. You were in coldsleep when the incident took place, weren't you?"

"Yep. Why?"

"Just wondering about Wallace. Fleischer suspected that he'd been with a woman, but do you know if he searched Wallace's bunk for hairs or other forensic evidence? I know the people who actually destroyed the embryos wore gloves, but maybe Wallace's woman..."

"If there *was* such a woman," said Carmichael. "I knew Wallace pretty well; he liked women, especially blondes, but I'll bet the only ones he had were in his fucking imagination."

"Maybe, but did Fleischer check?"

A pause. "It's not in his files?"

"No, not unless he left a back-up somewhere."

Carmichael sighed. "If he found anything, anything that might have been a clue, he would have checked it on the genescanner in the lab. The computer should still have a record of that—unless it was erased, which he couldn't have done without the A-G's clearance. I think you're wasting your time—even if Fleischer had found a woman's hair or whatever in Wallace's bunk, it wouldn't necessarily mean she'd been there that night, or with him—but if you like, I can ask Keys to let you examine the records."

"Thanks."

"Nothing," muttered Everett. "Either no material was ever scanned, or the records have been erased. Shit."

Carmichael shrugged. "I said I thought you were wasting your time—what're you doing now?"

"Just a hunch," he said. The sheriff looked around the lab, worried; they had clearance to be in the gene bank, it was kept under minimal security now that the embryos were already gone, but the cavernous room made him extremely nervous. It was, in its way, Ivory's answer to Ford's Theatre, Dealey Plaza, or Mitre Square.

"What sort of hunch? All you've got there are the records of scans already performed."

"I know—that's interesting... Three scans performed four days before the crime was committed, and not erased. Human, too."

"How can you tell?" asked Carmichael, peering at the screen.

"It's my job," replied Everett. "Just a second." He stared at a row of letters and figures, glad that the *Altair's* computer was recording everything he saw and heard. He checked the data on the screen against the memories in his headware, and whistled softly.

"What?"

"Can you call the ship, ask them to wake Dr Toure? I think I've found the answer."

"You know who killed the babies?"

"No, but I think I know *why*. But I need her to check this out against the ship's computer; I'd hate to be wrong about this."

Carmichael shrugged. "Okay. I'll meet you in my office when you're finished."

Toure breathed out slowly. "David, you're a genius."

Everett blushed. "Just dumb luck, more likely. I was looking for the wrong thing in the wrong place, and I saw this, and—"

"And you recognised it for what it was, and what it meant. Don't underestimate yourself. This changes everything."

"It doesn't tell us who destroyed the embryos... *if* they destroyed them. Maybe they hid a few amid the cattle or mammoth, as insurance. Embryos look pretty much alike, whatever species they're from, until they're much more advanced than these were."

Toure considered this. "The old purloined letter schtick, eh? Problem with that is that all of those embryos were meant to be spawned by now, and according to Schaefer's report, more than a third have been. Now, I'm not a medtech, but wouldn't it be easier to hide them in the coldsleep chambers?"

"I hadn't thought of that... can you dock with the *Forrest*, send someone in to look?"

"I'll have to clear it with the Ivorians, but I think so. Most of the crew are pretty bored."

"Okay. I want to talk to a few people, even if it is officially night here." He and Madelon had pretty much adjusted to the cold nights and the orange sunlight, but they were still finding it difficult to adjust to the sixty-hour Ivorian day with its twenty-hour sleep cycles. "Carmichael's been a great help, but I need to talk to Bennett, the geneticist. Pity his predecessor's dead."

"Unfortunate, that, both the sheriff who lead the investigation *and* the geneticist having died."

"It was more than nine standard years ago," said Everett, locking the door to the gene bank behind him and jogging across the courtyard, "and neither of them were young; people do die naturally, you know. Besides, Thompson, the old dean, was in coldsleep at the time, so he's not exactly a suspect. Not for destroying the embryos, anyway. I guess he'd have to have been involved in—" He stopped, seeing a flash in the darkness ahead. Toure had just enough time to register what it meant, too little to yell, not that it would have done any good. Everett threw himself to the ground, but the rocket had already locked on to his body heat and the shape-charge warhead, designed to kill mammoth, hit him in the back just below the ribs. The explosion tore him in half and Toure wept while she stared through his eyes, still open, at the cold soil of Ivory.

—III—

Carmichael turned the top half of the body over to look down into the face. He looked to be genuinely upset—unlike the deputies, who seemed confused, and Burgess and Keys, whose faces were rigid and cold. Madelon knelt by Everett's head, barely hearing Toure's voice as it was conducted through bone from her headware. "Ask how many of these guns they have," Toure insisted.

"How many of these guns do you have?" Madelon asked, a moment later.

Carmichael looked around at his deputies, who were armed only with their tasers and stunclubs. "Most of the farms have one, and there's, I don't know, a hundred or so in town. We don't register them; Hell, no-one's ever been killed by one before."

One of the deputies—Josh Wilkins—nodded. "Most folks prefer shotguns." Carmichael glared at him.

"Do you have any forensic tests that'll tell you who did this?" asked Madelon. "Serial numbers on the rocket? Rifling marks? A test to see which guns have been used, or who's handled one?"

"The last two, yes," said Carmichael. "Serial numbers, no; no rifling marks either, unless the gun's faulty. But people do use 'em for target practice—"

"It'll narrow it down," said Madelon.

"You're not giving orders here," said Keys, looking up to see more people approaching—John and Jessie Randolph, Harry Poulsen, Adam Bennett, and Pieter van Neukirk.

"She knows that," said Carmichael, gently. "And I think it's a perfectly reasonable request. Josh, see who's been signed up for target practice in the last thirty hours; those are the first people I'll want to see."

"Does that include deputies?"

"Yep. May as well get them out of the way first. John, you want to pronounce Mr Everett dead?"

The medtech nodded, his expression unreadable in the half-darkness. Madelon remained kneeling on the ground as Carmichael sketched a chalk outline around the corpse before the deputies and medtech-apprentices carried it away. A few minutes later, Carmichael sent the others away, and put an arm around her shoulders. She shrugged it off angrily.

"Sorry," he said. "Look, Miss Schaefer, I'm going to do all I can to get to the bottom of this, but I'm going to need your help." She nodded. "Even so, I can't promise to solve anything before your ship leaves. You're in touch with your captain, aren't you?" Another nod. "And Dr Toure? Good. Now, I'm guessing that Dave was murdered to stop him getting any closer to the people responsible for the killing of the babies in the gene lab. Do you agree?"

Madelon was silent for a moment. "Dr Toure says it's possible."

"Only possible?"

"She thinks it's more likely that he was murdered to help cover up another crime, one that's much older. She wants to know who you trust the most."

"What?" Carmichael stared down into her tear-streaked but still pretty face, and then shrugged. "Okay. Ben—that's Adam Bennett—my deputies, and Piet van Neukirk."

"Any women?"

"I don't know many... Aline, my sister, I guess; we disagree a lot, but yeah, I trust her."

"What about your wife?"

"Died three years ago," said Carmichael, softly. "In childbirth."

"I'm sorry."

He shrugged. "Yeah."

"You're sure you can trust your deputies?"

"Picked 'em myself."

"Okay, then. Can you deputize your other friends?"

"Sure."

"Good. Now, is there anywhere in town where you can address a few hundred people, and lock the doors if necessary? A church, or a hall?"

"There's a hall," replied Carmichael. "It's too small for baseball, but we use it for basketball games, meetings, dances, things like that. Why?"

"Can you call a meeting of all the people who were out of coldsleep when the foetuses were destroyed, plus a few others?"

"Those as are still alive and living in town, sure. Who're the others? And what the Hell is this about?"

Madelon looked at him bleakly, and listened to Toure's voice in her head. "Justice," she said.

Carmichael shrugged. "Okay. When do we start?"

"You may be wondering why I called you here," said Carmichael, staring around the hall. A deputy stood at each door, armed with taser and shotgun, giving them a dozen shots each if needed. He hoped it wouldn't come to that. "Well, I'll try to keep this short. As you all know, there was a murder earlier today. Don't panic, you're not all suspects in that. I know that many of you have already had your rocket pistols checked, and I apologise for any inconvenience. A few of you have also had your hands residue tested, and I apologise for that, too. And, of course, most of you were interviewed by Sheriff Fleischer nine years ago. Again, apologies. There's only three of you who've tested positive for residue *and* were out of coldsleep on the *Forrest* at the time someone killed ten thousand babies; two of you are deputies of mine, and the other has given me an adequate explanation. But there's at least one murderer in this room, and a few other criminals to boot. Now, I'd like you to listen to Miss Schaefer."

Madelon stood, and smiled thinly at Carmichael. It was a nice good-cop-bad-cop set-up, but after all, he would probably live here for the rest of his life, and she was leaving in less than twenty-four hours. "Good evening. I don't think any of you knew David Everett well; I'm sorry to say that I didn't, either. But I do know that he was a good medtech, good enough to look at a genescan readout and know what he was seeing." She looked around the room, knowing that Toure, Paratene and the *Altair*'s computer were all seeing through her eyes as well as the cameras that had been placed around the hall. "That's how he uncovered a crime. Four days before the embryos in your gene bank were destroyed, three of them were chosen and scanned. Why this was done then, I don't know; maybe someone had become suspicious. But I do know what they found, and I suspect it's why the embryos were obliterated. All three, certainly, and probably all ten thousand, were Negroid. African. Black. Use whatever word you like," she concluded, knowing that no-one would hear her over the ensuing uproar. A few seconds later, she heard cries of "Can you prove this?" from amid the crowd. She glanced at Carmichael, who stood, and called for silence.

"The only proof that remains is the result of those gene-scans on the computer," she said. "My captain requested permission to send crew from the *Altair* to search the *Forrest* for any more evidence—it occurred to us that the people responsible for the mass destruction might have kept a few embryos as a form of insurance—but this permission was denied.

"The next question, of course, is who would have chosen these embryos, and why?

"Sheriff Carmichael thought it might have been someone on Earth, attempting to sabotage your whites-only society." She took a deep breath. Aboard *Altair*, Toure, Paratene and Natsuki stared at the monitor, as the computer picked out the Ivorians who were showing the most stress—or who had suddenly relaxed. "And maybe this would have worked if no-one had gene-scanned the embryos before implanting them in the women here... but that didn't seem very likely. Any remotely competent geneticist would have scanned them before things reached that stage. Isn't that right, Dean Bennett?" Ben nodded.

"Strangely enough, the record shows that *none* of the human foetuses were scanned aboard the *Forrest* until those three were selected. The ship's chief geneticist, Dr Thompson, who'd been responsible for scanning and selecting the embryos before the *Forrest* was launched, was obviously confident that he had what he'd ordered. He might have implanted them into your women without any further checking, too. Now, nearly 1900 of your 2019 women became pregnant by traditional methods within nine months of your landing. If you'd trusted to Dr Thompson, he would have gifted you with two thousand black babies."

The uproar at this was too great for Madelon, or even Carmichael, to yell over; they waited until it had abated. "What would you have done with them?" Madelon asked. "Killed them all? Raised them as your own children? Or raised them to keep as slaves?"

The uproar at this was even louder; Carmichael stopped it by picking up a shotgun from behind the podium and pumping a round into the chamber for firing. "Miss Schaefer doesn't know you," he barked. "I do. I know most of you are decent people. Like me, you've probably never wanted to own slaves. But what would you do if somebody *gave* them to you? Especially if the alternatives are letting them die, or raising them like they were your equals? Now, that's not an easy decision for me to make—and it wouldn't even be *my* baby. But my *wife*, if she'd been in this situation..."

The audience was silent. "Unfortunately," Carmichael continued, "Dr Thompson isn't here to defend himself, and it pains me to see him accused in his absence. But it pains me even more to see his fellow conspirators get away with it. Thompson didn't choose those embryos alone, nor was he responsible for the efforts of Sheriff Fleischer *not* to find the people responsible for their destruction, because if he *had* found them, the secret might have come out. And how many of you women would choose to knowingly be implanted with a embryo that you would then have to carry, give birth to, feed, raise—and then see enslaved?" There was a low muttering. Carmichael drew a deep breath, then said, "Mr Mayor?"

Burgess turned to face him. "Yes?"

"Who else—apart from you and Thompson—chose those embryos? And why did you deny permission for a search of the

Forrest?" He waited for an answer, but Burgess was silent. "Okay. Until you choose to answer those questions, please consider yourself under arrest. I've also had Mr Earl arrested; he's on his way back here."

"*Who killed the babies?*"

Carmichael turned; an obviously pregnant woman had scrambled to her feet to call out the question. Before he could identify her, the shout had been picked up by others in the crowd. He turned to Schaefer. "You'd better tell them what you know," he said, softly. "It was still murder."

Toure stared at the monitor, shaking her head. Paratene looked at her inquisitively.

"They could have told people," Carmichael continued. "instead of killing ten thousand children."

"And done what?" muttered Toure. "Left them in a deep freeze for ever?"

"They could have let *us* make the choice," said Carmichael, as though he'd been able to hear her. "They're no better than the other conspirators."

Toure looked at the screen, and then at Paratene. "Do you know?" asked the Captain.

"All I have to go on is one good suspect, a gut feeling, and the computer's reading of people's vital signs, which aren't that reliable in a crowd that size. That's not enough to justify getting a woman lynched." Toure drummed her fingers on the console. "Schaefer? Tell Carmichael we don't have enough information."

Madelon's only reply was a slow pan of the angry crowd, ending with an equally angry Carmichael.

"Okay. I'll tell him what I know, but she's to be arrested and interviewed on suspicion of murdering David Everett, not lynched for destroying the embryos. I want his *word* on that."

Madelon passed that on to Carmichael, who nodded. "You have my word," he said grimly. "Who is it?"

"There's one woman who we've been watching closely since she walked in," said Toure. "She wasn't in coldsleep when the embryos were destroyed; neither was her husband, but the duty roster says he was on duty, so she doesn't have him as an alibi. It's my guess that she had the job of distracting Wallace; she was pretty then, still is, and Carmichael told us that Wallace liked blondes. She knew everyone, and asking questions was her job; Thompson or someone may have let something slip about the embryos. The computer says her heart skipped a beat and her face went pale when Schaefer mentioned the genescan, but *not* when he said what the genescan revealed, which suggests she knew what she was going to say. And she's fired a rocket pistol recently—on a target range, with witnesses, but that doesn't mean she didn't fire another round later; we just tend to assume that it does, the old purloined letter schtick again. Do I have to name her?"

Madelon relayed this information to Carmichael, who shook his head. "Jessie Randolph? She did it?"

"That's for a jury to decide," said Toure. "They do *have* juries on Ivory, don't they? I shouldn't worry too much, Schaefer. If she killed Everett, the bastards will probably give her a medal."

Carmichael and van Neukirk escorted her to the tilter which was to take her back to the shuttle. "I hope the town's still, uh, here when you get back," said van Neukirk, sourly. "You've stirred up a hornet's nest, Miss Schaefer. It's okay for you, but we're the ones who have to live there."

"You could come back with me," said Madelon, drily, as she climbed into the tilter. "There's room on the shuttle, and on the *Altair*."

van Neukirk laughed, and stepped back. "I'll think about it. Let me know when you find a habitable world that's even further out than this one—if that's okay with the censor, of course."

Carmichael nodded. "I don't see a problem with it."

"Hmm. Make sure you tell the new sheriff that. Who do you think people will want for mayor with Burgess, Keys, Earl and Poulsen all in jail on conspiracy charges?"

Carmichael shrugged, and climbed into the tilter. "Let's go," he snapped at the pilot.

"He's right, you know," he said, when they were airborne. "You've upset a lot of people; I just hope there's nobody on the flight path with a rocket pistol, because this thing isn't armoured.

I've had to deputize more people just to deal with the domestic disputes."

"Were any of them women?"

"Is that meant to be a joke?" He shuddered. "When we came here, we were hoping for a society without any divisions like this. Then you come along and create this huge gulf between men and women..."

Madelon shook her head. "We didn't stock that gene bank with prospective slaves, nor did we destroy the embryos."

"I know. Christopher Columbus wasn't the first man to discover America, either; he just told people it was there. He still got the credit and the blame."

They flew along for a few more miles, looking down at the landscape with neither of them speaking. "What's going to happen to Jessie Randolph?"

"I guess that depends on how many women Aline gets onto the jury during *voir dire*. She's admitted to shooting Everett, and to having masterminded the whole plot, though she won't tell us who else was involved; I guess she's planning to ask for mercy. Not all of the women agree with what she did, but they figure she did it for them. She told me to tell you why she did it, too; said she didn't want to be lied about on Earth or anywhere."

"What did she say?"

"Said she couldn't stand the idea of having a nigger baby growing inside her, and having to treat it like it was hers; said she'd rather kill millions of them than have that happen." Carmichael reached into a pocket on his khaki jacket and removed a data disk the size of a quarter, which he tossed to Madelon. "Said she figured every woman on the *Forrest* would feel the same way. I recorded it, if you don't believe me. Of course, I don't know what the others thought."

Madelon stared at the disk, then dropped it into her carry-bag.

"There's your shuttle," said Carmichael, nearly an hour later. "The ship that comes here in ten years time; do you figure to be on it?" She shook her head. "Well, then, I guess this is goodbye. I'm really sorry about David."

"Me too." The tilter landed, and she grabbed her bag and walked briskly to the shuttle. The ramp rolled down, and she walked up it without looking back. Carmichael waited until the shuttle had flown high enough to be invisible, and then he, too, flew home.

a sort of walking miracle

The room was dark, apart from the sick blue glow from the clock on the VCR, the reflection in the half-open eyes of the family Siamese, and a diffuse hint of light from underneath a closed door somewhere upstairs. The messenger stood for a moment, letting his eyes adjust, then reached into the pocket of his leather jacket for a penlight. A quick sweep of the room revealed thick carpet, an enormous television, a complicated stereo, shelves of books and tapes and trophies, a space heater, a leatherish-looking sofa and chairs, a vase full of roses... It all smelled clean and rich and respectable, and new. He calculated quickly, then noticed a newspaper folded on the seat of the largest chair, and grinned. He picked it up, careful not to rustle it, and a picture of the New York skyline and the word BOMB caught his eye simultaneously. He flinched, and then read the rest of the headline and the first paragraph. Just a car-bomb in the World Trade Centre. He sat down on the arm of the chair, drew a deep breath, and looked at the paper again. *The San Francisco Chronicle*, Friday, March 5th, 1993.

1993. *Jesus*, he thought, *I'm in the future. And San Francisco. Haven't been here since—*

The cat glanced at him, then went back to sleep. He pointed the penlight at the floor, and listened. He had excellent hearing, and had always been good at listening, which isn't quite the same thing. Outside, still suburban streets. Inside, only one other person in the house, upstairs, awake. He switched the penlight off, pocketed it, and walked carefully towards the stairs, making no more noise than a cat.

There was a thin line of light showing under only one of the doors; he padded along the corridor, and knocked lightly. He heard someone inside jump, and then a girl's voice called, "Who's there?"

"A friend."

There was a disbelieving gasp from the other side of the door, and then the voice, trying to sound older, snapped, "I've got a gun..."

He opened the door slowly, and looked inside. The girl was sitting on the bed, cross-legged, wide-eyed, dressed in designer jeans and a silk blouse with a small roll of puppyfat showing between them. There was a thin paperback face-down near her feet, with a sheet of notepaper tucked inside it. He guessed her age at fifteen, maybe younger. She saw his scuffed leather jacket, his dusty Levis and boots, his shaggy hair and beard, and recoiled. He hoped he didn't smell too bad; he could barely remember the last time he'd been able to take a hot shower. "If you've got a gun," he said, softly, "why d'you need the pills?"

"What?" She glanced at the open jar in her hand, as though noticing it for the first time, and then dropped it on the bed, spilling the pills. "I—who the Hell are you?"

"My name's Colin Patterson, if that helps. It probably doesn't, but I'm not a burglar, or a rapist. Can I come in?"

"How did you *get* in?"

"That's a long story. Can I sit down?" He shrugged his khaki pack off of his back, and slid it along the floor towards her. "There's a gun in *there*, if it makes you feel better. Survival rifle: it should only take you a minute or two to assemble it... And a knife."

She stared at the pack, then at Patterson. "Get out! Get the *fuck* out and leave me alone!"

He didn't move.

"Did you hear me? I said, get out!"

"I heard you," he replied. "You were going to take all of those pills, weren't you?"

She stood, her face white. "What the Hell business is that of yours?"

"There's been an accident. Your parents are going to be late."

"*What?*"

"That's all I know. I mean, they weren't *in* it, they're not *hurt*, they're just stuck in traffic. They'll be home an hour or so later than you expect them. That's all she told me."

"She?" She stared, seeing the grey at his temples and in his beard, the creases in his forehead, then sat down again, her face crimson. "You're a friend of my mother's," she said, despairingly.

He shook his head. "I've never met your mother. *She* is... can I sit down? Thanks. *She...* look, what do you want me to call you? I know your name's Genevieve, but—"

"Jenny."

"Fine." He noticed the can of Diet Pepsi on the bedside table, and asked, "Can I have some of that? It feels like years since I had anything to drink."

She handed it over. "If you're not a friend of Mum's, then how did you get in?"

"Well, that's—"

"A long story. Right. Do you do this often?"

"Oh, yes," he replied. "Yes, all the time." He took a long swig of the Pepsi, and grimaced; Jenny actually laughed, and then recoiled when she realised what she'd done. Patterson shook his head, and closed his eyes. "That's better," he said, and passed the can back. "Don't worry; I've left you enough."

"Huh?"

"To wash the pills down. If you still want to. But if you do, you'll die. I mean, *die*. Is that what you really want?"

She sat down, then curled up on the bed, kicking the jar and the paperback to the floor, and stared at the wallpaper that her mother had chosen years before. "Why else would I take a whole bottle of sleeping pills?"

"I don't know. Me, I've never wanted to die. That's sort of why I'm here—part of it, anyway."

"I've got reasons."

"Maybe you have. Want to talk about them?"

"Reasons you wouldn't understand."

"That's possible."

"And I don't have to explain myself to you!"

"I know."

Suddenly, she burst into tears. "Why *are* you here?"

"To help you," he said, softly. "If you really want to die, okay, I'll go; I think we all have the right to choose when we want to die. In my case, it was *never*, which was probably a mistake.

"And if you're trying to make a statement, if you think that the only way you can get people to care, to listen to you, to help you, whatever, is to try to kill yourself, or look like you tried... maybe you're right. You're probably not, but I don't really know. All I was told before I came here was that your parents were going to be—"

"In an accident," she repeated, dully. "Who told you that?"

"A girl. No-one you know... well, actually, she might be, I don't know. You see, there are these three women... or maybe it's only *one* woman, I... Did you ever see that movie of *Macbeth*?"

"What? The Polanski film? Yes; why?"

"Do you remember the three witches? One ancient, one middle-aged, one a teenager? That's what these three remind me of... but they're also a lot like each other, uncannily so. Maybe they're just grandmother, mother and daughter, but I really think they're the same woman, you know, like I was seeing them at thirty year intervals." He paused. "I know, that sounds bizarre, but they could do it. They send me through time, why the Hell not themselves?"

"They send you through time?"

"Well, yes and no... I really don't know, but... Have you ever heard of alternate worlds?"

"Like, what if the Nazis had won World War II? Or Kennedy hadn't been shot? That sort of thing?"

He nodded. "Most of them aren't *that* different—not the ones I've been to, anyway. Not that I've noticed, anyway; I haven't had time to study most of them. The way the woman—or women—explained it to me, the only things that change the worlds are deaths. Not all deaths—Hell, everyone's got to die *sometime*—but some deaths are..." He looked up at the light. "Jesus. I have to explain this nearly every time, you'd think I'd be good at it by now. Chloe warned me that I needed to practise... Anyway, most deaths are... maybe not inevitable, but... *fated*, I guess. Like in *Lawrence of Arabia*, you know, 'It is written that he should die'. Or at least *probable*. But some deaths can be prevented. Like yours."

She laughed sourly. "You mean I'm going to live forever? Shit."

Patterson shrugged. "I don't know how long you're going to live, or how you're going to die. I don't know what sort of difference you're going to make to the world. But the women sent me back here to talk to you, so they must think there's a chance." He grimaced. "Sometimes it doesn't work. If you really *want* to die, I can't stop you, and I won't. But most 'suicides' don't, and I don't think you do—"

"I—"

Patterson continued, ignoring the interruption. "Or maybe you're like Tom Sawyer, you want to 'die temporarily'. But there's no such thing. I don't think you know what dying means. Like most teenagers."

"And you do?" she said, sarcastically.

"I've seen people die," he replied, slowly. "Mostly when I was in Vietnam. I was drafted: I could—I *should*—have run away to Canada or somewhere, but I didn't. I guess going to war was a form of teenage suicide, too: fortunately, it's no longer fashionable.

"I saw suicides, there, too, including one Buddhist monk who set himself alight. I wouldn't have tried to stop him then, I wouldn't now, he chose the time and place of his death and that was his right, he may have been doing it as a gesture, a political statement, but I believe he *knew* what he was doing. He knew it was real. And when I saw that, *I* knew it was real. Never knew it before. Most teenagers don't. They think they're too young to die, just like they're too young to get pregnant, and they're *never* going to be like their parents, right?

"You can take those pills, if you want to. Like I said, I don't know what's worrying you. If you want to tell me, I'll listen; if I can help, I will. But I can't help you, *no-one* can help you, if you're dead... and I don't think you really want to be dead."

She sat up, and looked at him. "Haven't *you* ever wanted to die? I don't think I know anyone who hasn't—and a lot of my friends have tried."

"Not that I can remember. Maybe I did, when I was your age, but it was always too damn scary, even scarier than growing old. I just wanted to get away from home, have a life of my own. After that... well, the first time I saw Chloe, she—"

"Chloe?"

"The girl who sent me here. She calls herself Chloe Weaver, though I never believed that was her name. We were both staying in a backpacker's hostel, in Seattle, in 1985; some guy was doing tarot readings, and I asked if he could tell me where I was going to die. He asked why, and I said, so I could make sure I never went there.

"Chloe came up to me later—we were staying in the same dorm—and asked if I was serious about that. I said, sure I was serious. She said she could tell me where." He shrugged. "I liked her—don't get me wrong, she was too young for me, for one thing—so I called her bluff and said, 'Okay, tell me.'

"'Right here,' she said. 'Here in Seattle. This is where you're destined to die.'"

"I didn't laugh. She just looked at me, and asked if I believed her. I asked her *when*, and she said, 'tomorrow morning, a few minutes before noon.'

"'Okay,' I said. 'What can I do to avoid it—apart from not being here?'

"'Only that', she said—pretty coolly, I thought—and then, 'Were you planning to stay in town long?'

"'Not if I can get a lift somewhere. There doesn't seem to be anything going here.'

"'Are you looking for work?'

"'Well, it doesn't seem to be looking for me,' I told her. She smiled at that, and said, 'You might be wrong. I have a job for you. It doesn't pay well—but it'll get you out of town.'

"'Driving deadheads?'

"'What?'

"'Courier work?'

"'In a way,' she said. 'You like to travel, don't you?'

"I don't remember what I said to that—probably yes—but the next thing I knew, we were standing in a forest: no buildings, not even a road or a telegraph line in sight, I could see all the way out to Mount Rainier and no signs of human life at all except the two of us and I wasn't too sure about her... I don't know how she does it. I've never seen any sort of time machine or anything, but maybe it's back in the future somewhere, or another dimension, or maybe it's really small. And if you were going to travel through time, would you carry a big machine around with you and show it to everyone?

"Anyway, next thing I knew, we were back in our dorm in the hostel. She told me that she needed someone to take messages through time, occasionally—messages to people like you, suicides who didn't really want to commit suicide, who were just trying to make some sort of statement and things got out of hand... She said she was getting too old for the work; I thought, at the time, she was trying to make a joke."

Patterson shrugged. "I got to admit, I liked the idea. I'd never been a lot of use to anyone before, and I thought maybe I'd get to save people like Tchaikovsky, you know... I mean, I'd heard Tchaikovsky deliberately drank contaminated water to give himself cholera, because he was being blackmailed for being gay, and I always thought, how fucking horrible and what a fucking *waste*... or Alan Turing... I guess you could say I had a call. And, like she said, it was a chance to see the world, and if I was good at it and didn't quit, I could save a lot of lives, maybe even talk down a war...

"So I said sure, and went and spent the last of my cash on some gear I thought would be inconspicuous and useful—which is why there's a survival rifle in there, and a survival knife: there was a big war scare on at the time, *Rambo* was breaking box office records, and survivalist gear was everywhere...

"And the next day, I got up and got dressed, and suddenly I was in England, in a small apartment that reeked of gas. There was a woman there, who'd tried to seal the kitchen and turned the gas on, but she obviously didn't want to *die*; she knew there was a girl coming around at nine, and she'd left a note on the table with her doctor's name and number. Unfortunately, the gas had seeped into the room downstairs, so when the girl arrived and tried to get help, the man who lived there didn't wake up... if I hadn't unlocked the front door, I'm sure she would have died." He shook his head. "A moment later, I was back in Seattle. Chloe—at least, she said she was Chloe, she looked *ancient*—told me I'd just saved Sylvia Plath. I didn't even recognise the name.

"She was the first; there have been dozens since. A lot of teenagers and students, like you. Most of them listen. I don't know how many try again."

They sat there in silence, then Jenny asked, "These women... Chloe... do you know who they are?"

"No. They know the future, so I guess that's where they're from. I think they're the same woman at different ages, a time traveller— probably someone I've been sent to talk down at some time."

"Maybe," said Jenny. "But—do you know that Pretenders song, 'Hymn to Her'?"

"No."

"How about Greek mythology?"

"A little. Never read much as a kid; my parents weren't into books. Still don't."

"There's these three women in Greek myth, the Fates: Clotho, the young one, the maiden, spins the thread of each life; Lachesis, the mother, measures it out; and Atropos, the old crone, cuts it off. The three of them decide when it's someone's time to die, and they can't be defied, they're more powerful than all the Gods and..."

Jenny looked up, and saw that the room was empty. She sat there in silence for a moment, then knelt on the floor and began picking up the pills. When the jar was half-full, she muttered, "Oh, the Hell with it," and set it on the bedside table, where she knew her mother would find it in the morning, and began getting ready for bed.

The sun had just begun to rise when Patterson re-appeared in his scratched-out cave on the side of Mount Rainier; enough of its light broke through the perpetual cloud to turn the glassy, rain-filled crater that had once been Seattle from a sickly glowing blue pool into a dull red eye. As always, it reminded Patterson of the cauldron from *Macbeth*, full of dead things, which is what he would have been if he'd been there when the missiles hit... No matter how far he walked between trips, Chloe always brought him back here. All the other cities were the same, anyway.

Sighing, he reached into his backpack for his radio, his binoculars, his Geiger counter, and the AR-7 survival rifle. No sign of movement, nothing but static on the radio, radiation low enough for him to walk down to the ashen landscape that had once been a forest.

His own words echoed in his ears. *If you really want to die, okay, I think we all have the right to choose when we want to die. But if you're doing it as a gesture, a political statement, and you don't realise that it's real until it gets out of hand... you'll die. Is that what you really want?*

No, he thought. I guess it wasn't what any of us wanted. He assembled the rifle and walked warily, stubbornly, down towards the ruins, in search of food and some hint of life.

the vision of a vanished good

They call me mad: I smile, I weep,
Uncaring how or why:
Yea, when one's heart is laid asleep,
What better than to die?
So that the grave be dark and deep.

To die! To die? And yet, methinks,
I drink of life, to-day.

— Lewis Carroll, *Stolen Waters*

The Hatter sipped his vodka and stared owlishly through the window at the falling snow. He's a spectacularly ugly man even when he's sober, and after a few drinks, he makes Abraham Lincoln look like Darryl Hannah. "What are your plans for Christmas? Seeing your family?"

Barbara smiled. "Yes and no. My parents disowned me years ago, but I'll be having lunch with a pack of friends; they're about as close to family as I have."

"Good," said the Hatter. "Christmas is grim and horrible enough without having to spend it alone." He sipped at the vodka again, and turned to me. "What about you? Is your girlfriend back?"

"No. She's in California, with *her* family." Lee-Lin and I had met in Hong Kong three months before, spent as much of two days together as our schedules allowed, and had done most of our courting since by phone. She loved her job and her home, and while I couldn't say the same, I wasn't ready to move to Vancouver just yet. The Hatter shrugged, commiserating, then shambled over to the bar for another drink and stopped to chat with Midas Myers. I sipped at my Glenfiddich, stared at the snow, and pondered the four most important women in my life. One was gay, one lived half a world away, one had been murdered by her father nearly thirty years ago, and one was an eight-year-old vampire who'd inspired Lewis Carroll's *Alice* books.

I glanced at my watch: 9.05. "Drive you home?" asked Barbara, quietly.

"Okay." We said our goodbyes, then took the lift down to the carpark.

London is hideous in early winter. The trees are skeletal, the frozen fountains look eerie, and the first nocturnal snows melt during the day and turn into a corpse-coloured slush. The streets were deserted apart from a few sadomasochistic carol-singers, murdering 'Unto us, a child is given'. Though it was warm in the Jag, I caught myself shivering as I remembered that it was the winter solstice, the longest night of the year...

"'His soul swooned slowly as he heard the snow falling faintly through the universe and faintly falling, like the descent of their last end, upon all the living and the dead.'"

I blinked. "Eliot?"

Barbara tsked. "James Joyce. *Dubliners.*" She glanced in the mirror, and slowed down to let a drunk in a Volvo weave past us. "I used to love all of this, when I was a kid. I loved the snow, I loved Christmas, I thought the lights and the shops were beautiful and the presents really did appear by magic, I even believed in the virgin birth, which is pretty bizarre considering I was too innocent to know what a virgin was. Now, it seems so fake, so commercial and hypocritical and fucking patriarchal, but I look at kids and I know it isn't Christmas that's changed, it's me." She shook her head. "Sometimes, I almost wish I were a kid again. How about you?"

"Nah."

"Why not?" I was silent. "I mean, you're the one who collects Lewis Carroll books..."

I looked at the snow. "I think most of us have selective memories. We remember the fun, but not the fears—the things most adults know can't hurt them, but that still scare the shit out of kids. The nightmares, the boogeymen, the shadows and shapes, being a dwarf in a world of giants... and that's for the lucky ones. Some kids—too many—have good reasons to be scared; being a kid forever would be like... always being helpless, I guess. The eternal victim."

Barbara grimaced. "What d'you think it's like being a woman?"

I couldn't think of a good answer to that, so I said nothing until we were in the carpark. Before she could hand over the keys, I said, "I won't be needing the car for a few days: do you want to borrow it?"

"What?"

"Would you like the car? Pick me up Wednesday morning?"

She blinked—and then grinned. "Sure. Thanks."

"My pleasure. Merry Christmas; see you next Wednesday." I grabbed my briefcase and stepped out of the car, walking as jauntily as possible to the lift, giving a thumbs-up to the security cameras.

I pressed the button for EST on my watch: 1.30 P.M. Not a good time to call Lee-Lin. I was still toying with the idea of flying to L.A. when I reached the door, and so didn't notice anything strange until I was actually inside the flat.

There was a vampire in the room, waiting.

"Alice?"

"No." The voice was too deep for Alice's; a woman's voice, not a child's. I reached for the light switch, without closing the door behind me. She was reclining on the chaise-longue—a woman in her late twenties or early thirties, blonde with mousy roots and somewhere between plain and conventionally pretty, wearing a too-tight black dress. "I thought I had to invite you in."

She sat up slightly, and shrugged. "That's just a myth."

"Alice waited until I invited her."

The woman smiled sourly, without showing the tips of her teeth. "Alice likes the myths. Besides, she was well brought up. Are you going to stand there with the door open all night?"

I didn't budge. Vampire women prefer to call themselves succubi or sidhe, but they still drink blood, and sometimes they kill to get it. "Did Alice send you?"

"No, but she told me about you a couple of years ago. Don't worry, I won't hurt you, none of us will—you're sort of Alice's pet."

"Why are you here?"

"Friend of mine needs a lawyer."

I shut the door behind me and leaned against it. "Another sidhe?"

"Yes."

"Why?"

"She's been arrested; we need to get her out before sunrise."

I didn't bother asking why. "What's the charge?"

"Assaulting a police officer."

Oh, shit. "Did she bite him?"

"No, she just... I better start at the beginning. We met this girl tonight, in one of the squats. She's pregnant, and scared of her father, or maybe it was *the* father; I'm not sure. She said her mother died a few years ago. Anyway, she wanted a place to stay, and we said she could stay with us until morning, and then these cops blundered in. We disappeared as soon as they saw us, but one of them grabbed the girl, and she screamed out for Janet. So Janet came out of hiding... if there'd only been one cop, it wouldn't have been a problem, but you can't keep your eye on two. She had the WPC entranced, got her to let the girl go, and then the guy, knows something funny's going on even if he doesn't know what it is, grabs Janet and tries to put the cuffs on her..."

"And she hit him?"

"Well, the woman was snapping out of it; if she hadn't, the girl wouldn't have got away."

I rolled my eyes. "How hard did she hit him?"

"I think she broke his nose, but that's all... She kept struggling, made it difficult for them to get her to the car so I'd have time to hide the girl."

"Where's the girl now?"

"Safe."

"Does she have a name?"

"Ronnie," she replied, just quickly enough to be telling the truth. "Veronica, I guess. She wouldn't tell me her last name."

"How old is she?"

"I don't know. Twelve or thirteen, to look at her."

I nodded. "What's *your* name?"

"Kaarina."

"What're you going to do with her?"

"Huh?"

"Are you going to turn her into a—a Sidhe?"

Kaarina considered this, running her tongue over the edge of her teeth. "No, but..."

"Where—and how—is she going to live?"

No answer. I walked to the bar and poured myself a Glenfiddich, watching Kaarina closely, concentrating on her lips and eyes. Then I reached into my pocket for my penlight. "I want to see this girl, talk to her. On neutral ground, a cafe or somewhere, and after sunset, of course. Hold out your hand."

"What? Why?"

"Just a hunch. Where did they take Janet?"

Unexpectedly meeting a vampire is bad enough; bumping into Ross Bauer on the same night is more than anyone should have to stand. Bauer is nominally a private investigator, and he spends nearly all his time looking for women who've vanished. Nothing wrong with that, *per se*—but most of these women had good reason to vanish. Bauer found them, and took them back to their husbands, and at least two of them were subsequently beaten to death. I managed to convict one of the husbands, despite the best efforts of the judge, but no-one had been able to touch Bauer.

Bauer nodded civilly enough as I walked past him and approached the desk sergeant. "I'm here to see my client," I said.

"Janet Whittaker."

We went through the formalities, and then I was ushered into an interview room. Janet was a dark-skinned girl with dreadlocks and green eyes, wearing a badly scuffed waistcoat over a dirty *Tank Girl* t-shirt and threadbare jeans. She looked about seventeen or eighteen, and probably had for twenty years. She looked at me without any hint of friendliness, even when I told her I was going to get her out of there. "Are you ticklish?" I asked.

"Am I *what?*"

"The cops hit you, right? After I've gone, I want you to play dead. It shouldn't be that difficult—physically, you *are* dead." She stared. "I checked Kaarina out; she doesn't have a pulse, she doesn't breathe, her body temperature is cool, her pupils don't dilate. If you can keep still for long enough, they're going to assume you're dead and ship you off to the morgue. Can you get out of there?"

"Sure." She laughed. "Half of the night shift are vampires."

"*What?*"

"Well, not half, but some of them. Cleaners, mostly. As long as I can get out before sunrise... not that there's much chance of seeing the sun at this time of year. What's going to happen to you when they find I'm missing?"

"Nothing. You're homeless, and you died in police custody; they'll be much happier if you just disappear. Police credibility's pretty low at the moment." I glanced at my watch. "Let me know if you make it."

She smiled for the first time, showing teeth that would have scared a dentist into going straight. "Okay."

Bauer was still in the foyer when I left; he wished me a good evening and a merry Christmas. I wished him the same, trying to remember whether I'd ever seen him in daylight.

As soon as I was home and the door locked (much good it'd do me), I found my diary from two years before. There was a bookmark in late October, the time I'd met Alice; I guess it was the only part I ever bothered re-reading.

Kaarina, according to Alice, had met Sylvia Sullivan in a Greek Street bar, and taken her to the roof of a Canary Wharf high-rise for a vampire feast before letting her fall. Alice had been guest of honour.

I read that page of the diary twice, then began typing up a fax to send to a post office box in Manila.

I spent most of the next day reading some of Lee-Lin's books on Asian mythology. Kaarina phoned at six, to tell me that Janet and Ronnie were at the McDonalds in Paddington where they'd arranged to meet. "But I don't think she'll talk to you," she added. "She's scared that her father—or someone—is chasing her."

She didn't sound as though she was lying, but it's hard to tell over a phone. "They probably are. Where did she stay last night?"

"Somewhere safe," she said, flatly. "But... she's pretty crazy, pet. She might try to run away from us, too; she could do anything."

"Crazy how?"

"She thinks she's carrying the Christ child."

"*What?*"

"That's what she said."

I closed my eyes and tried to think. "She thought she was a virgin?"

"No, I think she knows who the father is... and she's only two, maybe three months gone, so she's not expecting it in time for Christmas, either."

"Barring miracles," I muttered. "Are you sure she's pregnant?"

Kaarina nodded. "We have better senses than you, pet—we hear better, smell better, see body heat... she's about two months pregnant. Apparently the father bought her one of those do-it-yourself pregnancy kits a few weeks ago; it sounds like he was *trying* to knock her up."

"That's—" I stopped short of belabouring the obvious. "*The* father or *her* father?"

"I'm not sure. It might even be 'the Father', a priest. She's talked a lot about a Lighthouse—I thought that showed she was really crazy, but Janet told me it's a church for teenagers, lots of hip-hop and movies and Armageddon; they hand out invitations which look like nightclub passes."

I nodded. "I've seen them." Leicester Square was usually littered with the damn things on Saturday and Sunday mornings.

There was an uncomfortable silence, then Kaarina said. "Look, pet, this is a public phone, and I don't want to take you back to the squat: I think we could talk a lot more easily in your car."

"I don't have a car at the moment; my secretary's borrowed it."

"Shit."

"I'll grab a cab; be there in a few minutes."

Sitting in the taxi, I wondered: was this all just a scam by Kaarina, a way to get money? After all, sidhe had to buy clothes, if nothing else...

No, that didn't add up. There were easier ways for sidhe to get money (and/or clothes); they were expert house-breakers, for one thing. Finding a safe place to stay during the day could be tougher for them, but not impossible.

The three of them were waiting in a booth, with the girl sitting between Janet and the wall. She was pretty but not quite beautiful, with long chestnut hair that would be difficult to disguise and pale green eyes in a face that had already lost most of its puppyfat. She was dressed for sleeping outside in a London winter, complete with gloves; under those clothes, she might have been plump, or voluptuous, or emaciated. Her anorak was unzipped, showing a large silver cross, which had no apparent effect on the sidhe. I slid in next to Kaarina and introduced myself. The girl looked up warily, but said nothing.

"You can trust him," said Kaarina, softly.

The girl took another bite of her burger, swallowed it, and then asked, "Who sent you?"

"No-one. Kaarina told me you were in trouble, and I want to help you."

Bite, chew, swallow, ponder. "Social worker?"

"No. I'm a barrister."

"Prosecutor?"

"Not usually: my specialty is libel."

Bite, chew, swallow; a nod at Kaarina. "What's she told you?"

"That your name is Ronnie, you're pregnant, and you're running away from home," I replied, hoping that wasn't saying too much.

Bite, chew, swallow. "What sort of help?"

"What sort do you need?"

She was silent for nearly a minute, and said, "You're not going to send me home?"

"I don't even know where your home is," I replied.

She reached for the cup in front of Janet and sucked on the straw. "I want... I want it not to be me. I don't want to have to do this."

"Do what?"

"Have this baby."

Kaarina, Janet and I were silent for nearly a minute, trying to think of something safe to say and hoping that the girl was going to continue. Finally, I asked, "Why not? I'm not arguing with you, but—why not?"

The girl jerked her head at Kaarina, and asked, "Did she tell you whose baby it is?"

"No."

She sucked on the straw for a few seconds, then asked, "Have you ever heard of the Merovingian kings?"

Kaarina and Janet looked blank. "It's a long time since I studied any history," I evaded. "They ruled parts of France and Germany in the fifth century until they were deposed by the Carolingians, but that's about all I know."

The girl looked gravely at us, and nodded. "Pepin the Fat murdered Dagobert, the last of the Merovingian Kings, under orders from the Pope. Dagobert's descendants fled and hid, which is why they were called the Lost Kings or the Hermit Princes, but they carried on their bloodline. The Pope wanted them dead because they knew a secret. They were known as the royal blood because they were all descended from Jesus Christ and his wife, Mary of Magdala. Mary had fled to Marseilles with at least one of her sons after Jesus was crucified, and Merovee—who the Merovingians were named after—married one of her descendants. That's why there was a legend that the Holy Grail, or *Sangreal*, was hidden in the south of France— 'san greal' means holy grail, but *Sang Real* is French for 'Royal Blood'. The Blood of Christ."

I had a strange feeling that I'd heard this story somewhere before, and then I remembered reading a book called *Holy Blood*,

Holy Grail. Presumably the girl's father had read it as well, and believed the bits that had suited him. "And your father's descended from the Merovingians?"

"Yes."

"How does he know? Did he tell you?"

She nodded. "He read some of it, and worked out the rest. He studied history at university, and he's a librarian at—" She stopped. "He has a birthmark on his chest, a red cross, which all the Merovingian men were supposed to have. It's why the Knights Templar wore a red cross on their tunics. And his mother would never tell him who his father was, but it wasn't her husband: Dad doesn't look anything like his brothers, and that's why his father— well, you know what I mean—really hated him. *He* doesn't have the mark, but Dad thinks his mother's father did. He came from Scotland, where the Templars weren't wiped out. He thinks his real father had sex with his mother when she was on holiday in France because they were both descendants, and that's why *he* had to get *me* pregnant; the blood is already so... uh, I forget the word, it's like polluted—"

"Diluted?"

"I think so. The only way he could preserve it was by—" Her voice tightened; I expected her to start crying, but she didn't. We sat there in silence until she'd recovered, and I asked, "And your father told you that, too?"

"Uh-huh." She said it without bitterness, or any other emotion that I could recognise. Kaarina glanced at me, her expression bleak, and nodded: the girl believed what she was saying. "He said he'd suspected it for a long time, but he knew for sure when my mother was raised from the dead."

Jesus. I looked around the restaurant surreptitiously; no-one seemed particularly interested in us, but it wasn't the ideal venue for a theological debate. "When he—"

"There was an accident," she said. "Mu-um was in the side that got hit..." She started snuffling. "Sorry. I don't remember her very well, I was only four..."

A few people were beginning to look around; time to move. I looked at Kaarina, who shrugged helplessly, and then at Janet, who was dressed in full Gothic kit, possibly to hide her sunburn. The four of us could probably pass as a family if need be, and there were plenty of small hotels in the area; it shouldn't be difficult to find one with a family room, small windows or heavy curtains, and a disinterested night clerk. "Finished your drink?"

I gave the clerk an excuse about having missed a train; that and a gold Amex card satisfied her curiosity. We steered Janet into the shower, and sat down with Ronnie in the double room. "Your father raised your mother from the dead?" She was silent. "Did you see this?"

"No. I was at home. He told me she died... but when the ambulance arrived, she wasn't in there. They said she'd *never* been in there, that she couldn't have just walked away, but she—he—"

"Okay." I refrained from rolling my eyes. I'd heard less credible stories before, often from my clients, but this was too elaborate to be a spur-of-the-moment fabrication, and I didn't know how much of it she believed. "Did you ever see her again?"

"No. I dream about her quite a lot, and my father always wants to know what I dream... He thinks dreams are very important." She sat there in silence for a moment, and then said, "He thinks she only stayed on Earth for a few more days, like Jesus, and she's in heaven now—in the flesh, like we're all going to be after the Rapture. He says he doesn't know whether he brought her back, or if it was just because she's the mother of Jesus' second mother... He used to think he might be Jesus, but he knows now he's too old; Jesus isn't going to be born again until next year, because it'll be two thousand years then... and probably at the summer solstice, he thinks, because it was winter last time." She was silent for a while, and then she continued, "He said I shouldn't tell people this; he said the unbelievers would persecute me. I haven't even told anyone from Church, because a lot of people go there to mock; he said it would be best if we waited until He was an adult." I wondered, fleetingly, what her father would say if the baby was a girl. "Our preacher keeps talking that way, too. He says that most people will refuse to believe and won't let themselves be saved, even if they see the miracles themselves...

"But I felt I had to tell somebody. I don't think I can do this any more; I just want to be like everybody else..."

When Janet returned, Kaarina and I retreated to the other bedroom to talk, and collapsed onto the bed. "I don't understand this," said Kaarina, "and I don't know what to do about it."

"Does she believe what she's saying?"

"I think so, pet. She's too upset for me to be sure—her heartbeat and temperature and smell are all wrong anyway—but I think she believes it. Some of it, anyway. Is any of that stuff about the kings true?"

"I don't know. I don't think it matters, either; what matters is that either her father believes it, or he's one Hell of a liar."

"What are you going to do?"

I shrugged. "She hasn't told you her surname?"

"No. I don't think she trusts us not to tell her father; she's more than a little paranoid." She grimaced. "I guess it'd be hard to trust anybody after what she's been through."

Betrayed by her father *and* her God... "Do you know anything about this church she goes to?"

"The Lighthouse? No, but Janet might. She hangs around the places kids go to, bites the boys and the occasional girl—never drinks deep, just takes what she needs."

I considered this. "Why didn't either of you bite Ronnie?"

Kaarina was silent for a moment, then replied, sourly, "We don't bite pregnant women. Succubi don't, anyway: I can't speak for the male vampires."

"Why not?"

"We don't know what it'll do to the foetus. Probably nothing, but we don't like to take the chance. You see, pet, we can't have babies of our own—except by turning them into vampires, and then they stay babies forever, which is a pain in the arse. Especially if they don't have teeth, you have to breast-feed them forever. So we have this superstitious respect for pregnant women." She smiled thinly. "Besides, we have to get new blood from somewhere, pet: we can't just go around biting each other."

I remembered Carroll's story about the island where everyone survived by doing their neighbour's laundry, and nodded. "Do you know how to turn your, ah, victims into vampires?"

"Yes, of course, pet. Why?"

"Alice didn't."

"Alice was probably too young when it happened to her to understand. I wasn't. Why, do you want to be a vampire?" I shook my head. "You're probably smart. It's a hell of a price to pay just to avoid dying. I heard of one billionaire in America got himself turned—he'd already been avoiding the sun for years—but even he couldn't get enough human blood to keep himself sane. I heard he finally died, but maybe that was staged; he could certainly afford it."

I shuddered. "How were you turned?"

"I was working nights, trying to save enough to get away from my husband—divorce was expensive, back then—and there was this kid I liked, a drummer. No-one you've ever heard of, pet. He kept asking me to go with him... I didn't know he was a vampire. One night I said yes—I think I may've been a bit drunk." She shrugged. "Anyway, it wasn't any worse than the way I'd been living before; he had a decent place, he managed to pay the rent and stuff without anyone knowing what he was... but one morning he didn't come home, and I never saw him again. I don't know if he found another girl, or whether the rippers got him."

"Rippers?"

"Vampire-killers. They kill one or two of us a month in a city this size, plus a few mortals—I don't know if they get the wrong person sometimes, or whether they think a bleeding body's bait. Maybe it is, for some of the vampires who've been living off rats and birds."

"How do they kill you?"

"Hit and runs, usually, or a shotgun blast to the head. We can heal most wounds, but decapitation always works; the stake through the heart is pretty hit and miss. 'Staking' used to mean staking us out in the sunshine to make sure we died and decomposed—it takes days, even weeks. Cremation is better, but it doesn't have the same sort of audience appeal."

I absorbed this, then said, "Thanks for trusting me."

She propped herself up on one elbow (with her back to the mirror) and showed her teeth. "Don't get carried away, pet. I'm not going to sleep with you."

"Yeah, well, that's mutual. I'll catch a cab home, be back before sunrise."

"Where can we stay tomorrow?"

"One of the partners flew out to Hawaii this morning; he'll be gone for two weeks. I know you can get into his place; can you smuggle Ronnie in?"

"Does he have a chimney?"

I stared, and then remembered that it was Christmas Eve and realised that Kaarina had actually made a joke. "We'll get her in, pet, " she replied. "Now go home, get some sleep."

I never remember my dreams when Alice isn't around, but I know I slept badly that night; I woke at six with the sheets wound around me like a strait-jacket. I stared at the clock for a long moment before remembering why I was getting up so early on a holiday, then I dressed hastily and called a minicab, trying to think of some credible excuse for retrieving the Jag from Barbara. By the time I arrived in Paddington, I'd decided to tell her that an old friend was returning to London unexpectedly that night, and I needed to drive her around: it had the advantage of being true. I told the cabbie to wait while I collected Kaarina, Janet and Ronnie, and then we headed for Midas's home in Highgate. I caught the tube home, grabbed another two hour's sleep, and then called Barbara and arranged to pick up the car.

I'd never visited Barbara at home before, and I wasn't sure what to expect. The only thing visibly out of the ordinary was an over-abundance of curious cats (none of whom, she assured me, was named Sappho) and a *Dykes to Watch Out For* calendar hanging beside the phone. "So, who's your friend?" she asked. "Not Lee-Lin?"

"An old girlfriend," I replied, and when she raised an eyebrow, I added, "*Very* old girlfriend—from my college days, in fact."

"Well, at least you won't be spending Christmas by yourself. Cup of tea?"

"Thanks," I said, suddenly wondering how I *would* be spending Christmas, and then asked, "Have you ever heard of a place called the Lighthouse?"

"The born-agains? Yeah; why?"

"What do you know about them?"

"Not a lot. I've never been there, but I get into arguments with them occasionally, when they try to convert me in the street. They get really flustered when you ask them where in the Bible it says lesbianism's a sin—because it doesn't, just as it never lists the punishment for a man who has sex with his own daughter." I blinked. "Mother, step-mother, daughter-in-law, sister, half-sister, aunt, another man's wife, another man, an animal, or a woman having her period, yes, but not his *daughter*. I guess it's because daughters were regarded as property—either that, or someone with a guilty conscience cut that bit out. It's in *Leviticus* 20... or rather, it's not, but it should be. Anyway, the Lighthouse kids are pretty reasonable, as fundamentalists go. All sweetness and light, at least on the surface, but they really do believe that these are the Last Days, and they expect to be bodily transported to Heaven, which, considering some of their bodies, is a pretty scary thought." She shrugged. "They seem happy enough, but it's sort of eerie. Why? Is one of our clients thinking of buying the place?"

I was trying to think of a safe answer when my pager suddenly beeped, rescuing me. "Sorry. Can I use your phone?"

"Sure."

The message said to call Kaarina, on Midas's home number. The phone rang once before being snatched up. "Hello?"

"Kaarina?"

There was a moment's hesitation, then, "You'd better get over here, pet."

"Okay. Why?"

"Ronnie's gone."

"*What?*"

"We couldn't stop her—the sun's out. I'll explain when—" I hung up. "I'd better be going," I told Barbara. "Thanks for the tea."

She nodded. "Merry Christmas."

"Yeah. You too."

The door opened before I could knock on it. "What happened?"

"Did you see her?" asked Kaarina.

"If I had, I'd have her with me. *What happened?*"

"She had an abortion." I stared. "A spontaneous abortion—a miscarriage, if you like. She was only in the second month, pet, it happens a lot..."

I shut the door behind me. "Jesus."

"No longer exists," said Janet, from somewhere in the next room. "Nothing but a bloody mess left."

"We didn't cause it," said Kaarina, hastily. "It happens a lot..."

"Yeah, you said." Where would she go now? Home? Not if she were rational; her father would probably just rape her again. The Lighthouse?

"She left her stuff here," Janet said, and appeared in the doorway carrying Ronnie's sports bag. "She was really freaked out—screamed and panicked all the way to the shower." Her eyes were gleaming red; maybe it was the memory of all the blood. "The water seemed to calm her down. I left her there, and she sneaked out."

I glanced at Kaarina, who nodded slightly. "What is she wearing?" I asked.

"I don't know," Janet replied. "She took her anorak... her jeans and knickers were soaked..."

"I saw her running down the street," said Kaarina. "I think she was wearing a skirt..."

That made sense—Midas had two daughters who were about Ronnie's size—but it didn't help. She might have had enough money for tube fare in her anorak; failing that, she might have hitched a ride. "What do we do now?" asked Kaarina.

"I don't know."

"There might be something in her bag," suggested Janet. "Something with her address on it, or her surname..." Before I could answer, she'd unzipped the bag and dumped its contents on the carpet. I stared at the mess, and noticed a vaguely box-shaped lump underneath a t-shirt. I picked up the shirt, and saw a yellow-covered book that closed with a strap and a tiny lock.

"A diary," I breathed, handing it to Kaarina. She poked at the lock with her fingernail, and it popped open. The first page showed a name—Veronica Stewart—a Norbiton address, and a phone number. I stared at it for a moment, and then turned to the end of the book, flipping back to the last entry. Her handwriting was painfully small, but no worse than that of most lawyers.

Thur Dec 22. I met 2 women in an alley today, Kaarina and Janet. (I read). J isn't much older than me, she looks like a junkie or something, but she's smart and acts friendly. K is older, but she says she doesn't have a home either. They knew an empty shop where nobody goes, and they took me there. They don't have any food, and J started to laugh when I asked, but it's warmer than the park. I told them about myself, but not who I am, and the baby, but not whose it really is. K went away to get some money, and came back about an hour later then bought me some food and brought me here to the hostel. They seem pretty strange, and I don't know why they're helping me or what they want, but they're not the sort of women Dad knows, and it must be better for the baby if I keep warm.

I stared at the page, and asked, "You think she was two months pregnant?"

"About that, yeah." I flipped back to October. *Fri Oct 21. Algebra Test OK. Went to church with Felicity, Dad and Pauline, but Zoe wasn't there. F thinks she has a boyfriend (Z not F), probly some friend of David's.*

Sat Oct 22. Bought new jeans. Went to church; still no Zoe. Period started.

It went on in that vein for several days—schoolwork, teenage gossip, church—and I started skimming, until I noticed the line *Dad says I'm fertile now, and he wants to try again.*

"This is a child!" Haigha replied eagerly, coming in front of Alice to introduce her, and spreading out both his hands towards her in an Anglo-Saxon attitude. "We only found it to-day. It's as large as life, and twice as natural!"

"I always thought they were fabulous monsters!" said the Unicorn. "Is it alive?"

"It can talk," said Haigha solemnly.

Lewis Carroll, *Through the Looking-Glass and What Alice Found There*

Alice's plane arrived at ten, only a few minutes late, but it took her nearly an hour to get through Customs, and I suspect I was still shaking when she came running through the crowd, dropped her suitcase at my feet and leapt into my arms. "Have you missed me?"

"Horribly," I replied.

"Liar. What about your girlfriend?"

I wrapped one arm around her, then bent down to grab her suitcase, nearly dislocating my shoulder in the process. She's so tiny and plays at being a child so convincingly, I sometimes forget she has a vampire's strength. "I've missed her too."

Alice leaned back to stare into my eyes. "Are you in love with her?"

"Yes," I said. "Yes, I really think I am."

"That's wonderful."

I nodded. "How's Manila?" I asked, softly, as soon as we were in the carpark.

"Horrible. The poverty's so bad that I almost feel guilty scaring tourists away from the brothels—especially when you know they're probably just going to Bangkok."

"How many sidhe did you leave in Bangkok?"

"Seven... but I don't know if they're making a difference *there*, either. Killing a few of the bastards isn't enough; what matters is frightening the others, and the Thais are covering it all up." She shook her head vigorously, like a child. "It feels like justice when we do it, but it's not *working*."

"Uh-huh." It's an old saw that justice must not only be done, it must be seen to be done. I let her into the Jag, and she clambered up onto the seat. "Home?" she asked.

"Home."

Kaarina was waiting at the flat, sprawled out on the chaise-longue, listening to the radio and reading Ronnie's diary. She and Alice looked at each other coolly. "Janet not back yet?" I asked.

"No."

"Where is she?" asked Alice.

"At the Lighthouse, in case she turns up there," I replied, and nodded at the diary. "Have you found anywhere else she's likely to go?"

"No. She has a few friends, but she never mentions their addresses or even their full names. Of course, I'm mostly reading it backwards..."

"Of course."

Kaarina stretched, and sat up. "Maybe I should go and check out the squats again, and if I see any other sidhe, I'll tell them to look out for her, tell them she's blood." I stared. "Family blood, not food blood," she explained. "Okay?"

"Sure," I said. Kaarina placed the diary gently on the coffee-table and walked to the door. Alice curled up in a chair and closed her eyes. "Jet-lag?" I asked.

"Bad. I feel like the sun should be up; day and night affects us more than you."

"Yeah, I guess it would. How was the flight?"

"Okay, except that they kept giving me colouring books and expecting me to eat. But the movie was okay—not as funny as *The Lost Boys* or *Interview with the Vampire*, but not bad."

"If you want to sleep, there's a bed in the guest room..."

"Yeah. That's not a bad idea." She uncurled, and staggered towards the bathroom, then stopped. "Is this Lee-Lin? This photo?"

"Yeah. I took it in Hong Kong."

"Very pretty. You still take many photos?"

"Not as many I used to, no." I used to take photos of young girls—harmless photos, and no, you don't want to know why.

She nodded. "How tall is she?"

"Huh? About five foot, I think."

"In high heels, I bet."

"Okay, so she's short."

"How old? Seventeen?"

"Thirty-three," I replied, dryly. "She's a lecturer at the University of British Columbia."

Alice studied the photo for a moment. "I saw a lot of beautiful women in Bangkok and Manila. They all seem to stay young forever... have you ever taken this woman out during the day?"

"Huh?" I tried to remember, and Alice laughed. "Only joking," she said. "We don't show up in photographs, remember? Sweet dreams."

I *did* dream—I always do, when Alice is around—but for once, I didn't wake in fright. I was wandering through Room 42 at the British Museum, the Medieval Room, admiring the Carolingian engravings, when I saw Irene, still eleven but very much alive, playing with the Lewis Chessmen inside a glass case. I rapped on the glass, and she looked up and smiled, holding up a white knight. "Lovely, isn't it?"

"Yes," I replied, and then added, inanely, "Walrus ivory."

"Yes," she replied. "Very old."

We looked at each other, and then I said, "Can you come out?"

She touched the glass with her empty hand, and then shook her head. "No."

"It's a beautiful day outside."

She shook her head. "I can't."

I hated to say it, but I asked, "Because of your father?"

"No," she replied, sadly (after all, it was her father who had murdered her before shooting himself). "Because of you. That's why I'm here—*in* here. Because of you."

"Me?" I asked. She opened her mouth to speak, but all I could hear was a strange buzzing sound. Everything went dark, and as I fumbled for the alarm clock, I realised that Irene had gone again, leaving me in my bed alone.

Alice knocked on the bedroom door a moment later, as I stared blearily at the clock. Six A.M.: Kaarina and Janet would be arriving soon. "Are you okay?"

"Yes," I said, and switched the light on. "Come in."

She was wearing a black happi coat—one of mine; it hung down past her wrists and ankles, making her look disturbingly bat-like.

"Nightmare?"

"No... I don't know." I reached for my robe. "I keep wondering what we're going to do with Ronnie, even if we do find her. Her mother's dead, and I don't think she has any other family apart from her father, any other home... Do you think the incest might stop if he realises that she's not going to have a baby? I've read some of Ronnie's diary, and the incest didn't start until after she'd started having her periods.

"Her father probably fantasised about being the second coming of Christ when he was a kid—a lot of boys do, and he had better reason than most. He didn't know who his real father was, it sounds as though his mother's husband beat him, and he had a birthmark shaped like a cross... but most boys grow out of it, and he didn't." I shrugged. "He read about the Merovingians somewhere, probably in *Holy Blood, Holy Grail*. And he wanted to have sex with his daughter, and this gave him the perfect excuse..."

Alice shook her head. "People will always find excuses to do the things they really wanted to do anyway: blaming the Bible is as silly as blaming porn. If Ronnie goes home to him, he'll—" She stopped as the french windows slid open (I *know* I locked them) and Kaarina and Janet hurried in just ahead of the dawn.

"Any news?" I asked.

They looked at each other, and Kaarina grimaced. "I went looking in every squat and hideyhole I knew, pet, and talked to every sidhe and male I could find, including those who work in the hospitals; nobody's seen her."

I turned to Alice. "Maybe she's already gone home."

"I don't think so," said Janet, slowly. "I went to the Lighthouse, I spoke to people who knew her, I even saw her father—miserable-looking little guy, thick John Lennon glasses and really long grey hair like some fossilised hippy, though he dresses like a first-class dweeb—and he had this little girl with him. Her name's Pauline; Ronnie mentions her in the diary, *she's her younger sister*. Eight or nine years old, I guess, still just a kid..."

I hid my head in my hands. Why the Hell had we assumed she was an only child?

"But the same blood," said Alice.

Jesus. More blood.

"I'll kill him," suggested Kaarina. "We can break into his house, take Samira and Anita and—"

"No!" I snapped, and they all turned to stare at me. "No," I repeated, quietly. "There has to be a way we can stop him ."

Janet nodded, very slowly. "How?"

I stared at the books in the library. "I don't know." I reached for Ronnie's diary, and suddenly sat bolt upright. "Yes I do."

"What?"

I waved the diary at them. "I can get this published. Or some of it, anyway. Cut out any surnames, change a few other details... I'll say I'm representing a client who wishes to remain anonymous. Then we send him a copy, he'll know that he's been found out, and he won't dare touch his other daughter..."

The sidhe stared at me, and finally Alice nodded. "I like it. Don't forget to send a copy to her school library."

"I'll send a copy to every school library in the country," I promised.

Kaarina took the diary from my hand, and leafed through it. "How long will it take to get a book like this published?" My face fell. "And I've got some more bad news. We're not the only ones looking for Ronnie. Samira told me there's some guy, who doesn't sound at all like Ronnie's father, going around to the squats and shelters with photos of her, asking if anybody's seen her..."

"What does he look like?"

"Tall, big, dark hair, sort of rough... like he was trying to look like Clint Eastwood."

Oh, shit. "Ross Bauer."

"She didn't remember his name. You know him?"

"Yeah, I know him. He's a hunter; he finds runaways, usually wives, and takes them back home. He's good at it, too; if he wasn't, a few more of them might still be alive."

"Could he find Ronnie for us?" suggested Janet.

"Can you follow him?"

"At night, not a problem."

I pondered this. "Okay. We need someone to watch Ronnie's home, someone to follow Bauer, maybe someone to watch the Lighthouse—is it going to be open tonight?"

"Sure," said Janet, dryly. "It's Sunday, isn't it?"

Sunday. Christmas Day. I remembered Barbara and the Hatter worrying that I was going to spend Christmas alone, and started laughing.

I slept most of the day, and slept well, despite the three vampires in the flat. It was dark before five, and they disappeared from my balcony silently, without leaving a footprint on the slushy snow.

The phone rang at five past seven, and an unfamiliar voice rasped, "Are you looking for Ronnie Stewart?"

"Who's calling, please?"

"Why are you looking for her?" the voice responded. It echoed as though she was calling from a booth; I listened to the background noise, but couldn't pick anything out. "I think she may be in danger," I replied.

There was a moment's quiet, then the voice said, "She's safe now."

"Where?"

"What sort of danger is she in?"

"She just miscarried," I replied. "She needs to see a doctor."

"Are you a doctor?"

"No; I'm just a... a middleman."

"Between who?"

"The sidhe, and the... rest of the world."

There was a quiet hiss, then, "Okay. Meet me at Baker Street station, the Circle line platform, in thirty minutes."

I glanced at my watch. Thirty minutes would give me time to pick up one of the sidhe on the way. "I'll be there."

There was a slim, chestnut-haired woman sitting on the platform when I arrived. She was wearing tight black leather pants and boots, and a dark fur coat. She was striking, but not beautiful, and she would have passed for twenty-five until you looked at her eyes. She looked vaguely familiar, but maybe that was just because she was so obviously another sidhe.

She raised an eyebrow at the sight of Alice. "You didn't tell me to come alone," I pointed out.

"No, I guess I didn't," she admitted, and picked up her shoulder bag. Her voice was softer than it had been on the telephone. "Shall we go?"

"Where is she?"

"My flat. It's only three blocks away."

She led the way to the escalator; Alice looked her up and down as she walked, watching her body language. "My name's Alice."

"Natasha," replied the woman.

I raised my eyebrows slightly at so un-English a name being said with such an obviously English accent. "You're a dominatrix?" asked Alice.

"It keeps me off the streets," the woman replied, without any apparent embarrassment. "I get to sleep days, I never have to do any housework, and some of them like being bitten." I shuddered; Alice merely nodded. "Don't worry; I don't have Ronnie in the dungeon or anything, she hasn't guessed what I am."

An uncomfortable silence followed. "How is she?" I asked.

"She's very weak, exhausted, and obviously terrified that somebody's chasing her; apart from that, I guess she's okay." She softened slightly. "She's been eating, she's stopped bleeding, and she was asleep when I left."

"Nightmares?" asked Alice.

"Some. What happened to her?"

I looked around the station; there was no-one else in earshot. "What did she tell you?"

"Just that she was running away from home. Her home must be pretty scary."

"It is."

"You said she was pregnant."

"She *was*, yes."

We walked on in silence until we reached the woman's flat. It wasn't quite as large as mine, but it was much bigger and more secure than Barbara's. The sitting room was aseptically and impersonally plush, with thick carpets, heavy drapes and black leather divans, and it reminded me obscurely of Madame Tussaud's: the Chamber of Horrors was presumably behind one of the doors down the hallway. No mirrors, of course. "Not what you expected?" she asked.

"I didn't know what to expect," I replied. "Is this what you did before—"

"Before I died? No. I was a housewife, and my husband wasn't... into this sort of thing. Neither was I, I'm still not, it's just a job. Tell me more about Ronnie."

"What about her?"

"Why is she running away?"

I sat down on one of the divans, and sighed. "Her father was having sex with her; that's how she became pregnant. He's crazy, he thinks he's descended from Jesus and that he brought his wife back from the—" I stopped, suddenly realising why Natasha looked familiar. It wasn't the other sidhe she resembled, it was Ronnie. "You're her mother?" I whispered.

Alice's eyes widened; Natasha was silent. "Is that how you escaped from the car?" I asked.

She nodded. "A vampire got there before the ambulance arrived. I probably would have died, otherwise... I mean..."

"I know what you mean," said Alice.

"Yeah. Anyway, that was years ago; I'd almost forgotten I *had* a family. I mean, it wasn't like I could go and see them, not like this, not when I'm some sort of monster." Natasha stared at us, dry-eyed: Alice had told me that sidhe can't cry. "Simon—my husband—would have had the crosses and holy water out in a second.

"And then I heard that the sidhe were looking for Ronnie, so I went hunting for her, and found her wandering around Leicester Square. She was so sleepy, entrancing her was easy; I don't think I could have done it otherwise." She shook her head. "Now you tell me her father is a monster, too."

There wasn't anything I could say to that.

"So what do we do now?" She laughed bitterly. "It's not like I could claim custody; I've been legally dead for three or four years, and look what I do for a liv—for money. You're a barrister; what would you say my chances were in court?"

There was a knock on the door, and we all jumped. "Are you expecting anyone?" I asked.

"On Christmas? No; most of my clients are home with their wives..." Natasha stood, walked unsteadily to the door, and looked through the peephole, shrugged, then put the chain on the door and opened it a few centimetres. "Yes?"

Someone kicked the door open; Alice and I leapt to our feet, just in time to see the muzzle of a gun come swinging up to point at Natasha's face. Natasha stepped back, and the gunman walked into the hallway and shut the door behind him. He looked startled to see me, and then a grin spread across his face. "Well, well. The things you see when you haven't got a—oh, damn, I *have* got a gun. The great defender of women's rights, here in a child brothel. You know," he continued, as he walked into the room, forcing Natasha back, "I'd heard some rumours about you liking little girls, but I never believed them. Guess I was too charitable. Sit down. You too—over there, next to him. Where's the other kid?"

I stared at the gun—a short-barrelled riot gun, probably a twelve-gauge. I have a hatred of shotguns bordering on phobia, and I remembered what Kaarina had told me about rippers. Natasha glanced at me as she sat down. "Who is this?"

"His name's Bauer," I said. "Stewart paid him to look for Ronnie. Normally, he finds runaway wives and takes them back so their husbands can beat them up." There was no point in trying to mollify him, and this situation was impossible to explain to someone that pragmatic.

Bauer snarled, then sat opposite us with the gun pointed at my chest. "What would you know about it? You ever been married?"

I raised my eyebrows slightly. Maybe Bauer wasn't just a mercenary; maybe he had a personal grudge against wives or women. "Have *you* ever been beaten to a bloody pulp?" I countered.

Bauer didn't answer; he just reached into his overcoat with his left hand and pulled out a mobile phone, which he placed on the cushion beside him. If he tried to fire the gun one-handed, it'd probably break his wrist, but that wouldn't help me. "Mr Bauer?" said Natasha, a strange, lilting tone in her voice.

"Yes?" he replied, a little thickly, trying to press the right buttons on the phone and watch all three of us at the same time.

"I don't think you really want to call the police."

Bauer's fingers stopped in mid-fumble. "Why—what do you mean?"

"Why do you think they've left me alone up to now? Think for a moment."

Bauer's eyes seemed to bug slightly, and perspiration beaded on his brow, as though thinking was an enormous effort. I glanced at Natasha; she was staring straight into his eyes, and smiling. I glanced back at Bauer; his finger was still on the trigger of the shotgun, which was still aimed in our direction.

"Mr Bauer?" Natasha crooned.

"Huh?"

"You've left the safety catch on your gun."

Bauer didn't even look; he just flicked the switch back into the other position with his thumb. Alice suddenly appeared beside him, grabbed the gun, and pointed it at the ceiling. Bauer seemed to snap out of it for an instant, and tried to pull the gun down again, and Alice grabbed his right wrist with her left hand. There was a hideous crunching sound, and Bauer turned very pale, screamed, and let go of the gun. Natasha leapt to her feet and was flying towards him when I yelled, "NO! STOP!"

She stopped, her fingers already around his neck, and glanced over her shoulder.

"Don't kill him. Please."

"Why not?" She smiled. "I'm hungry."

"He's no danger to us any more," I said. "He'll never dare talk about this. Having his arm broken by an eight year old girl? Who would he tell?"

Natasha hesitated. "What do we do with him?"

"Do you have any handcuffs?" I asked.

"Of course; how many, and what colour?"

Okay, so it was a dumb question. "We'll drop him outside a hospital. I just want to be sure he behaves—"

"He'll behave," said Natasha. She turned, stared into Bauer's terrified face, then slapped him across the mouth, breaking his jaw and knocking him out. "Insurance," she growled.

"What do we do about Ronnie?" asked Alice.

I sighed. "Why don't we ask her? Do you think she wants to stay here? Do you want her here? Or do you think she'd go home if her father promised not to hurt her again?"

"And if he doesn't?" asked Alice. "What then? Publish Ronnie's diary? And what if that doesn't stop him? Do we beat the crap out of him, too?"

Natasha shook her head. "You don't know Simon. He's not a masochist, but he'd love to be a martyr."

"We're talking about a fanatic who thinks he's descended from Jesus," Alice reminded me.

"I know that," I snapped. I looked at Bauer, feeling almost sorry for him. It was going to take him a long time to restore his self-esteem; he would probably rather have died than...

"Would he love to be a *vampire?*" I asked. The sidhe were silent. "You could threaten him with *that*," I continued, quietly. "Undead, undying, never going to heaven... I bet they wouldn't even let him into church. And no Rapture. Wouldn't that scare him more than death?"

Something hideously like a smile flickered across Natasha's lips. "Yes, I rather think it would."

We left Alice in the flat to watch over Ronnie, and Natasha carried Bauer down to my car. We took him to the emergency room at Middlesex Hospital, and then I drove to the Stewarts' house. "What are we doing here?"

"Go in," I said. "Talk to him, tell him who you are and what he is and what you'll do if—"

Kaarina, who'd been watching the house, suddenly appeared at my window. "What's happening, pet?"

Natasha stared at me, and then leaned over and kissed me. She tasted terrible, but it's the thought that counts. Then she stepped out of the Jag, and ran through the snow to the front door.

Kaarina slid in and onto the empty seat, and we watched as Stewart opened the door, and stepped back, startled. Natasha walked in, and closed the door behind her.

"Yet still before him as he flies
One pallid form shall ever rise,
And, bodying forth in glassy eyes

"The vision of a vanished good,
Low peering through the tangled wood,
Shall freeze the current of his blood."

— Lewis Carroll, *Three Voices*

I collapsed on the bed as soon as I reached home, but I'd barely closed my eyes when the phone rang. I fumbled for it, and managed to grab the receiver without knocking it to the floor. "Yes? Hello?"

"Merry Christmas!"

I must have still been asleep; it took me several seconds to recognise the voice. "Lee-Lin?"

"Did I wake you? I'm sorry."

I sat up, and switched the light on. "Don't be. Merry Christmas."

"Sorry I didn't call you earlier... the weather was just too bad in L.A., so we flew to Phoenix. Just my parents and my sister and I. Can you join us for a few days?"

"A few days?"

"It's wonderful and warm here," she said. "Not a cloud in the sky; nothing but sunshine."

I looked at the curtain, imagining the moonlit streets outside, the falling snow, the dismal wind, and the sidhe. "I'll catch the first plane I can," I promised. "I love the sunshine."

best-seller

"Hello, marketing department.

"Yes. Yes, I've read it, but I think it needs some changes.

"No, the opening story's fine. Great images, gets you in immediately. Maybe a little *too* much info-dump, and I don't think we need precise measurements of some of the settings, but that's just a quibble. Most of the others... great. Lots of sex, lots of violence, lots of magic, strong characters, good emotional stuff... some continuity problems, sure, but you can edit those out, can't you? Some of the genealogy stuff belongs in an appendix, it slows down the story, and we need a map, but those are easy to fix. Real problem is, it starts to get a bit tame by the end, and I think we need something stronger for the finale.

"No, the last few pieces. They're too... talky. Didactic. Anticlimactic. This thing should end with a *bang*. Besides, there's the cover to think of.

"Look. You've done a great job. No-one's disputing that. But we both want this thing to sell, don't we? Sure, the names will help, but we need something that catches the eye. It needs a dragon.

"Okay, maybe not a dragon, but a *monster*. Dragon-like if possible. And a woman in a skimpy costume.

"Hear me out, will you?

"You did *what?*

"In the *contract?*

"Okay, okay. If you promised that the cover would depict a scene from one of the stories, we can do this. I wish you'd cleared it with us, but you're the editor. Just let me think.

"No, a snake isn't good enough. Giving it legs doesn't turn it into a dragon... okay, maybe it does, but I want this book to be *big*. I want the cover to scream *imagination*. A dragon with lots of heads, maybe. What do they call those things? Oh, yeah. And horns. Do they have horns?

"Look, it's easy. Commission another story.

"That's right, one with a dragon.

"Yeah, and a woman in a skimpy costume. Or skin-tight, but skimpy is better. And exotic-looking. Girl next door and dragon just doesn't cut it.

"Look, the sketches have already been done, and they look great. We can show it to the writer and—

"I'm serious. I know it's a shared universe, I know there's a strict chronology, but why not take it a little further? Into the future? Wouldn't that be a great way to end?

"I don't know. Something dramatic. A war. A plague. Something like that.

"Well, what about asking John?

"Yes, I know he can be a bit obscure, a bit heavy, but he's got one hell of an imagination. Wonderful images. Very scary. Just what the book needs for a finale.

"Okay, so he's not easy to work with, but as long as he takes his medication, he never misses a—

"That's just a rumour. He was never charged. And it's not as though he *sells* the stuff.

"Look, *I* can call him if you prefer.

"Uh-huh. Talk to you later."

"John! How're they hanging?

"Uh-huh.

"Uh-huh.

"Uh-huh. Look, John, can you do me a story if I send you a copy of the cover art and the rest of the book?

"Yeah. Look, it's perfect for you; half-naked woman and a seven-headed dragon. With horns.

"Well, I really need a finale—something dramatic. I mean, you can't kill the other authors' characters off, it's in their contracts and we might be wanting a sequel, but... Yeah, apart from that, make the body count as high as you like.

"Oceans of blood? Shouldn't be a problem.

"Meteor strikes? Plagues of locusts? Sure. Whatever. Can I have it by the end of the month?

"Thanks, John. Thanks. You're a saint."

from whom all blessings flow

Kaarina Schroeder, the inventor of the Bifrost Bridge, was born in what later became known as World One, which was fine as long as the only other World discovered had a population of a few million humans and trillions of mutated rats. The next World contacted, however, was technologically advanced enough to build their end of a Bifrost Bridge, and they refused to accept the title of World Three. After a few months of (occasionally acrimonious) discussion, World One became World Green, and World Three, World Blue, largely because of the background colours of their respective U.N. flags. Their histories had diverged sharply in 1906, when the English Revolution didn't happen in World Blue—mostly because some of the ringleaders were already dead, or not in London. Historians had found minor divergences as far back as 1879, and some joked about the *real* divergence points being lost in prehistory.

World Two became World Cyan, but none of the rats were heard to complain—at least, not to the historians. Then there was World Azure, where Robert Kennedy had been *fatally* shot; and World Indigo, where there hadn't been a Great Fire of London; and then another cold ruin which was christened World Grey and quickly abandoned... and then, a world so different from World Green that none of their living languages were recognisable, which became known on the other Worlds as World Red. By this time, Schroeder had retired to an estate in Green-Nova Scotia, surrounding herself with the best sound system available in any of the Worlds and refusing to speak to *anyone*. Meanwhile, hundreds of lawyers, politicians and other bureaucrats were trying to write a set of interWorld trade laws that would give their own homeWorld the maximum share of any hitherto undiscovered uninhabited or underdeveloped Worlds... and then a delegate from World Red, speaking in perfect pre-Homeric Greek, made an offer which made the emerald mines of Cyan-Brazil look like a handful of change.

Dearborn finished washing his hands, and stepped over to the hot-air dryer. "I know it's none of my business," he said, "but it's just *too* good a deal. I don't trust them."

Anagnostakos, listening, wondered if all the decisions for *all* the inhabited Worlds were made in men's washrooms. Monsignor Whately, sitting in the cubicle at his right, said, "You're right. It *is* too good an offer—too good to refuse—and, as far as I'm concerned, it *is* none of your business."

"Are you sure the interpreters got it right? It wasn't the Donation of Constantine in Classical High Tibetan?"

Anagnostakos ignored the insult: he was more startled that Dearborn had *heard* of the Donation of Constantine. Maybe the Azure-American had a professional interest in fraud—or, more likely, some researcher in his staff had found the reference and expected it to embarrass the Jesuit. The *Constitutum Constantini* had supposedly given the Roman Catholic church authority over all Christianity, but was later proven to be a fairly poor forgery written four centuries after Constantine's death.

"I'm sure enough," replied Whately, mildly. "Of course, we don't need their help as badly as you do..."

Fifteen love, thought Anagnostakos, wincing inwardly. World Blue had a population of fewer than six billion people, as against World Green's eight and a half, World Azure's ten, and World Indigo's thirteen (most of them starving). World Blue could also boast blue whales, gorillas and tigers still living in the wild, and breathable air in all but its largest cities.

"Some *help*," snapped Dearborn. "Okay, so they're building their end of the Bridge, but we're supposed to give them *millions* of our people, and I bet *we* have to do the fucking paperwork! Where is this land they're offering them, anyway? Antarctica?"

"All over their World: Canada, Brazil, Indonesia, Australasia, Southern Africa, Eastern Russia, South-East Asia. Underpopulated areas, but arable with the right techniques."

"Sure," said Dearborn, sarcastically.

"Have you ever seen Indigo-Australia? It was settled by the Spanish and their Mediterranean allies, who saw it as a beautiful country—unlike the English who landed there in *our* Worlds, who regarded it as a desolate hellhole. Now it's supporting a quarter of a billion people—probably the best fed people in World Indigo. Green-Australia's not as crowded, but it's nearly as rich: after they broke with England, they encouraged immigration from countries with similar climates and soils."

"Slave labour," muttered Dearborn. Whately's only answer was to flush the toilet, loudly.

"I still don't like it."

"*You* don't have to go: they're asking for volunteers. I think they'll get them."

"Not if we say no to the Bridges, they won't," Dearborn replied, and walked out, slamming the door behind him.

"Whatever happened to 'Give me your poor, your tired, your huddled masses?'" asked Anagnostakos, emerging from his cubicle.

Whately laughed. "I take it you're going to vote 'yes'?"

"I'm just a humble interpreter: I don't get a vote."

"How's the translation going?"

"Slowly. We haven't even tried to learn each other's native language—apparently theirs, Arrinesh, is descended from Sumerian the same way English is descended from niederdeutsch—but we're fairly sure that we understand each other's Greek. Of course, there's a lot of modern abstractions which we're having trouble getting across. I know a certain amount of Red-Japanese, but their new Katakana are unrecognisable, and Japanese is easy enough to misunderstand at the best of times. Apart from that, there are a few Native American languages which are the same in all the Worlds except Indigo, but their written alphabets are completely unlike ours and there's almost nothing published in them anyway. The stuff we *need* has to be translated at least twice to be any use to anyone, and that's painfully slow."

"What about their Bible?"

Anagnostakos shrugged. "I'm afraid I don't know. Why?"

"I've seen a copy—untranslated, of course, but illuminated. Your opposite number, their interpreter—Dr Melle?—lent it to me. Their Old Testament is unrecognisable, as is much of the New, but the four Gospels are there. And since they *do* use arabic numerals, I've been able to count the chapters and verses, and there are some interesting discrepancies. Their 'Mark', for example ends at Chapter 16, Verse 9, but there are verses..." He stopped; Anagnostakos was shaking his head. "What's wrong?"

"Their 'Mark' is more likely 'Mary', Monsignor." said Anagnostakos, gently. "Matthew, Martha; Luke, Lucy; John, Joan. Their 'Old Testament' seems to be Sumerian or Babylonian—"

"But they believe in *Christ*," replied Whately. "Their interpreter wears a crucifix, almost identical to mine, and I've seen her cross herself. The crucifixion picture in their Bible is the same as ours, even down to the woman kneeling before the cross, and the Last Supper—"

"Their interpreter is a priestess. Their 'pope' is a woman, the 'World Mother'. How long has the Catholic Church in World Blue been ordaining women? Over here, it's been less than fifty years. Their 'Christ' may not even be the same person, or have said the same things—and if He did, they were translated into entirely different languages, and cross-referenced to different prophecies, a different mythos, maybe even a different *ethos*. Besides, do the Christians on *your* World always agree with each other?" The diminutive interpreter shook the water from his hands, and walked out. Whately followed him.

"Do you mind if I ask you a personal question?" he asked, quietly.

"No, I guess not."

"About your religion?"

Anagnostakos shrugged. "My grandmother was Greek Orthodox, and she used to drag me along to services until I was too heavy to drag—but I haven't been inside a church since her funeral, and that was nearly twenty years ago. I went to a Catholic college in Melbourne, on a scholarship, but I think they would have expelled me if I hadn't kept winning the language prize. I've been exposed to every major religion on Earth—well, Earth Green—and none of them have stuck. No, that's not quite true—some of them stuck in my craw. I've seen holy war, sanctified bigotry, sacramental starvation... Hell, even back home—in Green-Australia—there was a Muslim community that practiced what they euphemistically call 'female circumcision'. Let's say I'm an ethical atheist."

"Do you believe in Christ?"

"Only as an historical figure."

"I'm not going to act as an apologist for religion," said Whately, nodding rapidly. "Or even for Catholicism: I have family in Blue-Belfast. But none of the religious wars were *Christ's* fault.

"We've both seen World Red. It's cleaner than our homeWorlds, and less violent, and no-one seems to be starving or homeless—"

"True," said Anagnostakos, "but maybe they have the death penalty for everything from graffiti to speeding—not that it's easy to speed in those electric cars—or compulsory euthanasia, or a suicide cult... or maybe their medical science is a few centuries behind ours, or they're suffering from an epidemic which only kills the poor, or they expose their children. It would explain why they need their gene pool boosted..." He looked at the priest's ashen face, and then smiled gently. "Don't worry, Monsignor; I'm just playing Devil's Advocate. It's a hobby of mine. I *like* all the Reds I've met; they seem... peaceful, at home—the way Zen Buddhists are supposed to be," he added, teasingly; then, "It's almost as though they don't have the concept of 'foreign'."

The ambassador smiled. "I think I know what you mean. Wouldn't you be interested in learning *why*?"

"Of course, but—"

"Doesn't religion play a large part in shaping a society's attitudes and behaviour?"

"Yes, but—"

"We know the RedWorlders invented the printing press thousands of years ago. Their gospels may not have been misinterpreted, censored and rewritten like those of our homeWorlds," concluded Whately, hastily. "Wouldn't that be a logical place to start looking for the secret?"

Anagnostakos stared at him for several seconds, and then smiled broadly. "I always wondered what 'Jesuitical reasoning' was: now I think I know. But what if you don't like what you find?"

"Monsignor?"

Whately looked up from his newsfax, eyebrows raised. "Yes?"

"I've spoken to Dr Melle," said Anagnostakos. "She's offered to take us to meet a teacher of hers on World Red, a priestess who should have, or be able to find, a facsimile edition of their gospels."

"That's wonderful!" Whately dropped his fax, reached for the interpreter's hand, and pumped it vigorously. "Thank you *very* much."

Anagnostakos smiled, and tried to disengage his hand. "We'll have to leave on Wednesday afternoon, at two: the priestess has a very busy schedule—we're lucky she could find a few minutes to accommodate us—and the temple is quite a long drive from the Bridge. I wouldn't expect to be back before seven."

"I can leave Panosian in charge for an afternoon: he's good, and he disagrees with almost everything Dearborn is likely to say. Are there any strictures I should know about?"

"Melle didn't mention any. They don't seem to have a dress code in Ptolemaios, what we call Red-Alexandria—the outfit the delegates wear are part habit, part weatherproofing. Your mufti may look uncomfortable, but at least they'll know you're from out of town. Melle suggested that *I* not wear a tie or a vest: apparently, the Reds think they look ridiculous, and only seasoned diplomats could keep themselves from laughing at me.

"Besides, we won't be mixing with the populace; I don't speak Arrinesh that well, anyway. We're to let Melle act as guide and take us from the bridge to the car, from the car to the temple, and then back the same way."

"Thank you again. I wish there was some way I could repay you."

"Just vote 'yes' on Friday," replied Anagnostakos, smiling.

"Oh, I planned to." Whately gave the younger man's hand another enthusiastic shake, and then calmed himself down. "You know, you're much smarter than you give yourself credit for, Mr Anagnostakos. You'd be *much* better at my job than I am—let alone Dearborn."

Anagnostakos shrugged. "I'm a street kid. I can learn any language you want, but I still forget which fork I'm supposed to use, and I'm the world's worst—" he hesitated: he'd been about to say 'liar', but realised that the priest might misconstrue this as an insult. "Poker player," he finished, rather lamely, but just as accurately.

"That boss of yours isn't much better."

"Oh, don't let that smile fool you. Besides, he isn't one sixty-eight in stacked heels."

"168?"

"Centimetres—I think it's about five foot five in Olde English. Jimmy has a *granddaughter* who's taller than me." He glanced at his digital watch (an import from Japan-Azure), and swore mildly. "I'm late. See you Wednesday."

"Goodbye," said Whately, "and again—thank you."

Whately peered through the windows of the electric car at the suburban streets of Red-Alexandria. The houses, new or old (it was difficult to tell), seemed to be built of the same colourful material (ceramic? plastic? one-way glass?), in much the same style—plenty of parabolic arches, a minimum of straight lines, and no sharp corners. He noticed more greenery than he thought Egypt could support, and pristine statues that might have been new or centuries old, and though the road was wide, he saw very few cars. He was wondering how Red-Ireland must look, when Anagnostakos said, "Monsignor?"

"Yes?"

"Dr Melle would like to ask you a question."

"Certainly."

"Why are all the ambassadors at the summit, men? I've explained why for my World, as best I can, but maybe yours is different?"

"Well... there *are* female diplomats and ambassadors on World Blue, of course, many of them in the U.N... but unfortunately, few of them have any experience as trade envoys. Where would they get the experience? We can't send them to Blue-Japan, much less any of the OPEC countries: they'd think we were insulting them. And only rich countries can afford women's rights movements: women in the poor countries don't have the leisure or the access to communications.

"In fact, women had been without most rights for so many centuries in all of our Worlds, the little progress that *was* made in my World over the last century is something of a miracle. Women still can't vote in most countries in World Indigo, and while progress was being made in Azure, it was reversed in the 1980's and 90's when Azure-America went from World leader to... can you translate that?"

"I think so, though I'm not sure that I understand all of it."

"That makes two of us. Are we nearly there?"

"Yes: in fact, we're ahead of schedule. I'm sorry we've both been talking shop..."

Whately waved a hand as though brushing away flies. "Don't worry: I've been enjoying the scenery. Tell Dr Melle that she's lucky to live in such a lovely World."

Anagnostakos translated that, and then said, "That's the temple ahead. She says it'll be nearly twenty minutes before Dr Esa is free. Do you want to tour around, wait in her office, or would you rather see a service?"

"A service?"

"Yes: she'll be giving some people... I think 'communion' would be the right word. Dr Melle wondered if you, as another priest of Christ, might be interested."

Whately gulped. "Tell her that I'd be fascinated."

Whately sat in the back of the church, wishing that God might grant him—if only for an hour—the gift of tongues. Even Anagnostakos couldn't understand the World Red vernacular well enough to translate, and Whately was desperate to know whether Dr Esa's sermon was as Christian as the fittings of the temple. Faith, he told himself. Have faith.

Finally, a number of the congregation moved to the railing at the head of the church, and knelt before it—some with hands behind their backs, some with hands clasped in prayer, and Whately's eyes filled with tears of joy. Dr Esa, wearing a burgundy-coloured kimono-like robe, stepped towards them. "Take and eat it," translated Anagnostakos, in a murmur, "This is my body. Drink; this is my blood, poured out for many for the forgiveness of sins." Then, as the offWorlders watched, Dr Esa opened the divided skirt of her robe, and guided a boy's face towards her groin. Then she moved over to the girl beside him, and repeated the gesture.

The boy, feeling the pressure of Whately's stare, turned around. Whately saw blood on his lips, and screamed.

"They've voted against any migration," said Anagnostakos. "Unanimously."

Melle stared, and then translated for the ambassador and her staff. The ambassador's reply needed no interpretation: "Why?"

"Officially? I suspect they'll say it's because they need to do more research, to pick the right people, to prevent a violent clash between two dissimilar cultures... The truth is far more simple. Whately told them about your church service."

"I don't understand."

"On *our* Worlds, they perform the same ritual with bread symbolising the body, and wine symbolising the blood—"

"Wine?" Melle erupted with a most un-diplomatic fury. "But that's a *travesty!* It's—"

"Blasphemy?"

"Worse!"

"Obscenity, maybe? I suspect that's the word Whately used."

The ambassador cleared her throat, and asked a question. Melle translated. "What will happen to the millions starving on your Worlds? What will they tell them?"

Anagnostakos shrugged. "They'll think of some excuse. Dearborn suggested they be sent to World Cyan, that he'd rather deal with the rats—as though it were *his* problem. I'm not a scientist, so I don't know how feasible that is, but I suspect they'll try. Whately also recommended they close *all* the bridges to World Red."

Melle translated this, and the ambassador and her staff were silent. Finally, the ambassador spoke.

"What about you?"

"Me?"

"If they do close the bridge," Melle translated, "which side will you be on?"

"I don't understand."

"You have no home in your World," the ambassador continued. "You've not lived in the same city for as much as a year since you were twenty-three—and now you're thirty-six?"

"I like travelling."

"We have a *World* that you haven't seen, with a hundred new languages for you to learn. And you're an interpreter. Your job is helping people to understand each other. On our World, you could help us to understand thirty billion people..."

"And," added Melle, "if the bridge is re-opened, you could help them to understand *us.*"

"I'm really not sure that's possible..." Anagnostakos replied. He tried not to sound tempted, but he'd never been a good liar: Melle knew that he'd already accepted the offer.

"Think it over," she said, "but don't tell anyone. They may try to stop you."

"Of course, there's one other option," said Dearborn, wiping his hands.

Whately, who'd been staying drunk for days in an effort to avoid a near-lethal hangover, grunted non-committally. As far as he was concerned, now that all the Reds had returned to their home World, the Bridge apparatus should be dismantled without delay.

"Military. We invade."

Whately nodded, then suddenly sat bolt upright. "You're joking!"

"Hell, no! Move the bridge to one of their uninhabited areas and drop in a few million troops from each World, take one continent at a time..."

"But what about..." Whately tried to remember the word 'proselytising', failed, and finally blurted out, "cultural contamination?"

"Biowar?" Dearborn mused. "I don't think we know enough about their immune—"

"No!" snapped Whately, winced, and continued quietly, "No... I mean... their relig... uh, their cult? *You* know? What if some of the troops, uh, especially the women... what if they... learn about it, get converted to it—"

"So we lose a few sol-"

Whately finally found the words he wanted, and used them. "What if they bring it *back* with them, for Christ's sake?"

"Oh," said Dearborn, and considered this. "Oh. Well... we won't send any female troops over. The men won't... well, they just won't. Besides," he said, recovering his confidence, "the Reds *can't* corrupt us. None of them know our language, and vice versa—right?"

—II—

Anagnostakos closed the door behind him and locked it, then staggered the remaining few steps to the bed—taking great care, despite his fatigue, not to tread on any books—kicked off his boots, and collapsed, face down. He looked up a moment later, and realised that hours had passed; the room was dark, and someone was rattling the door. "Melle?"

"Yes."

"Come in," he said, rolling over and rubbing his eyes. The lights, sensitive to heat and motion, brightened as she entered the untidy room.

"Were you asleep?"

"Huh? Yeah." He stood, a little unsteadily. "Where are we going tonight?"

Melle regarded him carefully, and then shook her head. "Nowhere. Sleep is more important. I'll call for some food."

"You know, that's the longest speech in English I've heard all day," Anagnostakos replied, unlacing his jacket. "Where *are* we going? The theatre again?"

"The play will be on tomorrow night. Sophocles has been dead for centuries; *you* need to sleep. You've been working too much."

"I was a teacher for years. That's how I managed to see the world—one World, anyway. I'll admit, I've never had class where everyone was so bright *and* enthusiastic, and that's as tiring as herding cats... but I'll cope." He stepped out of his trousers, and pulled on another pair with practised haste. As far as he could tell, RedWorlders didn't have any nudity tabus, but he hadn't quite lost his own. "What time's the show? Can we eat first?"

"How long did you sleep in the night?"

"I don't know. About five hours—call it eight *tou.*" She looked at him dubiously, and then glanced at the books beside the bed. "Okay, maybe seven. I read for a while. There's so much I don't *know* yet. Anywhere else I go, I know *something* about the tabus and the customs, what I can and can't do and say and wear and eat, where I can and can't go, and when, how rich or poor the people are..."

"I understand that," replied Melle.

"I'm not sure you do. All I know of your geography is that Wa is Japan and Nura is Australia, and a little about the Concordat. I know some Arrinesh, though not as well as you know English, but there's hundreds of languages, thousands of years worth of history, millions of books and plays... *we've* only had the printing press for a few centuries, not four millenia. We probably lost half a million books when the Library of Alexandria burnt down—hundreds of plays by Sophocles and Aeschylus and Aristophanes and Euripides, the complete works of Berossus and Hecataeus and Hypatia, all stuff you take for granted and that academics on Green would murder their grandmothers for... And the beautiful things the women here have done, books and paintings that never existed on our Worlds at all, except maybe in someone's head... In any of the other Worlds, I'm a well-travelled and educated man; here, I'm an ignorant barbarian. And I'm a Greek: we *invented* the term barbarian, to describe everyone else!"

Melle laughed. "The Arrinesh word 'hort' means roughly the same, and is probably even older—but I haven't heard anyone use it to describe you. Is that all?"

"No. I really do love what I've seen of this World. All the time I've been here, I don't think I've seen anything ugly or dangerous; I *know* I haven't seen anyone who looks beaten, or frightened, or hungry, or even seriously angry. I was scared, for a while, that the men might be treated as badly here as women are in the other Worlds, but if they are, I haven't seen it. I *have* wondered why there are so few men in my classes—"

"There are very few men in the Councils, at present," Melle admitted. "The Concordat, and most of its member-states, has been led by a coalition of religious and women-only parties for the past eleven years—and, of course, they appoint ambassadors who will agree with their policies. So most of the women in your classes are diplomats, while nearly all the men are teachers or linguists—there are plenty of men in the universities, especially the sciences, and even in the church; they can do anything but give the sacrament."

"And become Worldmother."

"The Worldmother must actually have *been* a mother, with at least one son and one daughter… but that's mostly symbolic, like most of her powers. Some people have tried to change it, but most accept that it isn't important."

"Maybe that's what I like about this world," said Anagnostakos. "You believe in a mother whose first priority is feeding her children; we pray to a father who seems more concerned with punishing them."

Melle smiled. "That's a lovely idea, but unfortunately, it isn't quite true. Not everyone is as well-fed as the people you've seen in Ptolemaios and Erech. There was a famine in Punt before you arrived; *thousands* starved before we could send enough food.

"And there are people here, even whole countries, which worship male gods. There are even some, including a few Buddhists sects, who believe women don't have souls, but who are still known for their good works. *All* of our religions teach that you should never refuse food to anyone hungrier than yourself; life is just too valuable.

"On the other hand, not all Christians will turn the other cheek. All clergy are forbidden to bear arms, preach violence, or even raise a hand against a child or a cat—but the same law doesn't apply to the laity, many of whom serve with the army when required. And there have always been those who worship the Mother by sacrificing innocent victims— one of the oldest prayers in the Bible, by Enheduanna, praises the Goddess for 'filling the rivers with blood', and they say there are *still* devotees of Kali Ma in Maurya and Harappa."

Anagnostakos nodded, thinking hard. "You mentioned the army. Do you still have wars?"

"Yes, of course—though not *here*. The Concordat hasn't been attacked for centuries. But the war in Funan is still going on, though both sides signed a treaty nearly twenty years ago—"

"*That's* why I need more time to study. I didn't even know you still had *armies*—"

"Do *you* still have wars? On World Green?"

"Yes—"

"How large are your armies? What weapons do your soldiers have? What about the other Worlds?"

"I don't know the precise—"

"But *you* do know they're larger than ours, and probably better armed."

"I don't know about your weapons, but the other four Worlds have—" He calculated quickly. "Nearly forty billion people between them. Most countries have between one or two per cent of their population in the armed forces during peacetime, so that's about half a billion. If you could get them all to fight on the same side, which is unlikely... say five billion if you throw in the reserves."

"That's more than twice our total population," said Melle, softly. "That's why we *need* you to teach English. A third of your students are diplomats; the rest are teachers, who'll teach more diplomats and more teachers. When they're fluent enough to take the beginners' classes, then we'll be able to reduce the tou you have to work, and you'll have more time to study. But if we're invaded, we're going to need—"

"You don't really believe that's going to happen, do you?"

Melle shrugged. "It's possible, and that possibility makes you uniquely valuable to us."

Anagnostakos looked at the books on the floor, and then sat down. "Well, since you put it like *that*..."

Whately grunted a greeting to Brother Luke as the younger monk dashed past him on their way to chapel. Brother Luke was an explosively devout redhead from Cork, who seemed better suited to the I.R.A. than to monastic life; he always ran, as though his need to confess something was unbearably urgent.

The Church should have copyrighted confession centuries ago, Whately thought; Alcoholics Anonymous would owe us a fortune in royalties. And that was all they ever asked *him* about; had he had a drink? had he craved a drink? as though that were the only thing he'd come to the monastery to avoid. Which suited Whately perfectly; let them believe that, he could answer *those* questions with a smile and a clear conscience. The other thing was...

"Brother John?"

He looked up slightly, recognising the abbot's Chicago accent. The abbot was a short man, who reminded Whately vaguely of someone else he'd known, once. "Yes, Excellency?"

"Another letter for you. I was requested to deliver this one to you personally, and to be sure that you read it and replied. The request," he added, with a slightly sour edge to his voice, "came from the secretary of His Holiness. Apparently you've been remiss in answering your mail."

Whately blinked, and then stared at the envelope. There was neither stamp nor postmark. He'd received enough mail in recent weeks to arouse the curiosity of his fellow monks, especially as most of it had come from World Azure. Nervously, he opened it, and read through it quickly.

"Bad news?" asked the abbot, sympathetically.

Whately nodded. "It says I'm to leave at once."

"Are you surprised?"

"I wasn't expecting a papal edict," replied Whately, choosing his words with great care.

"Weren't you? You must have realised that you couldn't hide here forever."

"You think I've been hiding?"

"Yes," replied the abbot, simply. "I don't really know why, and I'm not about to ask—oh, I know you've been bitten hard by the bottle, but that's never the whole story and I suspect you could have beaten that yourself. You were a delegate to the interWorld trade talks, weren't you, before they burnt all the bridges to Red?"

Whately glanced at the letter again, and said nothing.

"And the delegate from Azure-Washington is now sitting in the White House... Have you been to Azure-America, John?"

"No. Have you?"

"No, but I try to keep up with the news. They're having terrible troubles there, economic and environmental, and all of them can be blamed on overpopulation, though that's an oversimplification. Even the U.S.A. thinks of itself as overpopulated; the irony is that they regard their poor as the excess, when it's their rich who consume more than—but that's by the by. What's disturbing is that the Church is being used as a scapegoat, because of *Humanae vitae*, which was never repealed over there. Widely ignored, maybe, but never actually repealed. Now, your friend Dearborn—" ("He's not my *friend*," muttered Whately.) "—has gotten where he's gotten largely by scaremongering and pandering to prejudices. He knows there's a lot he could do to hurt the Church in Azure without it rebounding on him. On the other hand, he has no good reason to do so—which makes it an excellent bargaining chip. His people call Azure-Rome, and..."

Whately nodded. "Things were so much simpler when there was only one Pope."

"Amen to that. At least we all worship the same God." He sighed. "The helicopter will be picking you up tomorrow—after matins, I expect. Where were you going, confession?"

"Yes."

"Then I won't keep you. Goodbye, Brother."

Whately bowed his head, and walked slowly towards chapel, in time to hear Brother Luke burst out of the confessional and crash onto a pew. Out into the Worlds again, he thought, wearily, and realised he was shaking; he leaned against the back of a pew, but never looked up, not here, not in chapel.

He could feel the image of the virgin Mary staring at him from behind the altar, and the mere thought, the idea of a woman in the front of a church, was enough to remind him of—

He doubled over and vomited on his sandals. Bless me Father, for I have...

He heard other monks running towards them, Brother Luke in the lead. Let them believe it's the alcohol that scares me, he told himself again, not the... Bless me, Father, for I... Not the obscenity, the uncleanness, the blood, the Whore of Babylon Mother of Abominations... Bless me, Father, for...

'Let your women keep silence in the churches; for it is not permitted unto them to speak'

Bless me, Father, for...

'For the man is not of the woman but the woman of the man.'

Bless me, Father...

'These are they that were not defiled with women'

Bless me, Father, for...

'And the woman was arrayed in purple and scarlet colour, and decked with gold and precious stones and pearls, having a golden cup in her hand full of abominations and filthiness of her fornication'

Father...

After weeks of dropping hints, Melle finally came out and said it. "If you're scared of violating tabus, you can stop worrying. All of your students are adults. If you want to sex with them, you can ask; it's not forbidden, as long as you're polite and respect their right to say 'no'." While Anagnostakos was still staring, his fork halfway to his mouth, she hurried on. "I shouldn't worry unduly. Mati seems to be as attracted to you as you are to her, and we have an old saying that the best place to learn a new language is in bed."

"We have the same saying," replied Anagnostakos, a moment later. "Though I can't vouch for its antiquity. Look, I'd better ask this now, before I make a complete fool of myself—what are the marriage customs here?"

Melle almost choked on a mouthful of salad. "I don't think she'll agree to *marry* you," she said, cautiously, after regaining her composure. "I wasn't suggesting you ask her *that*; you've only known each other for a few months. But you've been here for just over a year, now, and that's a long time to be without sex; I would have spoken sooner, but I wasn't sure of *your* tabus."

"I meant, is she already married, and does marriage mean—?" He tried to think of the Arrinesh for 'monogamy'. Melle stared at him, and then smiled. "Oh. I don't think she's married, I'm fairly sure she hasn't any children, and she's not wearing any warn-offs or fetishes, so it's safe to ask. For sex, I mean."

"What if she *were* married?" he pressed on. "I haven't seen a wedding here, and haven't even heard anything about them, until now. Our traditional marriage vows require the partners to 'forsake all others, until death us do part.'"

"Forsake? As in *abandon?*" Melle sounded horrified. "All others? The entire *world?*"

Anagnostakos shook his head. "Okay, so it was a bad choice of words. It mostly means 'don't have sex with', not 'don't help'..."

"Why not?"

"What? Oh... well, originally, I suppose it's because men used to want to be sure their heirs were also their biological children, and not someone else's—passing on their own genes, as the sociobiologists would put it. So they made sure their wives were faithf... didn't have sex with anyone else. If a married woman was raped, she was stoned to death. It was supposed to cut both ways, but it didn't; look at the *Odyssey*. Odysseus sleeps with Kirke and Kalypso and Goddess knows who else, while Penelope sits at home and spins for eleven years. At its most extreme, of course, some Muslim sects practice clitoridectomy or 'female circumcision', mutilating women so that they can't have orgasms." He grimaced.

Melle stared at him. "I'm sorry," she said, softly "but I don't think I understood a single thing you just said."

Dearborn looked beefier than he had at the trade talks, though the muscles he'd built up for the campaign were already starting to turn to flab after barely a month in office. "Johnny boy!" he chortled, as Whately was ushered into the room. "Good to see you again. How're things on Blue?"

Whately was too experienced a diplomat to frown, but his voice was cool as he replied, "I haven't seen very much of it, lately, I'm afraid. I've been on retreat."

Dearborn's smile broadened into something even less pleasant. "Yeah, I heard. Doing the Lord's work. I like to think I'm doing the same." Whately grunted non-committally. "And that's why I've called for you. I've spoken to all the other delegates from the trade talks. Remember what I said, just before we closed the Bridges to Red, about the military option?" Whately stared at him. "Okay, so it was a little premature. But you musta heard what happened to our colonies on Cyan and Grey." Whately nodded. There were still a few off-shore oilrigs on both of the Blasted Worlds (as the press had taken to calling them), but they were barely paying for the energy to keep the Bridges up. "Fortunately, I'm on the record as being against it from the beginning. I mean, frankly, we might as well try to put men on the fucking moon. Even if you succeed, who the Hell wants to live on the *moon*? We haven't found any more Worlds since then, and that goddamn Schroeder woman refuses to help. But Red—Red could be the Promised Land. The Land of Milk and Honey. The Garden of Eden. You know what it looked like; none of us saw as much of it as you did."

"I saw it," replied Whately. "And you already know that I believe any contact is just too great a risk."

"Never underestimate a good publicity machine; just ask the man who's ridden one. We just tell our boys that the Reds'll cut their balls off if they let any get close enough to talk to them; Hell, it's probably true. You missed out on the Gulf War, didn't you? Shit, it was like a video game; all anybody ever saw was blips on a screen." He grinned. "So what makes you think they can beat us?"

"Because they already have," said Whately, solemnly. "On all of our Worlds, we defeated them thousands of years ago. But on Red, they won."

"I think I understood *some* of that," said Melle, uncertainly, after Anagnostakos had spent nearly quarter of an hour explaining. "You take the family names of your fathers?"

"Yes."

"Why?"

"Because men still own nearly everything, and it used to be almost impossible for women to bring up their children without a father's financial support."

"Why would anyone have children they knew they couldn't feed?"

"Well, they probably didn't intend to, unless the man convinced them that he was going to marry them or something."

"But if they didn't intend to—"

Anagnostakos stared at her. "Don't women here ever become pregnant by accident?"

"No! Almost *never*; it's about as unlikely as having triplets..." They both sat there in stunned silence, until he asked, "Since when?"

"For as long as anyone knows!" replied Melle. "Some of the oldest printed books we have, maybe the first ever written in Demotic, are herbal recipes for young girls who haven't learn how to control their fertility by—I don't know if you even have a word for it, the closest I can think of is 'faith healing'..."

"Biofeedback?" guessed Anagnostakos.

Melle broke the word into its roots, then nodded. "Yes. That sounds right. How long have *you* known it?"

"If we ever knew it at all, we've forgotten it," he said, softly. "For a long time, we didn't even admit that women were anything more than incubators, sure that all life came from the male, that every sperm was a miniature human waiting to be born... We still have some of that attitude, but now we blame the women."

"Is that why you have nearly nine billion people?"

"It's *how*; I'm not sure about *why*. Partly because we spent most of the past few millenia expecting most of our children to die, and having as many as we could to compensate. Partly because most of our rulers wanted men for their armies. And, probably because of the first two reasons, men were taught that they weren't really men until they'd fathered sons, and women were never told that they had a choice."

"Do you mean a choice of not having children, or just a choice of not having sons?"

"You can choose the sex of your children, too?"

"We can choose not to have *sons*," she replied. "Choosing to have them is more difficult. Sperm with the male message—I'm sorry, I don't know your word for it—"

"Chromosome."

"They're very sensitive to heat and chemical changes, very easily killed. Females are much, much tougher. It's just as well; how many men does a World need, after all?"

"The Sumerians and Babylonians, the Minoan culture, the ancient Egyptians and Greeks, even the Celts... they all worshipped a Mother-Goddess," said Whately. "Inanna. Ishtar. Isis. Astarte. Anahita. Artemis. Aphrodite. Athena. Danu. The myth is probably as old as language; a lot of primitive cultures even claim that a goddess taught them writing, or call the goddess 'The Great Scribe'. We don't know much about their rites, except that they used poisonous snakes; I shudder to think how. The priests, the soldiers, the judges, sometimes even the rulers, were women. They probably had no idea how babies were conceived, didn't realise men were important.

"Our ancestors—Aryans, Caucasians, whatever you choose to call them; what's important is that they worshipped God, a *male* God—came from the north into Mesopotamia about four thousand years ago, with their own laws. It was inevitable that the two cultures would clash. In our Worlds, *we* won, destroyed the temples and the idols, enforced our laws... but in Red, somehow, we lost." Whately took a deep breath. "To beat them this time, we would have to kill every single one of them. It may take even more than that; we have to destroy every *trace* of their religion. At the very least, we'd have to burn every book, unread, and even if it were possible, it wouldn't be popular with the academics. More likely, we'd have to nuke every city—*Deuteronomy* 12:2; 'Ye shall utterly destroy all the places, wherein the nations which ye shall possess served their gods, upon the high mountains, and upon the hills, and under every green tree.' Not even neutron bombs would do; we'd need to turn the planet into a cinder like Cyan or Grey. Hell, that may even be what *happened* to Cyan and Grey! Even if you were prepared to kill that many people—and I'm not—what would it profit you?"

"We still have famines, but they are minor and isolated; no-one intentionally has more children than they can feed.

"We still have wars, occasionally—but women who are against the war make sure the next generation hasn't enough surplus males for an army. Invaders may capture a country—but if they oppress the people, they have to go home to breed or die out.

"Slavery died out thousands of years ago. It wasn't economically viable, because the slaves wouldn't breed.

"There is still rape, but no woman has to bear her rapist's child.

"We created and we continue the human race. We taught you your first words. We are the source of life and language. And all we ask is that *you remember where you began.*"

Dearborn sat back in the enormous leather chair and suppressed a yawn. "Is that your official position?"

"I no longer hold an official position," replied Whately. "I've retired from the U.N., and I intend to stay retired; I'm here at the request of your Pope."

Dearborn nodded. "Well, Monsignor, thanks for your input. It's been good to see you again; give my regards to World Blue."

Whately stood. "You're going to do it, aren't you?"

Dearborn stared at the Oval Office ceiling for a moment, then shrugged. "Yeah. If I don't, the Indigos will beat me to it; besides, we've spent billions just getting ready. The Bridges are built, the troops are trained, the logistics are all worked out, the news releases have been written... Hey, chill out! There's no need to worry." He grinned. "God is on Our side, remember?"

Three years later, when he caught his daughter giving communion in the Lincoln Bedroom, it occurred to Dearborn that he might have been wrong.

twenty views of hokosai by fuji

Figure in a Landscape

A person stands alone on a low-lying hill, around is little but dips and mounds of mud and rock. Small pools of dark water reflect the grey sky. It looks to be an abandoned battlefield from some forgotten conflict. Desolation is the word that comes to mind from a passive observer. The figure standing in the centre of this scene knows full well the power deep within the soil. It is only dormant for those who do not know how to awake it.

Figure in a Memoryscape

Standing in line to buy a ticket to a random session of a sci-fi film festival of classics, sleepers, blockbusters and turkeys. Someone steps up behind to join the queue. He is wearing a bowler hat, dark make-up around one eye and striped overalls. He holds a cane and is not conservative with which way it swings and thrusts. You feel compelled to ask, "Are you are droog?" You get the response, "Congratulations, you've just won an extra five minutes on your life."

Figure in a Timescape

The robot probe materializes in front of a ruined stone monument somewhere deep in a sandy desert. The ruin can best

be described as two vast legs of stone. The probe receives a signal—
that has traveled thousands of years—instructing it to pan its little
stereoscopic camera down to the base of the ruin. There, finely
chiseled, is an inscription:

> My name is Ozymandias, King of Kings:
> Look on my works, ye mighty, and despair!

But as soon as a technician—some other place, some other time—
has read the transcription, a large bulk passes in view swiftly and
out-of-focus. Nothing of the mysterious creature is seen again, but
when the probe is instructed to pan further down to the ground at
the monument's base, it focuses on a deep impression in the soil. It
is a large three toed foot print, triangular in shape and the toes end
with the deep incisions of long, curled talons as sharp as a razor.

Figure in a Memoryscape

A photo rests on a table near a pile of second-hand SF novels
stacked ready to go back for exchange. Looking more closely at the
photo, it is of a bearded gentleman in a dramatic pose dressed as
Dr Frankenfurter. After just the brief look, one feels compelled to
gently slide the photo under the stack of books.

Figures in a Dreamscape

Ray Bradbury and Harlan Ellison are drinking at a bar. The
alcohol makes them a only little more loquacious than normal.

"So, Ray," asks Harlan. "Why did you call *Silver Locusts* the
Martian Chronicles?"

"So, Harlan," asks Ray. "Why did you call anything?"

Suddenly, the ghost of Edgar Allan Poe appears over the bar.
"I'm here to warn you of the Apocrypha yet to come."

Ray and Harlan look up, both with bemused eyes.

"So Edgar," voiced both the aging enfants terribles. "How's
Lovecraft doin' up there?"

Figure in a Timescape

Midnight, a cobbled street, the worn bricks glisten in the moonlight.
A tall figure in gentleman's suit and top hat hides within the
descending fog and the shadows of an alleyway. Also hidden is a

long, scalpel sharp, blade within his thick cloak. He remains still in the darkness and watches the prostitutes under the pools of gaslight as they call to the passing gents. This figure believes in his divine immunity and the surety that no one watches him. But, oh, he is being watched. Forever shall he be watched.

Figure in a Memoryscape

Next to an old computer, whirring and clunking as the ancient drive tries to read a disk, are a stack of letters. Starting at the bottom, one pulls out a page and reads. It is short and to the point. An editor's rejection slip. The next letter is also a rejection. This too is short. The third letter from the bottom is again a rejection, but not so short. A little further up the stack, we pull another page. Although a rejection, it is not a short letter. The next one is also long. Now we pull out a sheet from the top third of the stack. Short and to the point, it is an acceptance. The next one is also short and positive. And although the writer is more fond of the letters toward the top of the stack, he has as much respect for the letters near the bottom. The latter don't mean so much without the former.

Figures in a Timescape

Michelangelo and Raphael are hangin' at a strip joint drinking cheap beer. A pair of shapely female legs in fish-net stocking and stilettos dance on the table by their seats. They are being entranced by the dancer when Raphael has a thought.

"Hey Mick!" shouts Raphael above the thump thump of the dance music, the end of a feather boa softly lashing across his face. "You think Leonardo got to do the Mona Lisa?"

But before Michelangelo can answer, the dancer crouches down, and seductively holds a finger under Raphael's chin.

"How do you think he got me to smile."

Figures in a Memoryscape

A young couple enter a bookshop, a science fiction and fantasy specialty bookshop. They go to the man behind the counter who cheerfully puts down the book he's reading. The couple say they recently enjoyed The Hobbit and Lord of the Rings and ask if he could suggest something else they'd like. With enthusiasm he jumps off his stool and proceeds to select books off the shelf. He selects thin books, thick books, trilogies, collections of short gems, stories of warriors, of angels, of princes, of magic, of political intrigue, of great journeys, of family sagas, of long lost love. As he presents each book, describing the richness within the pages, the couple look more and more disconcerted. When he has presented all his choices and laid them to rest on the counter, the couple ask, "Are there hobbits in any of them?". As the disappointed couple leave, the bookseller heaves a sigh and slowly returns each book to its respective nook.

Figures in a Dreamscape

The dawn arrives but he remains sleeping as the sun moves across his face. She floats above him. Her night vigil once again over. She descends slowly and kisses his lips as gently as a hint of breeze before the light of the sun dissipates her form

Figure in a Landscape

A backpacker is walking along a trail of stone at the bottom of a deep gorge. Looking up would show a strip of bright blue between walls of dark grey slate. Over the many years, those walls have slowly crumbled and the shards of stone form ramps of loose rock on either side of the narrow pathway. Eventually the traveler comes to a split that forms two canyons veering right and left. Looking down both paths, the backpacker gives a shrug. Taking a pair of dice from a pocket in the pack, the traveler crouches down and rolls them on the chasm floor.

Figures in a Timescape

The man steps carefully within the dank catacomb. The inky darkness only kept at bay by the lantern he holds in an out-stretched hand. His objective is ahead. An ornate coffin carved and painted with bright little flowers. Carefully, he lifts the lid to reveal a gentleman with pallid face, black hair falling around his white neck, a pin-stripe suit and a large silk handkerchief erupting from his breast pocket. The carnation in the lapel looks freshly picked. Trying not to shake, the man places the lantern on a corner of the coffin and probes his coat for the hammer and stake hidden within. He holds the wooden stake over the resting figure's heart and raises the hammer high. But before he can strike, a pale hand reaches up and grabs the stake. The reclining form opens his eyes and looks upon the person leaning over him. From the coffin he calmly smiles, showing a hint of his pointed teeth.

"My dear Mr Stoker," says the vampire.

"My dear Mr Wilde," whispers the vampire hunter.

"Bram, my dear fellow," sighs Oscar. "To lose one's mortality can be deemed an accident, but to lose one's immortality would be carelessness."

Figures in a Mindscape

A pair of eyes stare, unblinking, full of all the world's joys and all the world's pain. The person to which those eyes belong could easily weep, but chooses to laugh. This person understands that one can always forgive, but should never forget.

Figure on a Deskscape

Deinonychus; "terrible claw", fleet of foot, flesh-ripper, hunter of many, adversary to all. With a firm yank of her powerful legs, she pries herself off the little display stand and begins to roam her domain. She climbs a hill of manila folders, walks through a canyon of books, almost slips on a raft of pens. She passes a big pale structure, rumbling like some underground stream, having to climb over a rocky terrain that continually gives a little under her claws. She takes scant notice to the line of markings extending on the dark side of the cube. She walks around the corner of a wall of large, thick books and several folders to spot her prey. Tenontosaurus stands on his pedestal by the edge of the desk, oblivious to the dangers. Deinonychus wishes she was in the pack right now, but being on her own won't stop her from the hunt. She ducks down and slowly moves up behind the stack of editor's letters. She pauses for just a moment, then leaping high above the paper, she strikes.

Figures in a Timescape

"Excuse me," said the tourist. "Could you please turn around for a moment?"

The artist looked behind him to see a man in strange clothes holding a small box to his face. The sound like the single click of a cicada came from the shiny black box.

"Thank you," said the time traveler.

The artist grunted at the bizarre nature of the fellow and returned to his sketching.

"You're Katsushika Hokusai, aren't you?"

The artist tired to ignore him.

"You're sketching Mt Fuji, aren't you."

"What if I am," replied the artist.

"You're going all round Mt Fuji sketching different views, aren't you?"

The artist tried to ignore him again.

"Then you'll go back home and use them for your series of wood prints that you'll call a 'Hundred Views of Mount Fuji'. And those wood prints will become famous and influence artists of the impressionist and post-impressionist era."

Not understanding half of what he was taking about, the artist looked back at the strange person and grunted his irritation.

"Oh, don't mind me," said the tourist. "You keep on drawing, I just want to take a few more snaps."

Although annoyed, the artist eventually got back to his drawing and even the clicking of the small box wasn't so distracting once he imagined it was just the cicadas.

Figure in a Dreamscape

Humphrey Bogart in his pristine white suit jacket stands up from the table and strolls over to the bar. He grabs a match out of holder, lighting it in the process and calls to Walter Brennan, the bar tender, to fix him a whiskey. As he lights his cigarette, he glances over to the end of the bar. "And a vanilla milkshake for my friend over there."

Figures in a landscape

TRAVELER ONE: Wait a minute.

TRAVELER TWO: Wait what minute?

TRAVELER ONE: When did Walter Brennan ever play a bartender?

TRAVELER TWO: You tell me.

TRAVELER ONE: And does Ellison drink? I didn't think he did.

TRAVELER TWO: So?

TRAVELER ONE: And why would Michelangelo be doing in a strip joint? Wasn't he gay or something?

TRAVELER TWO: And?

TRAVELER ONE: And there were twenty-four views of Mount Fuji, not just twenty.

TRAVELER TWO: Thirty six, actually?

TRAVELER ONE: Then why did they say otherwise.

TRAVELER TWO: Your point being?

TRAVELER ONE: How come they got it all wrong when they probably knew all that.

TRAVELER TWO: My good man, it's good to know your facts, but you don't let them get in the way of a good story.

TRAVELER ONE: Why is it so important to know the facts if you change them to fit the story.

TRAVELER TWO: So you can reply to stupid questions like yours.

TRAVELER ONE: Did you make that "getting in the way of a good story" stuff up?

TRAVELER TWO: No, it's a paraphrase.

TRAVELER ONE: Paraphrased from who?

TRAVELER TWO: D.W. Griffith or Cecil B. De Mille, I think. Anyway, one or the other.

TRAVELER ONE: Whichever makes the story sound better, you mean?

TRAVELER TWO: You're learning.

Figure in a Memoryscape

The waiter places the tray on the table. We check the pot of Earl Grey to see how the tea has brewed. Needs to wait a minute more. Both of us look out the large window of the lounge in the hotel. It's raining hard on the busy street, but little can be heard inside, except the light chatter of other patrons. Fellow friends and associates pass by our table, but they understand we are doing "the catching up" so leave us to our own company. I take off my name badge, it seems out of place at this moment. Nothing is said, it doesn't need to be. My colleague checks the pot again. He smiles and prepares to pour.

Figure in a Futurescape

The module lands silently on the icy surface of Pluto, its little weight making a negligible change to the planetoid's orbit around the sun. The three man team take their first steps out onto this tiny world and, over the course of several days, take samples and measurements. When the time looms to head home, they erect a sign; Welcome to Sol—Pop. 200 Billion. Before take off they drop various empty containers and other items used up on the outgoing voyage. One item that slowly falls to the ice is a well thumbed paperback about ancient demons, vampires and adventurous ninjas. It comes to rest on the frozen ground and proceeds to circle the sun.

Figure in a Landscape

A person stands alone on a low-lying hill, around is little but dips and mounds of mud and rock. Small pools of dark water reflect the grey sky. It looks to be an abandoned battlefield from some forgotten conflict. The figure closes their eyes. And around them is the lush green of grass and the smell of distant pine. Above is the blue sky barely broken by the white clouds. And somewhere over one of the small hills can be heard the sounds of children playing

.*for Stephen, naturally.*

—ROBIN PEN

story acknowledgements

First edition acknowledgements

For invaluable assistance in the production of this collection and for continuing support, Ticonderoga Publications sincerely wish to thank:

Grant Stone;

and

Stephen Dedman, Van Ikin, Sean Williams, Robin Pen, Russell Blackford, Simon Brown, Jonathan Strahan, Jack Dann, Janeen Webb, Karen Logan, Christine Logan, Elaine Logan, Al Chan, Lyall Griffiths, Tania Griffiths, Kate Armitage, Michelle Cook, Michele Stambulich, Lisa Green, Terry Dowling, Mel & Phil, Jeremy G Byrne, Annette Curtis, Peter & Pat Swallow, Shay Telfer, Altair, Jason Bleckly, Julian & Susan Ackermann, Optima Press, Gigi Boudville, Cathy Cupitt, Scot Snow, Marianne S. Jablon, Erika Maria Lacey, Danny Heap, Mitch, Brian Clarke, Peter Cooper, Victoria Stein, Jason Kennedy, Chris Lawson, Jim & Trish Farr, Helen Binks, Eve Johnson, Bruce Anderson, Brian & Isabella Farr...

and especially you.

Second edition acknowledgements

In preparing this second edition, the publisher also wishes to thank:

Liz Grzyb, Alisa Krasnostein, Angela Challis, Shane Jiraiya Cummings, the Mt Lawley Mafia, the Nedlands Yakuza, Sue Manning, Grant Watson, Simon Oxwell...

and still, especially you.

www.ingramcontent.com/pod-product-compliance
Lightning Source LLC
Chambersburg PA
CBHW031942240626
47153CB00003B/832